D1562069

THE GOVERNESS'S EARL
Grace-By-The-Sea, Book 4

Cover Design and Interior Format
© The Killion Group, Inc.

The Governess's Earl

REGINA SCOTT

To those who dare to be themselves—thank you for the gift you offer the world. And to the Lord, who made us all wonderfully and uniquely.

CHAPTER ONE

Castle How, Grace-by-the-Sea
Dorset, England, early September 1804

HE MIGHT BE EARL, BUT he would never be his father.

Standing in his dressing room of the castle his family had used as a hunting lodge, Drake, Earl of Howland, pulled away from the well-meaning attentions of his new valet. Pierson had been, until recently, a moderately successful under-footman, but Drake's former valet had refused to leave London for the wilds of Dorset, and promoting Pierson had meant one less servant he would have to discharge.

If his cravat looked as if it had been trod upon by a herd of hungry hippopotami, that was a small price to pay for household harmony.

Somewhere a door slammed, and Drake flinched, imagining the fit Miranda was likely throwing in front of some unfortunate maid.

"Too tight, my lord?" Pierson asked, pale blue eyes liquid with anxiety as he gazed at the ruined cravat.

"It's fine," he assured the manservant yet again as he regarded himself in the standing mirror. Pierson had combed his blond hair back from his face and trimmed the ends to rest neatly above his ears on the sides and collar at the back. Few would notice that one sideburn was slightly shorter than the other. Then too, few here in the little spa village of Grace-by-the-Sea would notice that he was wearing the same waistcoat as the day before and the day before that.

Did Pierson have some sort of affinity for the striped wine-colored silk? He would have to remind the fellow he possessed several waistcoats, in different colors and textures, as well as more than the brown breeches Pierson persisted in pairing it with. At least his wardrobe hadn't had to be sold at auction like their townhouse and country estate. Then again, what did it matter what he wore? It wasn't as if he had anyone left to impress.

A knock sounded at the dressing room door. Pierson froze, eyes wide in indecision. A footman answered doors. But a valet? "Should I...?" he started.

"Please," Drake said.

As soon as the servant turned, he snatched a different coat off the hook and shrugged himself into it.

Pierson opened the door, then scuttled back like a crab on the shore so that Jonas, the family butler, might enter. Now, there was a fellow designed to impress. Black hair pomaded in place around an impassive face, the butler advanced into the room with stately tread. He was the third butler that Drake remembered, the other two having been discharged by his father for not representing the House of Howland with sufficient aplomb. No one would ever level such an accusation at Jonas. Drake suspected that spine, which never bent, and that air of command stemmed from the days his butler had served under General Cuyler.

Now Jonas stood just behind Drake, his head only an inch or two higher, and kept his grey gaze respectfully in the middle distance until Drake recognized his presence.

"What is it, Jonas?" he dutifully asked.

"The next candidate has arrived for her interview, my

lord."

Another one? Already he was regretting putting the advertisement in the *Upper Grace Gazette* for a governess for Miranda. She had pouted for hours when she'd learned he intended to locate someone to care for her. And he'd sat through four interviews so far, finding any number of reasons why not one of the women was clever enough, devoted enough, and kind enough to see to his daughter's needs.

He eyed the butler. "I don't recall scheduling an interview for this morning."

Jonas kept his gaze over Drake's left shoulder. Why did he still feel a touch of impatience? "Nevertheless, Miss Denby is waiting downstairs in the study."

"Perhaps a cravat pin, my lord?" Pierson fussed. "Or a different coat?"

Drake waved him back. "I am sufficient, thank you. Jonas, you may tell Miss Denby I will be right down."

Now that regal face hinted of disapproval, dark brows gathering over his long nose. "I'm sure Miss Denby will be willing to wait until you are pleased to see her, my lord." He remained still. Drake nodded. He inclined his head and left.

This Miss Denby would have had to wait on his father's pleasure. How he had relished any display of power—making the staff wait, making callers wait. Making Drake wait. He would never be his father—the fact had been drummed into him since birth.

And he couldn't mind in the least. The real question was—was he enough to be the earl?

"Boots, perhaps?" he suggested to Pierson, who immediately went to fetch a shiny black pair.

He found Miss Denby seated in one of the heavy-armed chairs in the study. Felicity had laughed at the pretentious red and black dragons entwined on the velvet seat, but then again, his late wife had had a way of making the darkest day seem bright.

He made himself smile at the waiting lady. "Miss Denby. Forgive me for keeping you."

"Punctuality is a prize few attain," she replied, and he had to stop himself from apologizing again. Odd. She wasn't imposing or stern-faced. Indeed, her gown of sea-green wool was tailored to a trim figure, and the patterned shawl over her shoulders might have graced any young miss in London. The only things about her that were the least intimidating was the way her warm brown hair had been pulled back into a severe bun behind her head and the lorgnette hanging from a black ribbon about her neck, as if she would raise it to her clear blue eyes to study his character.

But he was the master here, the one intent on hiring a governess. He would be the one asking the questions.

"Indeed," he said, taking the seat beside her. "Is punctuality a lesson you generally impart to your charges?"

She regarded him. "I have no need to impart it, my lord. My charges are seldom late."

Slippery. He kept the smile on his face. He'd learned a few tricks from his father, after all. Never let your guard down. Never allow them to become aware of your indecision. "I see. I assume you brought references to such, from previous employers."

She clucked her tongue. "I would never advise making assumptions on such short acquaintance."

Drake opened his mouth, then shut it again. What was it about this woman that put him in so defensive a position?

He gathered his dignity with difficulty, raising his chin and squaring his shoulders. "Exactly how much experience do you have as a governess?"

She glanced up at the ceiling as if counting the beams that crossed it. "Six years, three months, and eighteen days."

Well, that was something, both the amount and the precision. Though she must have started rather young. She could not be much beyond five and twenty. "And how many charges have you schooled during that time?"

"One."

Drake raised his brows. "One?"

She cocked her head. "Yes. I distinctly said as much. Have you a difficulty with hearing or recall?"

Though the question was said with all solicitation, it was still just this side of impertinent.

"One child is insufficient experience for this position," he explained.

Her eyes widened. "But you only have one child. Why would you need a governess with experience schooling more? In any event, if you require additional evidence as to my capabilities, I started the dame school in Upper Grace and developed its curriculum before leaving it in my older sister's capable hands."

So she hadn't actually taught there either? He felt as if the bookshelf-lined walls were closing in around him. "Miss Denby, you seem unsuited for the role of caring for my daughter. She has been through a great deal for having only attained nine years. She requires encouragement, nurturing."

"Precisely why I applied," she insisted. "Lady Miranda and I have much in common. She lost her dear mother a year ago, I understand. I lost my father when I was eight."

The memory of Felicity's death was all too vivid. He would not have wished such an experience on any child. "My condolences."

She did not pause to acknowledge his comment. "Furthermore, through a change in circumstances, Lady Miranda finds herself in a new home in a new location. I too had to leave our home in Kent for Dorset to live with my uncle after my father's death."

Perhaps she had something to teach after all. He leaned

forward. "How did you manage?"

She spread her hands. "As you can see, I grew into an educated woman capable of managing her own future. I would like to help Lady Miranda reach a similar happy state."

Felicity would approve. She had refused to hire a nanny or governess, preferring to care for Miranda herself. He had never seen such love and devotion, even if she tended to let their daughter do whatever she liked. He had been desperately trying to act in her stead for the last year.

Now that he was earl, he no longer had the luxury of spending all his time with his daughter. He must find a way out of the financial chasm his father had dug for them, do his duty in Parliament when it started up again in the fall, and help his cousin James safeguard the village from the impending French invasion. Why, a French ship rested in the caverns below the castle even now, waiting for someone. Therefore, another must step in and care for Miranda.

Could Miss Denby be exactly what he needed?

Rosemary Denby counted off the seconds. The new Earl of Howland must grant her the position. Truly, what other recourse did she have near Grace-by-the-Sea? She hadn't the ever-pleasant aspect of a spa hostess to serve in the Grand Pump Room in the village, and her highly competent sister-in-law Jesslyn held that position in any event. The local fathers were distressingly uneasy with a young, unmarried woman teaching their sons, so she had yielded her place at the dame school in Upper Grace to her older, widowed sister, Hester. And she would never have the patience to work in a shop.

"I don't understand why you must work at all," her

mother had lamented only this morning when Rosemary had begged the gig to drive herself to the castle. "Your uncle left us with enough income that we need never worry."

"It isn't the income, Mother," Rosemary had tried to explain. "Hester has the school and little Rebecca; you have uncle's properties to manage. I just want something of my own."

Her mother's face had bunched. "And a husband won't do?"

The words had been like a lash across her back. As if she hadn't attended nearly every assembly the last four years, accepted the attentions of any number of shopkeepers and farmers in Upper Grace, the young officers stationed at West Creech. The one man she'd hoped, prayed, might be interested had made it abundantly plain she was not the woman for him.

"I'm not certain I wish to be a wife, Mother," she'd said. "And there are few gentlemen here interested in taking a bluestocking for a bride."

But perhaps a governess.

And so she had brazened her way into this interview, claiming an appointment the earl had never made. So what if she'd only ever cared for her niece, Rebecca? She remembered what it was like to be a girl whose world had suddenly been upended. Her uncle had encouraged and supported her dreams of learning. She could pass that along to another. It seemed her best objective in life.

"I can see you are passionate about your profession, Miss Denby," the earl said, leaning toward her. He looked so much like their magistrate, Mr. Howland—same golden blond hair waving back from a strong-jawed face, the same piercing blue eyes. But the magistrate was all cool logic and determination. If she had been forced to find one word to describe his cousin, the earl, it would be…

Lost.

"I live to serve, my lord," she assured him, leaning toward him as well.

The way he held his slender body—controlled, still—told her he was not convinced. "But Lady Miranda, I have been informed, can be a challenge."

"A challenge I welcome," she promised, fingers closing around her lorgnette.

They were nearly nose to nose now, and she caught herself holding her breath. Still he studied her. Would he see more than the fathers who had rejected her as a teacher? Would he see more than Captain St. Claire when he'd refused her admiration?

The click of the door sent them both upright in their seats. A blond-haired girl flounced into the room, ruffled pink muslin skirts dancing about her matching kid-leather slippers.

"There you are, Father," she declared as if he were late for some state function. "You said we could visit Mr. Carroll's Curiosities today and pick a new book. I'm ready."

"So I see," her father said with a fond smile. "I will take you when I have finished my interview with Miss Denby."

Lady Miranda glanced her way. Rosemary knew that set to her chin, that light in her hazel eyes. On any given day, she might have seen such an attitude in her own mirror.

"But I want to go now," Lady Miranda said.

Lord Howland looked to Rosemary. She did not so much as straighten a finger. This was a test. She had never failed one yet.

"Certainly you should go now," Rosemary said. "All your father has to do is agree to hire me as your new governess."

Her father frowned.

So did the little girl. "But I don't need a governess."

"Now, Miranda," her father started.

She turned to put both hands on his arm and gaze up at him beseechingly. At least Rosemary had never stooped so low, but then, she'd seldom had to do more than argue with her uncle. He had been one to appreciate logic.

"But Father," Lady Miranda wheedled, "I only want to be with you. I love you."

His face melted. Truly, it was an extraordinary sight. Any resemblance to their stern magistrate vanished. In its place was a man who cared: deeply, desperately. A man who would have done anything to see his daughter smile.

And the little wretch knew it.

"I love you too, Miranda," he murmured. "And I want you to grow up into the accomplished woman your mother hoped you would be. That's why I'm searching for the perfect governess."

Such a creature did not exist. No one was perfect. But Rosemary knew she could do good in this house. Er, castle.

"I don't need a governess," Miranda repeated, and now her face and tone were mulish.

"Ah," Rosemary interjected, lifting her lorgnette to her nose and gazing at the girl through it. "Then you know the difference between *elephas* and *crocodylus*."

The girl turned her way. "No. I don't know what they are."

And didn't like that. Good.

The earl was watching her again. Rosemary tried to focus on Lady Miranda.

"I'd be delighted to explain," she told the girl. "My uncle, Flavius Montgomery, the famous geologist, taught me everything he knew. I can tell you why fossils appear in limestone and where the ancient elephants lived in this area." She leaned closer to the girl and lowered her voice. "I can even lead you to their last remains."

Hazel eyes met hers, calculating, curious. "I'd like that.

What about mathematics?"

"The square root of twenty and four is approximately four point eight nine eight nine eight."

She swung her gaze to her father once more. "You didn't teach me to do square roots. Is she right?"

"Yes," he said, lips hinting of a smile. "And square roots might be a bit beyond your skills at this point."

"Nonsense," Rosemary and Lady Miranda said at the same time.

Lady Miranda beamed at her. "I like her. Hire her, Father, so we can go."

"There's a bit more to hiring than merely giving my word," he told his daughter. "We must agree on when she starts, her salary, half days off, and requirements for room and board."

"I'll start tomorrow," Rosemary said as fast as she could, lorgnette slipping from her fingers. "I can bring my things and spend the night tonight. I'll accept twenty-five pounds per quarter. Sunday after services and Wednesday evenings off. A bedchamber and sitting room here at the castle with meals with the family most days. And I dress as I like. No uniforms."

"Fine," Lady Miranda said. She grabbed her father's hand and gave it a tug. "Now, come along, Father."

He rose slowly, but his gaze was on Rosemary. "Ask Jonas to fetch you a bonnet, Miranda," he said, and she released him to scamper from the room.

He waited for Rosemary to rise, then closed the distance, and she had to lift her lorgnette once more to stop herself from falling into the blue of his eyes.

"I am devoted to my daughter, Miss Denby," he said, as if she could have had any doubts on the matter. "As you can see, I deny her little. So, I will agree to your terms, but only for the next fortnight. You will have to prove to me you can do this job. And I won't be nearly as easy on you as I am on my daughter."

CHAPTER TWO

SHE'D DONE IT. IT WAS all Rosemary could do not to skip down the steps fronting the castle's massive oak door and kiss her family's horse Daphne on the tip of her velvety nose. But she had a reputation to maintain—governess to Lady Miranda, daughter of the Earl of Howland. So she kept her head high and smile no more than satisfied as she glided up to the stable hand who was holding the reins.

"I'll return this evening around six," she told him, taking the long ribbons of leather from him. "Will someone be available to fetch my things into the castle?"

The Castle How servants must be particularly good about sharing news, for he didn't so much as look surprised as he handed her into the gig. He even knew her name. "Yes, Miss Denby. Just as you like."

She waited until she had turned the gig and headed away from the castle before letting her grin out. And if she gave a whoop of delight as well, the only ones who noticed were a pair of doves that wheeled out of the trees near the edge of the drive.

Mother listened to her tale of triumph with a brow that grew more furrowed with each word. Her hair was grey now, crimped around her face and pulled back behind her head, but she carried herself with the dignity of a queen in her spruce-colored wool gown.

"So, you're determined, then," she said, lines evident around her brown eyes, when Rosemary finished.

"I *left* here determined, Mother," Rosemary reminded her. "The deed is done. I achieved my goal."

"I suppose you could look at it that way," her mother allowed.

Rosemary shook her head, then enfolded her mother in a hug. "I do look at it that way. I know I wasn't the easiest child to raise. If you cannot be happy for me, be happy you no longer have to worry."

"Well, of course I worry." She pulled back with a gentle smile that tugged at Rosemary's heart. "I worry about your sister too, a widow so young with a daughter to raise. I worry about your brother. His work as Riding Surveyor is dangerous. I couldn't bear to lose any of you."

The pit inside her that was never entirely closed threatened to swallow her. Rosemary drew in a breath, shoved down the memories, and turned for the stairs. "You won't lose me, Mother. You won't lose any of us. We remember what it was like after Father was taken. Now, I must pack. I promised to return by six."

Her mother offered to help, but Rosemary waved her off. Just this moment, just *for* a moment, she wanted to think about the future, not the past.

But that proved impossible as she began gathering her things. Other, better memories beckoned. The coverlet with the hearts her mother had stitched along the edges. The bonnet her sister had encouraged her to buy because it brought out the blue of her eyes. Why was she surprised to feel such a connection to these things? She'd lived in the sprawling manor house since she'd been eight.

And had never traveled farther than the Dorset shore, less than a mile away, since then. That meant she had no trunk, no bags of her own. But she knew where her uncle had stored his. Surely he wouldn't have minded her using them.

"You've a keen mind, Rosemary," he'd say, one green eye looking misshapen behind the magnifying glass he held over his latest specimen. "Never let anyone claim you shouldn't use it."

His study was nearly empty now, the desk and worktable so bare it seemed a blasphemy. He'd left his collection to the British Museum in his will, and two staff members had come to carry away the delicate bones encased in stone, the chunks of ancient rock veined with fossil leaves, the white and gold swirls of Ammon's horn. She'd had to fight to keep a few of his books and journals.

"She was very fond of her uncle," her mother had explained to the indignant men. "You must allow her some remembrance."

Now, she pulled the battered leather trunk from the cupboard on the far wall. Uncle Montgomery had used it to carry his specimens between their discovery and the house. Debris still speckled the bottom—chips of limestone, bits of bark. She tipped it on one side, shook out the contents on a piece of paper for disposal, then dragged the trunk down to her room for filling.

Still the memories came calling—the day he'd first let her hold one of the spiral-shelled Ammon's horn, now turned to stone; the day she'd accompanied him on a hunt along the shore only to spy the frond of a fern etched in the earth; when she'd begun assisting him with his cataloging, amazed by both the number and the variety of his collection. It was hard to focus on folding cloth, sliding in books, packing her lorgnette in its leather case, setting it and her Bible in a spot where she could find them easily. She was nearly finished, the lid firmly on the past, when her sister looked in.

"You did it."

There was a smile of pride she could bask in. "You are looking at Lady Miranda's new governess."

"Congratulations!" Hester moved into the room to hug

Rosemary, arms warm and soft. Hester and their brother shared the same golden-brown hair, though Hester had blue-green eyes. She alone of the family seemed content with where she was, what she had.

Unlike Rosemary.

She pulled back to smile at her older sister. "Thank you. I'm beyond delighted."

Hester eyed the bulging trunk, and her light dimmed. "Rebecca and I will miss you terribly."

The mention of her little niece made her own heart constrict, as if in protest. "We'll still see each other," she said, striding for the wardrobe to pull out her cloak. "I requested Sunday afternoon and Wednesday evening off, so plan to see me for dinner after services and at assemblies. Though you will likely have to send the carriage for me."

"Leave it to me," Hester said. "Do you want any of the books from the school for Lady Miranda?"

Rosemary shook her head. "There should be a library at the castle. And she was asking her father about a book today, so he can buy her more if needed." She slung the cloak about her shoulders, every bit as if she knew her own mind. But her fingers fumbled on the silver clasp.

"Let me." Hester stepped forward and fastened the cloak, then smoothed the green wool over Rosemary's shoulders. Those blue-green eyes were dipping at the corners. How many times had Hester smoothed things over for her—softening disapproval, calming fears? After their father's death, their mother had been so consumed with managing the move that Hester and Rosemary had learned to rely on each other. Always Hester had been the one to protect her. From bullying in the village where they'd lived in Kent, from more than one heartbreak here in Upper Grace.

Of course, Hester had been the one to pull away first, after that wretch Rob Peverell had turned her head.

Her fascination for the fellow had been the only time Hester had fallen from grace. She'd returned to the path their mother espoused by marrying Lieutenant Todd and bringing Rebecca into their lives.

"It will be all right," Rosemary told her sister. "You'll see."

Hester stepped back with a smile. "Of course it will. Will you allow me the honor of driving you back?"

Her throat tightened, and she swallowed. "It's all right. Jem can drive me. Rebecca will need you."

Hester hugged her again, and Rosemary breathed in the dry sachet that always smelled a little like spiced apple cider. Then she went to take her leave of her mother and niece. She didn't feel any more regrets until Jem, their man-of-all-work, stopped the family carriage on the drive in front of the castle.

The stable hand had been waiting for her, but someone else had claimed his attention first. She remembered the roan horse just before she recognized the black-haired heartbreaker swinging down from the saddle. Before she thought better of it, her hand was raised to knock on the roof so she could order Jem to leave, immediately. She could not face that man on the drive. Not here, not now.

Coward!

She lowered her hand without signaling their coachman. Quillan St. Claire had haunted her dreams for too long. She wasn't about to allow him to steal this future from her too.

She lowered the window, turned the outside latch to open the door, and kicked out the stairs before Jem could climb down from the bench and assist her. She was halfway to the door before the captain reached her side.

"Miss Denby, what a delightful surprise," he said, doffing his tricorn.

It wasn't delightful in the least. But she would not look in those mesmerizing brown eyes. "Captain. Don't allow me to detain you."

The stout oak door brought her up short. She didn't feel comfortable waltzing through it when she couldn't claim the house her home just yet. She hadn't even moved in, after all. As she hesitated, he reached a muscular arm around her and slapped the dragon's head knocker on the brass fitting.

A footman immediately opened the door.

Rosemary pushed past him. "Thank you. Is Mr. Jonas about?"

"In the kitchen, Miss Denby," he said before turning to Quillan St. Claire. "May I help you, sir?"

"I believe the lady takes precedence," he said gallantly.

Rosemary was already moving. "Not at all. I live here, sir. You are the stranger." And she swept from the room before he could give her more than a startled look.

"What business do you have with Rosemary Denby?"

From the landing at the top of the stairs, Drake raised a brow at the gentleman who had just been shown into his home along with Miss Denby, who was disappearing down the wing that held the kitchen. He'd seen the famous captain at the recent annual regatta, when he'd taken second place without much effort. And he knew the former naval officer was friends with his cousin, James, the village magistrate. But he was unaccustomed to anyone demanding anything of him.

Except, of course, Miranda.

"Captain St. Claire, isn't it?" he asked, coming down the stairs to meet the fellow in the great hall of the castle. He offered a hand while their footman Giles grimaced apologetically behind the visitor. "I wasn't expecting you this evening."

The captain seemed to collect himself, bending in a bow. "My lord. Apologies. It is a matter of some urgency."

Involving Rosemary Denby? Curiosity had him agreeing to see the fellow in his study. Giles escorted them to the room, then Drake nodded his visitor into one of the dragon-patterned seats in front of the desk before taking the chair behind it. With his coal-black hair and hooded eyes, black greatcoat thrown back as if he'd ridden through highwaymen to reach the castle, St. Claire seemed rather suited to the chair.

"Thank you," he said. "I thought it time we had a conversation."

"About Miss Denby?" Drake prompted.

"Yes. No." He shook his head as if to clear it, then made a show of leaning back in the chair. "This should be a private conversation, if you take my meaning."

Not in the slightest, but Drake tipped his chin, and Giles melted from the room.

"Go on," Drake said.

He cocked his head, look assessing. "You're new here. I thought you should know which way the wind blows."

Drake crossed his arms over his chest. "I've spent part of every summer at this castle since I was ten. I know the wind blows predominantly toward the east-northeast, in from the Atlantic and veering eventually toward France."

Something kindled behind his dark eyes. "Aye. That it does, until recently. Now France is following it back, right to your doorstep. I understand there's a French boat in the caves below the castle."

Had James told him, or did the captain have another source of information?

"There is a boat," Drake acknowledged. "How do you know it came from France?"

"I'd have thought the apprehension of a French spy attempting to escape in it sufficient evidence."

So, he knew about the capture. It had given Drake a

few bad moments. Miranda had a fascination with the vast caverns that underlay the headland on which Castle How was built. She'd stumbled upon a fleeing spy and had nearly been taken captive. Only the timely intervention of Dr. Bennett from the spa and his new wife, Abigail, had saved Drake's daughter.

And still the boat waited. For whom?

"The boat may belong to the French," Drake allowed. "But it could just as well belong to the Lord of the Smugglers, the brigand who used my caverns as a landing spot before we returned."

"I can assure you it isn't his."

Drake raised a brow. "On such good terms with him, are you?"

"Excellent terms." He stood and sketched a bow. "The Lord of the Smugglers, at your service."

Drake stared at him. "You're a former Navy man. I won't believe you'd betray your country by smuggling."

He brought both hands down on the desk and glared at Drake. "Never. I may travel between here and France, but any goods I carry are at the request and service of the War Office."

"A spy, then," Drake realized.

He straightened. "I prefer privateer. I've been performing the service since my leg healed of its injury at the Battle of the Nile. When the castle was empty, your caverns made a safe place to pull ashore, with your cousin's permission, of course."

James had been steward of the Howland holdings in Dorset since the passing of his own father. "But my return has put a wrinkle in things," Drake surmised.

"Indeed." He returned to his chair and put one booted foot up on the other knee. "So, I'd like your permission to continue using your cavern, at night and at the whim of the tides."

The entrance to the caves from the Channel could only

be navigated safely as the tide turned to incoming. And when the tide was at its lowest, the water was so shallow it was possible to walk from the shore into the caves, potentially leaving a ship stranded for hours or days. But there was one other way to access the hideaway.

"You'll also need permission to use my kitchen, then," Drake pointed out, "where the stairs open down into the caves."

"Only after dark," he promised. "Your kitchen staff will be abed when we slip up the stairs and out the rear door. Though if you employ a night watchman, you might pass the word to look the other way, for his own safety."

Drake frowned. "Safety? Are you bringing danger to my home, Captain St. Claire?"

He held up one hand. "Not that will threaten you directly. But it's best for the people I carry that no one recognize or remember seeing them."

Drake leaned forward. "James will vouch for you?"

"He will. He's the one who insisted I speak to you about the matter."

And very likely the captain would have insisted on using the caverns without speaking to him, given a choice. As usual, his cousin had been looking out for Drake.

"Very well," Drake said. "Under those conditions and in aid of the war effort, you may use my caves. But if I learn you are employing them for other purposes, that offer will be terminated, with prejudice."

He nodded. "Understood. Thank you."

"Good. Now, what has this to do with Miss Denby?"

He studied his boot as if it held a map to some fabled treasure. "Nothing, to tell the truth. I was only surprised to find her making herself free to your home."

His father would have deterred his presumption with a smile that dripped ice. Drake merely let the silence stretch until St. Claire was forced to look his way.

"And what business is that of yours?" Drake asked

politely.

He dropped his foot to the floor. "I'm acquainted with her brother, Larkin Denby, the Riding Surveyor for this area."

Of course he would be. Riding Surveyors and their Riding Officers kept watch along a stretch of coastline for the type of irregularities Captain St. Claire created with his smuggling. Did he fear Rosemary would carry tales of what she'd seen?

"I doubt Miss Denby will have much time to contact her brother," Drake said. "Nor will she be up at night at the time you'll be using the caverns."

He chuckled. "Oh, you're a sly one."

If that wasn't the pot calling the kettle black! "I believe we're finished here, Captain St. Claire."

He looked at Drake as if trying to decide whether to mount an argument. Drake regarded him back. He wasn't sure why the privateer rose and bowed. "My lord."

Drake rose as well and watched him stride out. Then he shook his head. Perhaps he should have simply explained Rosemary Denby's position in his household, but he'd seen the look his new governess had sent the Lord of the Smugglers before turning her back on him. Captain St. Claire had aroused far more emotion in her than her verbal clash with Drake earlier ever had. He could not believe she would want Drake to confide in the fellow.

But the incident gave him yet another reason to keep an eye on her.

CHAPTER THREE

THANK GOODNESS SHE HADN'T HAD to say more to Captain St. Claire. If she never saw the man again, it would be too soon. But as she hurried down the corridor for the kitchen, her steps slowed. What, did some part of her want to turn back, beg his forgiveness? Did the man have some sort of hold on her?

She'd certainly been willing to let him. Quillan St. Claire was a legend. The hero of the Battle of the Nile, tragically wounded in service to his country. Dark hair, dark eyes, a sort of smolder to him, like a banked fire ready to blaze at any moment. Every unmarried lady sighed when he walked into a room, preening and primping to catch his attention. She hadn't been immune. She was clever. Surely she could find a way to make him notice her.

She nearly cringed remembering that day, a little over a month ago, when she'd accosted him after her brother's wedding. There had been dancing in the assembly rooms at the top of the hill as part of the celebration. He'd asked her friend Abigail to dance, and Abigail had declined. Why shouldn't Rosemary claim the honor instead?

She'd emboldened herself to sashay up to him, lorgnette swinging. "Captain St. Claire, you appear to be a gentleman who values bravery and tenacity. Allow me, then, to say that I have admired you for some time, and I would very much like to further your acquaintance."

Those dark eyes had gazed back at her with something akin to pity in them. "I'm afraid, Miss Denby, you're mistaken. A difficult thing for a bluestocking to accept, I'm sure. Your first error was assuming I'm a gentleman. Your second was that I would like to further the acquaintance of any lady. In short, my dear, you aren't the sort I'd choose to pursue."

It was as if someone had doused her in seawater. For once in her life, words had failed her. She'd pivoted on her heels and retreated to her mother's side.

She had wanted nothing more than to leave the assembly, run away and lick her wounds. Why had she thought he might be different? That he would see her for who she was and value her? The best she could do was hold her head high while inside her heart shriveled away in pain and sorrow.

She'd known then she couldn't keep on the path her mother wanted. She couldn't continue to pretend there was a man for her, if she just looked hard enough, smiled brightly enough, danced gracefully enough. She had to find her own place, her own purpose.

She'd done that by becoming governess to Lady Miranda Howland. Time to show her true colors.

So, she went in search of Mr. Jonas, the butler. Afterall, she had no idea where the earl intended to house Lady Miranda's governess. For all his home looked like a white-stone medieval fortress with rounded turrets at each of the four corners, it had been built as a hunting lodge and used as a summer house by his father. Very likely there was no schoolroom, much less quarters for a governess.

"Miss Denby," the butler greeted her when she found him in the wide kitchen. "Welcome to the staff. I'll show you your domain."

He led her to the chamber story and down a long corridor to a bedchamber and sitting room overlooking the inner courtyard.

"His lordship thought it best if you were close to her ladyship," he said. "Lady Miranda's room is next door, and the schoolroom is across the corridor. I believe you will find it a suitable arrangement."

She did, but his tone suggested she should not find fault regardless. She glanced around at the poster bed with its cheery red and white chintz hangings, the dual walnut wardrobes along the silk-draped wall, the thick carpet patterned in cream and ruby. Through the door on one side, she made out a cozy sitting room with bookcases, upholstered chairs, and a white marble fireplace.

"Imminently suitable," she said. "Does Lady Miranda have a schedule?"

His lips twitched a moment before he answered. "She does not. I encourage you to attempt to set one."

"First thing," Rosemary promised. "Where might I find her nursemaid, the woman who tends to her meals and dresses and undresses her?"

"Regrettably, she has none at the moment. Her ladyship has definite preferences in that area, and we've yet to find someone who meets them to her satisfaction."

Well that could be trying. She hadn't expected to have to deal with the girl's personal needs. Then again, she'd helped Hester care for Rebecca for years.

"If you would send up someone to tend the fire and bring her meals, that would be very helpful," she told the butler. "But my wages cover only being a governess. If I'm to play her nursemaid as well, I expect to be compensated accordingly."

His gaze narrowed just the slightest. "I'll see what can be done. But make no mistake, Miss Denby. This household runs according to Lady Miranda's whim. You will find your position second to none but my own."

Responsibility indeed! Rosemary inclined her head. "Then I am honored by the trust I have been given and will do my best to live up to it."

He did not look impressed. "If everything is sufficient, I will leave you to unpack. Warren, one of our maids, has agreed to help you with dressing. I will ask her to assist with Lady Miranda as well."

"Please ask her to come to me at half past six tomorrow morning," Rosemary advised. "I'll be ready for her by then."

She was, nerves tingling, lorgnette about her neck on a satin ribbon, but when she and the older maid poked their heads into Lady Miranda's room at seven with great anticipation, they found it empty.

Warren's sturdy frame sagged. Like Rosemary's mother, her hair was grey, her cheeks round, and her eyes brown. Rosemary had had no trouble warming to her.

"Not again," she said with a sigh, hands worrying in the apron covering her navy uniform. Then she glanced at Rosemary. "Begging your pardon, miss."

Rosemary moved to the fine walnut bed and peeled off her day glove to lay her hand on the sheets. "Still warm. She can't have been gone long. I take it this happens often?"

"Too often." Warren hastily bowed her head as if to hide her frustration.

"Where does she go?" Rosemary asked, the rustle of her muslin skirts loud as she strode for the door to the corridor. "To her father?"

"Sometimes," Warren allowed, following her. "Other times she wanders all over. Exploring, she calls it, as if the castle was some wild foreign land."

"It might seem so to her, picked up and deposited here after living in London all her life." Pulling on her glove, Rosemary glanced up and down the corridor, head cocked as she listened. Somewhere, a door shut, and voices murmured. Female? Definitely more mature than a nine-year-old girl.

"Who else has rooms in this wing?" she asked the maid, who had come out to stand beside her.

"The countess. Miss Marjorie has a room too, but she mostly stays in the village now with Master James and his wife."

James Howland and his bride Eva lived in Butterfly Manor in the village. His mother, Marjorie, had been the countess's companion in London.

"Ask if her ladyship has seen her granddaughter," Rosemary told the maid. "I'll check the schoolroom."

Warren hurried off.

Rosemary ventured across the corridor. The long room looking out over the grounds had probably been a gallery at one time. Now bookcases and cupboards had been pressed against three of the walls, leaving narrow strips of green and cream wallpaper in sight, as if a forest lay just beyond. Two teak desks faced each other over a carpet patterned in green leaves. The only open wall held the window flanked by a map of England and a more detailed map of Dorset. Nearby, a globe made of various kinds of polished stone stood on a brass stand.

"Nicely done," she said aloud.

No one answered.

Warren bustled back in. "The countess's maid, Davis, says she hasn't seen her. But I ran into Mr. Pierson, the earl's valet, in the corridor, and he says Cook's in a bit of a bother about Lady Miranda. There's food missing from the pantry again."

Rosemary frowned. "Why would the daughter of an earl need to steal food from her own pantry?"

Warren's round face sagged. "Her last nursemaid tried stronger measures to persuade Lady Miranda to behave, making her go to bed without her supper and such. When her ladyship complained to her father, he sacked the woman. Perhaps, knowing you were arriving, Lady Miranda decided to stock up just in case."

"Perhaps," Rosemary allowed. "We'll search her room for any food, after we locate her."

Warren sighed. "Shall I ask Mr. Jonas to turn out the staff again?"

"And give her so much attention? Certainly not." Rosemary gathered her skirts. "I will check every room on this floor and this wing. And then I will apply to the one person she cannot gainsay—her father."

Once more in the wine-colored waistcoat and side-burns that were beginning to look more lopsided every day, Drake glanced up from his plate to find Miss Denby in the doorway of the breakfast room near the front of the castle. She had dressed in a softer gown today—green-sprigged muslin with a white ruff that kept her chin high. Or perhaps it was her attitude straightening her spine so much the lorgnette on a ribbon around her neck lay perfectly aligned with her nose.

"Yes, Miss Denby?" he asked, rising. "Did you have a question about Miranda's studies?"

She moved into the room and somehow made it feel smaller. Even Giles, waiting to serve along the wall, edged away from her.

"Not her studies, my lord," she said. "Her location. She is missing from her room."

Not again. His daughter delighted in playing games with the staff, who did not appear as enamored with the idea. He couldn't blame them. The first two times she'd gone missing since they'd arrived, he'd turned out every member of the household in a panic. This would be, what, the tenth time in the last fortnight?

Still, one of the reasons he'd hired a governess was to marshal his daughter's considerable energy toward something more edifying then scaring him half to death.

"I see," he said. "So, on your first day of duty, you have misplaced your only charge."

She did not so much as blush. "Nonsense. I know exactly where she is. I came to inquire whether you had the same knowledge."

Well, that was a facer. Giles looked similarly nonplussed.

"I regret that I do not," Drake told her.

She moved closer, skirts swishing across the hardwood floor. "Then you likely are also unaware that your kitchen staff accused her of stealing food from the pantry."

Giles started, then quickly resumed his position.

Drake frowned. "Why would Miranda steal food? She has all she needs. If she wants more, she has only to ask."

"Perhaps it is the quantity," she acknowledged, fingers toying with the glass frame hanging on her chest. "Perhaps it is the type of food, such as sweets or salty things. With your permission, I'd like to speak to the cook about her diet, see if we can't prevent more theft while satisfying her."

"Agreed."

"And, while the schoolroom you arranged is well suited to its purpose, it's clear your daughter will require more variety to stimulate her. I propose lessons in biology and geology outdoors when at all possible and a daily regimen of healthful exercise. When there are events in the community, such as the upcoming Harvest Fair, I suggest we attend."

He couldn't help his smile. "Hoping to tire her out, are you?"

For the first time, she smiled back, and the room warmed. "Tire her out, thoroughly engage her mind, help her find activities at which she can excel."

It was all he had hoped. "I approve. It's what her mother, my wife, would have wanted."

"Then I know the approach will succeed." She inclined

her head, hand dropping. "I'll send word if we have any trouble."

He nodded, and she turned and left, taking some of the light with her. He thought Giles sighed as Drake resumed his seat.

Drake had sighed often enough since Felicity had died. She would have been sitting beside him now, telling him all the things she had planned for the day. And every bite would be sweeter, listening to her.

From the moment he'd been introduced to her in a crowded London ballroom, he'd known she was the only woman for his bride. Felicity was laughter, music, dance. She dominated every setting, captivated every heart. He'd been the proudest man on earth when she'd accepted his proposal of the many she'd received, including one from James.

It had only been later that he'd learned what that acceptance had cost her. The knowledge had never made him love her less. He'd thought she'd grown to care for him as well. Certainly, she'd poured her life into their daughter.

Who appeared to be missing. Again. What if Miss Denby was mistaken, and she didn't know where Miranda had gone? What if this time was no game? There had been that nasty business with the French agent and the caverns. The boat was still waiting for its unknown owner. If the French had returned for it at last, Miranda could be in danger.

He surged to his feet, and Giles jumped off the wall.

"Yes, my lord? Were you in need?"

"I'm finished here," he told the footman before storming from the room.

Unlike most of the other times Miranda had disappeared, no one had called out the staff. He passed a maid dusting a suit of armor in an alcove near the breakfast room and their other footman, Dawson, bringing in coal for the fire in the great hall hearth with its flanking statues of Grecian maidens. Neither of his staff deigned to notice him. He was not supposed to notice them. But he tried to notice every nook and cranny. Any hiding place might be fair game for Miranda. He must be vigilant.

And he would have to speak to Miss Denby. It had been too much to hope she could handle such an assignment. He had been right—she had insufficient experience to deal with a girl of Miranda's spirit, her boundless energy. Somewhere, there had to be a governess who would appreciate his daughter's unique personality, her amazing nature.

Something clanked from the music room, a jarring note quite unlike the sounds that usually floated through the great hall when his mother was at the harpsichord.

"Miranda?" he called, heading that way.

"Yes, Father?"

He strode through the withdrawing room and stopped in the doorway of the music room beyond. His aunt's harp had been moved to Butterfly Manor, leaving an open spot in the sunlight streaming through the drapes. Closer to the hearth, surrounded by little gilt chairs, stood his mother's black lacquered harpsichord. At the moment, the lid and flutes lay open, the brass strings on the soundboard exposed.

Miranda stood peering down at them with Miss Denby at her side. His daughter glanced up at him. "Did you know the harpsichord is a percussion instrument? The vibration of the strings when they are plucked is what makes the music." As if to prove it, she tugged on the nearest set with her fingers.

Drake winced at the cacophony. "How interesting. I understand you went missing this morning, Miranda."

She moved around to sit on the bench and craned her neck as if to see the strings as well as the keys. "I wasn't missing. I woke up and decided to take a walk before breakfast." She tapped at a few keys and watched the strings.

"Lady Miranda was in the library," Miss Denby put in between notes. "She located several books of interest. Her grandmother encountered us on the stairs and reminded her that she needed to practice."

If that noise was any indication of her proficiency, she needed to practice more often. "My mother has instructed Miranda from time to time," he explained to the governess.

"I like the harpsichord better than the harp," Miranda announced, bringing all ten fingers down at once.

Drake rubbed an ear, deeming the other a lost cause at the moment. "Do you play, Miss Denby?"

She raised her voice over the din. "I do not, my lord, but I will inquire of the countess as to when she'd like to offer further instruction. Lady Miranda."

His daughter's name held no more emphasis than the other words, but Miranda mercifully paused.

"It is a lovely day," Miss Denby said in the quiet, fingers once more clutching her lorgnette. "Let's fetch your bonnet and see what things of interest we can find on the grounds."

Miranda hopped off the bench. "Yes, Miss Denby. I'll ask Warren." She ran past Drake as if he wasn't there. A part of him wilted. The other part exalted to see her so engaged.

He looked to Miss Denby as she came around the instrument. "What, exactly, have you done to my daughter?"

"Not enough yet," she said, and she sailed out of the room.

CHAPTER FOUR

SO FAR, SO GOOD. ROSEMARY took a deep breath of the cool September air. Autumn was just beginning to make itself known in Dorset. The summer heat, such as it was, had faded, and the rain was creeping in. Thankfully, not enough to ruin the harvest and its attendant fair later this month.

And not enough to ruin today's outing with Lady Miranda.

The sea breeze played with their bonnets as they cut across the graveled drive. The castle sat on a headland looking out over the Channel. Emerald lawns dotted by late wildflowers surrounded the white stone building, with a ring of trees farther out. Dew clung to their skirts as they started toward the nearest copse, Rosemary doing her best not to think about the flowers.

Miranda seemed content, for once, to gaze about her, giving Rosemary a few moments for thought. The earl had given her a scare this morning, first when she'd gone to see if he knew Miranda's location and then when he'd discovered them in the music room after she'd found the girl trying to climb the tall bookcases in the library. She'd wanted to give him no reason to doubt her, and now he had two. Her ladyship clearly required stimulation, for Rosemary's peace of mind and the earl's.

A butterfly danced past to land on a Michaelmas daisy,

coppery-colored wings dotted by brown and edged in grey. Rosemary stuck out an arm to stop Lady Miranda and forced herself to look only at the specimen, not the petals below it.

"See that?" she asked her charge. "It's a *Lycaena phlaeas*, locally known as a small copper."

Lady Miranda regarded it. "It's very small. Father read a book to me about ones in the Jamaican plantations. Their wings are as big as saucers."

"Well, that is impressive," Rosemary allowed, lowering her arm so they could continue across the lawns.

Lady Miranda pouted, lower lip stuck out so far the small copper could have landed on it. "I thought you knew about such things."

"Dorset things," Rosemary stressed. "Though I have tried to keep up with discoveries on the Continent and in America as well. As you live in Dorset now, Dorset things would appear to be the most important for you to learn."

Lady Miranda hopped over a root as they moved into the shadows of the trees. "Grandmother says we won't be in Dorset long. Father will figure out how to return us to London."

Interesting. It was late in the year for the Howlands to arrive at the castle, but she'd thought perhaps the earl had retreated here after the death of his father to clear his mind before taking his seat in the House of Lords. And she'd heard the rumors that he intended to make the castle his country estate now. She'd thought that meant Lady Miranda would live here year-round. If he returned his mother and daughter to London, would Rosemary be expected to go too? It might be fun living in a great metropolis that boasted many museums and libraries.

They wandered through the trees, and Rosemary pointed out various plants and animals, like the mushrooms clustered in a circle and the beetle scurrying up the bark. They even located a hedgehog asleep under a bush. Rosemary dissuaded the girl from bringing it in to show her grandmother. It wasn't until they had returned to the schoolroom that she learned from Warren that Lady Miranda's grandmother had been seeking the girl.

"The countess expects her to visit from time to time," the maid confided in Rosemary after taking her and her charge's bonnets.

Warren made it sound as if Rosemary should prepare Lady Miranda for a great journey through bandit territory.

"A short visit only, then," she told the maid. "I need to assess where Lady Miranda stands in her various studies."

Warren's eyes widened. "You'd deny the countess's wishes?"

"No one says no to Grandmother," Lady Miranda declared blithely, giving the globe such a spin it wobbled on its axis. "I favor her, Father says."

She did indeed, Rosemary saw when she and her charge arrived at the countess's suite a short time later. Though the countess wasn't as animated as her granddaughter, she still liked things just so.

Her sitting room was paneled in dark colors, the wood polished to a high sheen so that Rosemary's reflection paced her across the Aubusson carpet. The two wingback chairs flanking the hearth were upholstered in satin-striped gold fabric, and gold and black Chinese vases stood on either side of the fire. The lady herself wore her silvery hair piled up in a high peak over her head as her mother might have done, and her gown, though the high-waisted style now favored, was black silk embroidered in gold and silver. Rather much for a visit with her granddaughter, but Lady Miranda seemed to take it in stride as she went to kiss the lady on her cheek.

"Miranda," the countess acknowledged. "You may sit there. Introduce your governess to me."

"This is Miss Denby," Lady Miranda said, plopping herself down on one of the golden chairs.

The countess tsked. "Sit up properly, if you please. And that is not the correct form."

The girl scowled at her as she wiggled herself higher on the chair's seat.

"Indeed not," Rosemary said. "One always introduces the lower-ranking person to the higher ranked and always a gentleman to a lady, regardless of rank." She looked to the girl's grandmother. "Lady Howland, allow me to present your granddaughter, Lady Miranda."

The countess inclined her head. "Nicely done."

Lady Miranda's scowl only grew. "But that means Grandmother has a higher rank than I do."

"That is correct," her grandmother intoned.

Lady Miranda hopped off the chair. "That's not fair. My father is an earl."

"As was my husband, your grandfather," the countess reminded her. She nodded to her maid, who drew up a hard-backed chair for Rosemary to sit. "One takes one's precedence from both one's father and one's husband."

"And occasionally one's mother," Rosemary felt compelled to put in. "If your mother had been born a princess or a duchess in her own right, for example."

Lady Miranda stuck her nose in the air. "Father says Mother was the most important person in his life, and now I am."

"Yes, dear," the countess said as if she'd heard the statement too many times. "Now, tell me what you've learned today."

The girl's frown turned inward, then she brightened. "Your harpsichord is a percussion instrument, and the vibrations of the strings make the sound we hear."

"Why, I suppose they do," the countess allowed. "And geography? I asked Jonas to have the maps and globe moved from the library for you."

"I like the globe," Lady Miranda said.

Her grandmother nodded. "Good. Just remember your sphere is not confined to this dismal stretch of coastline."

Rosemary tried not to take umbrage. After the fine establishments the countess must have frequented, Grace-by-the-Sea might indeed look dismal.

"And you, Miss Denby?" The older woman turned her gaze her way. "What lessons do you intend to impart to my granddaughter?"

"She promised to show me the last remains of elephants," Lady Miranda offered, deigning to be seated again.

"Do not interrupt, Miranda," her grandmother scolded. "And do not embellish. Clearly, there are no remains of elephants in Britain."

"*Elephas*," Rosemary corrected her. "The family of elephants, and there were members here in England in ancient times."

My, but that scowl looked like Miranda's. "What nonsense is this?"

"It has been shown through the study of geology and comparative anatomy that other plants and animals once lived here in England," Rosemary explained. "But to answer your original question, Lady Howland, I hope to teach Lady Miranda that she has many spheres to make her mark—society, politics, natural history and philosophy, art, literature, and music."

They both looked to Rosemary's charge, who was wiggling on her seat, gaze out the window and tuneless hum sounding from her throat.

"That would be quite a feat," the countess said. "I wish you the best of luck."

Drake found himself looking forward to dinner that evening. It must be the opportunity to spend time with his daughter and mother after working most of the day on the new evacuation plans for the area with his cousin. The lord-lieutenant for Dorset required that each village have such a plan in case of a French landing. Grace-by-the-Sea's original plan had been tested recently and found to be severely lacking.

But he knew it wasn't just Miranda and his mother whose company he anticipated. Some part of him was eager to match wits with Miss Denby again. The woman certainly knew how to keep him on his toes.

"Perhaps another coat, my lord?" Pierson asked when he came upstairs to refresh himself before dinner. He seemed to have become a bit more sure of his role but had decided Drake must go about dressed in sartorial splendor on all occasions, no matter how humble.

"This is sufficient," he assured the new valet. He had stopped changing for the evening. It was Dorset, after all, not dinner with the king. His mother alone persisted in the practice of changing for dinner. Tonight, she arrived in the great hall resplendent in an amethyst-colored silk evening gown with jewels glittering at her neck and ears. As Miranda clattered down the stairs to join them, he caught sight of Miss Denby in her wake. The governess glanced down at her own muslin gown.

Drake moved to meet his daughter, who kissed him and then ran to do the same to his mother.

"You are perfectly attired for dinner in Dorset," he murmured to Miss Denby.

Miranda led her grandmother past, chatting happily, so Drake offered her governess his arm to proceed to the dining room.

She took his arm so cautiously she might have expected him to yank it out from under her. "Thank you, my lord. Would you like me to have Lady Miranda change in the future?"

"Not unless she's dirtied her day dress or we have company," he told her, leading her toward the dining room on the other side of the great hall.

It was not as large a room as the ones in the country estate he had been forced to sell to pay his father's debts, but the teak table down the center could seat a dozen easily. Drake took his place at the head, with his mother on his right and Miranda at his left. Miss Denby seated herself beyond Miranda.

"Do tell me you've found a way to rescue us from this rustication," his mother said after he'd asked the blessing and the staff began to serve.

"I plan on staying in Grace-by-the-Sea for the foreseeable future," Drake told her, accepting some of the salmon fillet. He nodded to Giles as the footman moved on to serving the countess. "My compliments to Mrs. Hillers. She certainly knows how to bring out the flavor in the fish."

His mother made a face, reminding him of his daughter, and Giles hastily continued to Miranda and Miss Denby. "How am I to maintain my social standing from the wilderness?" she complained.

"Hardly a wilderness," Drake protested as Dawson, their other footman, brought forth Brussels sprouts in cream sauce. "People flock to Grace-by-the-Sea from all over the land to take the waters."

His mother sniffed. "I am not an invalid."

"Neither are many others at the spa, from what I've heard," he said. "Though I suspect Miss Denby could tell us more about the wonders of the area."

She swallowed her bite of salmon before answering. "Aristocrats and gentry come to the spa to socialize as much as for the medicinal waters. There's an assembly every Wednesday evening and special events each month. The next will be the annual Harvest Fair."

"Rock heaving and cart driving, I suppose," his mother said balefully, stabbing at a Brussels sprout.

"More like prizes for the largest and highest-quality produce and animals, baked goods, and crafts," Miss Denby explained. "And there will be booths selling cider and pastries and all kinds of locally made items plus exhibits of various trades. Every family of any consequence in Grace-by-the-Sea and Upper Grace sponsors a display. Very likely Jesslyn, my brother's wife and spa hostess, will ask the earl for support as well."

And very likely he would have to refuse. Only James knew how the purse strings had tightened. He had had to forego some improvements to the castle to afford Miss Denby's wages as it was.

"We should go," Miranda put in. She'd already cleaned her plate and was looking for more. He nodded to Giles, who offered her the platter of salmon again.

"I'll take that under advisement," Drake said.

She turned to Miss Denby. "That means yes."

Was he so predictable? "That means I will evaluate the possibility," Drake informed her.

"And then you'll say yes," Miranda told him before looking to her new governess again. "He always does, you know." She switched subjects before he could correct her. "We have big caves under the castle. Tomorrow, I'll show them to you."

"Gracious no," his mother said, setting down her fork. "Haven't you learned by now the dangers they pose?"

Dangers his daughter could not conceive. But surely Quillan St. Claire and his crew would be long gone by the time Miranda ventured down.

His daughter frowned. "They aren't dangerous now that Dr. Bennett and the baker captured that horrid man who tried to take me to France with him."

They had managed to keep the details of Miranda's kidnapping mostly quiet. He didn't want it widely known his daughter escaped on occasion. Then too, the War Office agents had advised caution when they'd come to take Owens, the French agent, in hand. And James had hoped the silence would lure any remaining French agents or sympathizers out of hiding.

Yet there was that boat.

"The caverns are still dangerous, Miranda," he said before Miss Denby could question him about his daughter's story. "Falling rock, rising tides. I would prefer that you stay away from them."

She sat up on her chair. "But I want to show them to Miss Denby. She's going to teach me about what's in them."

That's what he feared. "I deem it unwise at this time."

Miranda's lower lip trembled. "But Father, just once? Just so Miss Denby can see the danger too? Then she'd know how to take care of me."

Miss Denby dropped her gaze and shifted on her chair, fingers toying with the lorgnette. She wanted to intercede, which way he could not say, but she was giving him room to make his decision.

His mother wasn't. "Stop whining, Miranda. It is most unattractive. I've a mind to tell Cook you will forego breakfast tomorrow morning."

"No," Drake said, and everyone looked up at him, clearly surprised. "Food is not to be used as punishment in this house. It isn't healthy." For some reason, he glanced at Miss Denby only to find a commiserating smile on her face. Perhaps, in the matter of these caverns, he should appeal to the one person who had shown him support.

"Miss Denby, do you feel a need to acquaint yourself with these caves?" he asked.

"I do," she said, lowering her fingers. "If only to determine how to prevent Lady Miranda from accessing them by herself."

His daughter's smile had blossomed at the initial answer,

but it withered as her governess reached the end of the statement.

"However," Miss Denby continued undaunted, "we will not be able to go tomorrow. We will have services at St. Andrew's in the morning and afterward I have my half day off."

"So soon?" his mother demanded.

Drake held up a hand. "An agreement is an agreement."

Miss Denby inclined her head. "Thank you, my lord. I believe we could visit the caverns on Monday. Would you be available to accompany us?"

Warmth pressed up inside him. His father, his mother, and his friends had all questioned why he wanted to take so active a part in his daughter's life. Even Felicity had forgotten to include him in her plans on occasion. None of them seemed to understand how important Miranda was to him. She was his daughter, his first responsibility, even though he now had many more to contend with. Yet Miss Denby appeared to have realized his need on short acquaintance. Clever woman.

"I'd be delighted," he said. "Say ten?"

"Perfect," she said. "Isn't that kind of your father, Miranda?"

"Yes," Miranda said, eyeing him. "Thank you, Father."

"You're welcome," he said.

But his daughter continued to watch him for the rest of the meal, as if she couldn't decide who was the greater attraction on this upcoming outing—her, the caves, or her governess.

CHAPTER FIVE

ROSEMARY TUCKED MIRANDA INTO BED that night, after Warren had helped the little girl into her nightgown. The maid had expanded her duties, which gave Rosemary some moments of peace.

"I will expect to find you here in the morning," she told her charge, arranging the embroidered coverlet around her slender frame.

Lady Miranda snuggled under the covers. "Why?"

"Because when you are not where you are expected to be, those who care about you worry."

Her mouth tightened a moment, as if she struggled to digest that fact. "Why should they worry? I'm grown enough to take care of myself."

Not in the slightest, but then, her life would have been so sheltered that she didn't perceive any sort of danger. Look at how she viewed these caverns. Only the bravest souls in the area attempted to sail in through the Dragon's Maw, the entrance to the caves from the sea. Rosemary wouldn't have tried it even if she'd known how to sail.

"It is enough that they worry," she said, straightening away from the bed. "I will see you in the morning."

Lady Miranda rolled over as if she intended to stay there all night.

Rosemary exited through the connecting door to her room, picked up the porcelain washbasin, and went out into the corridor to position it in front of Lady Miranda's door. Warren, who had been waiting to help her change, stared at her as Rosemary returned to her room.

"Please alert the other staff to leave the basin where it is until I retrieve it," she instructed the maid.

Warren grinned. "So she makes a racket when she escapes."

"That's the idea," Rosemary told her.

Warren helped her change, then she lay awake for a while, listening. She heard nothing from the corridor. Perhaps it had been their busy day, perhaps her admonition, but Lady Miranda was still in bed when Rosemary and Warren went to wake her in the morning, and Rosemary could return the basin to its proper place.

"Bring out Lady Miranda's best day dress and bonnet for church today," Rosemary told the maid. "But we'll finish breakfast before changing."

Lady Miranda raised her chin, blond curls a riot about her face. "I'm not a baby. I don't spill."

Rosemary regarded her through her lorgnette. "It never hurts to be cautious."

"You're already dressed," the girl pointed out. "Though I suppose that might not be your best."

Despite herself, Rosemary glanced down. She'd thought the yellow muslin gown, which draped across her chest to fall gracefully to her feet, was the height of fashion with its triangles embroidered along every edge. The cinnamon-colored ribbon under her breast matched the color of the hat she'd don for church. Hester had complimented her on her choice.

"This will suffice," she said firmly, "but I'll put an apron over it, just in case."

She was glad she did, for her skirts were still immaculate when she led Lady Miranda downstairs later that morning. The little girl wore a blue lustring gown with puffed sleeves and a double flounce along the hem. The material was so iridescent it shimmered when she skipped.

"The carriage will be here shortly," Mr. Jonas told Rosemary as he watched over the great hall. His narrowed gaze kept coming back to her charge, as if he expected her to dash over and rip down the tapestry along one high wall. But Lady Miranda stayed by her side, fidgeting only a little, the lamplight flashing on her polished leather slippers.

Suddenly, she broke away. "Father!" She darted to meet him as he came down the stairs.

He had finally decided to set aside the wine-colored waistcoat, it seemed, for he wore a navy cutaway coat with brass buttons; a satin-striped, cream-colored waistcoat; and cream-colored breeches. His cravat seemed a bit rumpled, but his smile was bright as he bent and hefted his daughter up into his arms.

"Good morning, Miranda," he said. Then he nodded to Rosemary. "Miss Denby."

Rosemary dipped a curtsey. "My lord."

"Why must we wait for Grandmother?" Lady Miranda asked, fingers playing with the high collar of his coat. His blond hair was cut over his ears, unfashionably short, but Rosemary caught herself wondering whether it felt as soft as it looked.

She snapped her gaze to the butler, who was watching her with hooded eyes, as if he could see each thought. She would not blush!

"Have patience, Miranda," the countess said on the landing. Her black gown, with its insert of pearly white around the neck, swept the stairs as she descended. The ostrich plume tucked into her black and white satin bandeau bobbed a welcome.

"Mother," the earl greeted as she reached their sides. He bent to peck her on the cheek. Miranda offered a lopsided hug. Rosemary turned to follow Mr. Jonas out to the carriage.

She generally worshipped with her mother, sister, and niece at St. Mary's in Upper Grace, but she'd attended weddings at St. Andrew's, so she was familiar with the chapel. The simple church had seen an unusual number of marriages since Jesslyn had been appointed spa hostess. She was something of a matchmaker. Rosemary's friend Abigail, the painter, and the spa physician, Dr. Linus Bennett, had married here only a fortnight ago by special license.

She held Lady Miranda's hand as they entered through the wrought-iron gate, passed the stone grave markers, and climbed the steps to the long white church with its three-story tower. Did the girl know her great-grandfather had bequeathed the slender silver cross on top? The previous earl had helped pay for the stained-glass windows on the south side. The light coming through now left jewel-like patterns on the dark wood box pews as she followed her employer and his mother up to the very first pew on the left of the center aisle, which was reserved for the Howland family.

The countess entered the pew first, then the earl, then Lady Miranda with Rosemary, who closed the door on the box behind her. Lady Miranda perched on the pew, but she started wiggling immediately. Rosemary cast her a look as she sat, then clasped her hands and directed her gaze to the cross behind the altar. Out of the corners of her eyes, she saw Lady Miranda do the same.

Thankfully, the hymns were particularly engaging, and the vicar's sermon on doing unto others what you would have done unto you proved inspiring. Lady Miranda listened intently, as if memorizing every word, each gesture.

"That's why you wanted me to stay in bed," she told Rosemary after they'd exited the church. "I wouldn't like not knowing where Father was."

"Exactly," Rosemary said.

"May I go say good morning to Uncle James, please,

Father?" Lady Miranda asked.

He nodded. "I'll join you shortly. Stay with your grandmother."

She and the countess moved away.

He turned to Rosemary. "You astound me, Miss Denby. Miranda has seldom sat so still or taken anything from the sermon, especially to apply it to her life. My compliments."

Warmth filled her. "Thank you, my lord, but it was your daughter's own intellect that drew the connection. She is very bright."

"Like her mother," he said. His gaze wandered after his daughter, but she saw sadness in it.

"Excuse me," he said and went to join his family.

For a moment, Rosemary stood alone. All around the churchyard, families and friends gathered, chatting in the September sunlight. She felt as if she were inside a glass bottle, separated from them. It was unsettling, as if she'd wandered into town in her shift. All her life, her mother and sister had been there waiting. She'd chosen to step out on her own, but she hadn't thought that would mean leaving them behind.

"Just the lady we need," Abigail Bennett declared, sailing up to her with green muslin skirts flapping.

Rosemary's smile of welcome broadened when she saw her sister-in-law Jesslyn was with the painter. Abigail and Jesslyn had been the best of friends since they were children in the village together, and now they welcomed Eva Howland as well. The outspoken redhead, pretty blond, and curly-haired bundle of energy had recently admitted Rosemary and Hester into their circle too.

"And how might I be of service?" Rosemary asked them now.

"Mother Denby told us you'd taken the position as governess to Lady Miranda," Jesslyn said, smoothing down her white muslin skirts. "Do you have any time to yourself?"

"Sundays after church and Wednesday evenings off," Rosemary told them. "Why? What are you two up to now?"

Abigail and Jesslyn glanced around, and Rosemary's interest leaped. Abigail had founded a shop where she sold her paintings along with items created by families all over the area. Hester contributed tatted collars to support the school in Upper Grace. The income had helped many a family through the winter. And Jesslyn was always envisioning new ways to attract people to the spa.

"A militia," Jesslyn whispered.

Rosemary blinked. "But Grace-by-the-Sea formed a militia earlier this summer. Wasn't Lark helping to train the men?"

"He is," Jesslyn agreed. "And they are gradually improving."

"But after the scare at the regatta, it's clear they need assistance," Abigail added.

Everyone had been terrified that day when a sloop flying the French flag had appeared in the middle of a race at the Grace-by-the-Sea regatta, then taken up a position opposite the entrance to the horseshoe-shaped cove as if intending to fire on the village. Fearing an invasion, the militia had attempted to evacuate the area, but the results had been disappointing to say the least. Only the quick thinking of Abigail and Dr. Bennett had turned the tide and kept the villagers and their guests safe.

"So, will you be recruiting additional members to join them?" Rosemary asked.

"In a way," Jesslyn hedged.

Abigail had never had much appreciation for roundaboutation. "We are chartering a Women's Militia," she announced.

Several heads turned their way. Jesslyn took Rosemary's and Abigail's arms and led them deeper into the churchyard, as if the lichen-covered stones would be less judgmental.

"Yes, a Women's Militia," she confirmed. "But we must go carefully."

"Jesslyn fears some will consider the effort scandalous, and we don't want to frighten off potential recruits," Abigail explained.

"Or spa guests," Jesslyn reminded her sternly.

"What sort of militia?" Rosemary interrupted. "Would we march? Use weapons? Attempt fighting?"

Jesslyn cast Abigail a glance, and the painter pressed her lips shut.

"We hope to drill at least once a week," her sister-in-law explained. "I'm not sure marching is necessary, but it would be good to instill the idea of obeying orders."

"I suppose some of us need more practice in that than others," Rosemary observed with a look to Abigail, who was turning a shade of red that clashed with her hair.

"We probably won't attempt firearms," Jesslyn continued, "but we must be able to do our part to protect the village should the French land next time."

"Including how to use everyday items to protect ourselves," Abigail put in as if she could be silent no longer. "Brooms, frying pans, rolling pins, hat pins for that matter. And I would be delighted to show everyone how to use a sword."

Rosemary looked from Abigail's determined face to Jesslyn's concerned frown. "You're going to train and arm the women of Grace-by-the-Sea to repel the French?"

Abigail raised her chin. "Yes."

Jesslyn nodded more slowly. "I suppose that's exactly what we're proposing."

Rosemary nodded. "Count me in."

How eager she looked. Drake had never seen the polished and professional Miss Denby appear so animated as when she stood in conversion with her sister-in-law, Mrs. Denby, and the physician's wife, Mrs. Bennett. As he glanced her way again, she threw her arms around first one, then the other. What could have caused such a reaction?

Miranda tugged on his hand. "Father, you are not attending."

He brought himself back to the group surrounding them. James, who looked enough like him to be his brother; his wife Eva, dark hair confined in a bonnet decked out in feathers an astonishing shade of pink; Drake's aunt Marjorie; and his mother were all gazing at him, looks ranging from amusement to annoyance.

"Forgive me," he said. "Woolgathering."

"Well, I know when I've overstayed my welcome," Eva said with a smile. "Come, ladies. I persuaded Mr. Ellison to bake cinnamon buns yesterday, and I would be delighted to share my hoard with you."

Miranda happily abandoned him to accompany her grandmother and Eva out of the churchyard.

"It's only next door," James reminded him as if he'd seen Drake watching the girl. "She can't get into trouble in such a short distance."

"You'd be surprised," he said, gaze going once more to Miss Denby. She had collected a number of other ladies around her now, and they stood with heads close together as if confiding secrets. If she had been with Miranda, he wouldn't have worried. Astonishing how she'd proven herself to him.

"I take it your new governess is working out well," James ventured.

"Remarkably well," Drake allowed, purposely turning his back on her distracting presence. "She's only been with us a day and a half, and already I see positive changes in Miranda."

"Excellent." James glanced up at the headland on the other side of the village, where the castle dominated the horizon. "Just keep them close until we're sure this business with France is settled."

Drake shook his head. "*Will* we be sure it's settled? The War Office swore us to secrecy when the agent came to take charge of the fellow masquerading at the spa."

"Worse luck," James agreed. "*We* don't know if any of his cohorts remain, and *they* don't know what happened to him, so they won't realize his plans came to naught."

"Meaning the French may still be determined to land an invasion force near Grace-by-the-Sea," Drake concluded.

"We are the only stretch of low bank along this part of the coast," James acknowledged, gaze returning to his. "Have you had a chance to look over my last changes on the evacuation plans?"

"I'll have any suggestions to you tomorrow," Drake promised. "Though I can hope the plan will never be needed."

"I share that hope, but I'd prefer to prepare for the worst." He glanced around the churchyard as if expecting to see French soldiers popping up behind every gravestone. "Eva still helps at the spa twice a week. She says we have more Newcomers than expected."

His cousin's wife had explained the taxonomy to Drake. Regulars at the spa at Grace-by-the-Sea were those who came frequently or even spent the summer or a good part of the year in the village. Irregulars visited on occasion. Newcomers were those appearing for the first time. They were generally friends, but a few had proven themselves foes of late.

"Isn't having an excess of Newcomers usually good for the village?" he asked his cousin. "More visitors mean business is improving, even with the threat of Napoleon's invasion. And more people leasing houses means more rent." Funny how he'd never had to care about that before. But, as earl, he owned half the land and half the establishments in the village, and the rent from them was his main source of income now.

"Perhaps," James said darkly. "But I'd rather know they *were* visitors and not part of some advance guard, hiding in plain sight. You still have a boat waiting for someone."

"I know," Drake said. "And it keeps me awake some nights. Part of me would like to sail the thing out, see if anyone comes looking for it."

James shook his head. "I don't want to make it that easy for them to escape. With it inside the castle, we have some assurance we can catch them if they seek it out."

"Still," Drake said, "short of questioning every visitor mercilessly, which I cannot believe would be good for business, I see no way to be certain who may be in league with the French."

James regarded him a moment, jaw thrust out as if aiming it at him. "There might be a way. You could visit the spa, see what you think of the Newcomers."

He had enough on his hands. "Why don't you visit? You're the magistrate, trained to see the truth."

James chuckled. "I wouldn't make that claim. And I don't visit often. It would be remarked upon, perhaps scare off our quarry. You have the excuse of escorting the countess."

Who would likely refuse to accompany him, but he didn't want to burden James with how little his mother enjoyed the village.

"I'll take that under advisement," Drake promised. "Grace-by-the-Sea is my home now. I'll do all I can to protect it."

CHAPTER SIX

HER MOTHER, HESTER, AND REBECCA came down to Lark and Jesslyn's house, Shell Cottage, for an early dinner Sunday, so Rosemary was able to be part of a family again. She couldn't completely forget how lonely she'd felt at the church, but she wasn't about to give up her position at the castle. Even the earl had noticed the changes in his daughter, and that after only a short time.

Monday proved she had far to go.

Her bedchamber was still dark when her eyes snapped open. Had that been a movement beside her bed? Surely another person was in the room with her. Her heart started beating faster.

"Oh, good," Lady Miranda said, and Rosemary made out her silhouette beside the bed. "You're awake."

"Apparently," Rosemary said, sitting up. "I thought we agreed you would stay in bed."

"I didn't worry anyone," Lady Miranda protested. "You have charge of me. Father said so. I came straight to you."

And was obviously rather pleased with herself.

Rosemary stifled a yawn. "We might as well get up, then. What time is it?"

"A quarter past five," the girl offered helpfully, scrambling away from the bed as Rosemary swung her feet over the side. "I looked at the clock in my room. I can tell time, you know."

"I know now," Rosemary said. "Warren can tell time too. She won't be up to help us for at least another hour." She bent to light a lamp. "But I can see to your dressing."

Easier said than done. The girl was a squirming mass, darting after a hair ribbon to show Rosemary one moment, a different pair of shoes the next. Rosemary stopped trying to tie the satin bow at the waist of her charge's muslin gown.

"Let's play a game," she told Miranda, who looked up eagerly. "Can you run to the opposite side of the room and back by the time I count to ten?"

"That's easy," Miranda scoffed.

"One, two…"

Miranda dashed across the rug to touch the far wall and was standing triumphantly in front of Rosemary again before she reached nine.

"Very good," Rosemary said. "How many times can you hop while I count?"

Twenty-five times, as it turned out. Miranda's face was now as pink as her gown.

"How long can you stand perfectly still?" Rosemary asked.

Miranda went rigid. The faint fluttering of the flounce on her chest was the only indication she was even breathing.

Rosemary started counting and tied Lady Miranda's ribbon, buckled her shoes, and pulled up her stockings in the process.

She reached forty-two before Miranda collapsed on the rug. "That was hard!"

"I would imagine," Rosemary said. "Perhaps some lessons on geography until Warren arrives."

They had studied the English coastline and completed a page of arithmetic when the maid appeared in the doorway.

"Breakfast first," Rosemary told Warren as she gaped. "Then you can help me change while Lady Miranda finishes eating."

Rosemary also went to reposition the washbasin once more.

It was only eight when she and Miranda started down the stairs for the great hall. Unsure what to expect in the caves, Rosemary had donned the gown she'd had designed for hunting fossils with her uncle. The green wool tied snuggly under her chest then draped in wide folds to just mid-shin. It was easy to gather up, easy to move in, and the skirts hid two deep, leather-lined pockets for carrying her tools. Her uncle had approved of it.

"Can't have you climbing up and down cliffs in muslin and slippers," he'd said before taking her to the village cobbler to have stout leather boots made for her. He'd dictated the height as well—just under her knees. But he'd let her pick the color of the leather—blue-green, like the Channel at sunrise. With her lorgnette on a ribbon around her neck, she always felt like she was ready for anything.

She fully expected to have to explain her attire to the earl, but they found the breakfast room empty. In fact, they found the entire ground floor of the castle quiet as they wandered, with only servants here and there going about their duties. They met Mr. Jonas as they were coming back through the great hall.

"Where's Father?" Miranda demanded.

The butler looked down his long nose at her. "Alas, his lordship has not risen as yet. Perhaps another hour or two."

Miranda sagged. "That's so long!"

For her charge, most definitely. "Perhaps we could go down for a moment," she told the girl. "Just to see that everything is ready for the longer visit with your father."

Miranda grabbed her hand and towed her toward the

kitchen.

Mrs. Hillers, the cook, took one look at the pair of them, snatched the loaf of bread off the worktable, and hugged it close to her apron-covered chest.

"We are not here for sustenance," Rosemary assured her, the younger assistant cook, and the pot boy, who had also both stopped work to stare.

Oblivious to their concern, Miranda traipsed over to a door in the wall by the hearth and opened it for Rosemary.

"You'll have to light the lamp," she said, pointing to a brass lantern hanging from the wall on a hook. "It's too high for me to reach. Someone else was down in the caves the last time I came."

Rosemary frowned as she lowered the lantern and turned back to the kitchen to light it. It seemed unlikely other members of Lord Howland's staff would make a habit of visiting the caves. Who else would have used the lantern?

Belatedly, she remembered the girl's story from the other night. Something about a horrid fellow in the caverns. Was there more reason for concern about this place than she knew?

Miranda shut the door and started down the stone steps. Rosemary made herself follow, ears tuned to any noise from below. Rough walls surrounded them as they descended, the air cooling, becoming damper. Moisture congealed on Rosemary's cheeks. The scent of brine drifted up.

"It's very dark," Miranda cautioned as they neared the bottom. "You'll have to hold up the lantern."

They stepped down onto the floor of a vast cavern. Raising the light, Rosemary gazed around at fallen rock, smooth patches of sandy ground, and a roof that arched away into darkness.

"Hear that?" Miranda asked, hopping from one of

the larger rocks to another. "That's the sea. It comes in through a hole just there. The boat sailed in that way."

Rosemary could see the craft as she ventured deeper into the cave. The tide must be out, for the black water lapped a fair distance from the two-man vessel that lay waiting on a stretch of sand. How long had it been here? Who had sailed it in?

Why hadn't they sailed it out?

Miranda lifted a rock. "What's this called?"

Rosemary peered closer. "Limestone. Centuries old."

Miranda nodded as if satisfied and hurled it into the shallows, where it splashed before settling.

"I see why you like it here," Rosemary said, gazing about. "The stratigraphy alone is intriguing, and it's all rather mysterious."

"Noisy too," Miranda said. "Listen." She cupped her hands around her mouth and shouted, "Lacy lollipops!"

"Lacy lollipops, lacy lollipops," the cave echoed back.

Rosemary grinned. "Howland's homecoming," she tried.

"Howland's homecoming," the cave agreed.

"Great green gobs!" Miranda yelled.

The hard Gs made it sound as if the cave was laughing.

"Sibilant syllabub," Rosemary called.

Miranda giggled. "It sounds like a snake hissing."

"We can discuss why during our lessons this morning," Rosemary said. "And why the rocks fall from the roof." She bent to pick up a good specimen.

"And how all this came to be?" Miranda suggested, moving back to her.

"Excellent idea. That too."

As if satisfied, Miranda turned for the stairs. Then she jerked to a stop. "Someone's been here."

Rosemary turned as well, half expecting to see the earl on the stair, ready to scold her for daring to come down without him. But the archway leading upward yawned empty.

"What do you mean, Lady Miranda?" she asked.

Her charge pointed to some of the larger rocks. "They weren't in a circle before."

Rosemary went to look. Three stones about the size of chair cushions were arranged in more of a triangle than a circle, as if prepared to have a good coz.

"Are you certain?" she asked the girl, who joined her. "They might have fallen that way or perhaps been pushed by a particularly rough tide."

"Father says the tide only goes to there," she said, pointing to a jagged line of ground that appeared lighter.

"Interesting," Rosemary said. "We should show your father when we bring him down."

"Yes, let's." She started for the stairs at her usual clip. Rosemary followed.

Less than a half hour had passed since they'd left the ground floor, but she was pleased to find his lordship up, dressed, and at his breakfast. He stood at the sight of them. He did not comment on her outfit, but he listened as his daughter told him her suspicions.

"I wish I'd been there to see it with you," he remarked when she finished. "I seem to recall we'd agreed we would go together."

"You weren't ready," Miranda informed him with a look that implied she was disappointed in him. "Uncle James says the tide waits for no man."

"But a daughter should wait for her father," he countered. "Keeping your word is important, Miranda. It's one of the ways others know we can be relied upon."

She leaned against him. "I'm terribly sorry, Father. We only went down for a moment, just to make sure everything was ready for you. We can go together as soon as you've finished."

His smile softened. "Very good. Why don't you practice your scales on your grandmother's harpsichord until I'm ready? I want a word with Miss Denby."

Rosemary drew in a breath. Miranda had no concerns, for she turned and skipped past her. Rosemary waited until the sound of the girl's boots faded down the corridor before meeting the earl's gaze. That blue was brighter than sunlight on the sea.

"Yes, my lord?" she asked dutifully.

He regarded her a moment, mouth set. "You couldn't wait?"

She'd blundered. She'd been so focused on harnessing Miranda's endless energy that she hadn't stopped to think about how he might feel to be left behind. Only to be expected, she supposed. She'd only just discovered how wretched being alone felt.

Before, she'd brazened her way through his comments. She saw one way forward now.

"I'm sorry, my lord," she said. "I thought only of Lady Miranda. Please forgive me."

She was apologizing? He'd been ready to argue, to match wits. He'd determined his strategy. For once, he'd take a leaf from his father's book and remind her of his position—in the village, in this household, in his daughter's life.

She'd taken the wind from his sails instead.

How could he berate her for thinking of Miranda first? He'd been putting Miranda first since the day she'd been born.

"Your zeal for my daughter's interests is commendable," he allowed. "But had I been with you, I would have been able to explain just such a circumstance that Miranda described, allaying any concerns."

"I understand," she said. "I told her it was quite possible

the position of the rocks was natural. Perhaps a lesson in probabilities is in order."

Neither James nor St. Claire would thank him for inviting her into their confidence, but if he was to ensure Miranda was protected, Miss Denby needed to know all. And this situation had given him an unexpected opportunity to learn her connection with the captain.

"By all means, teach her about probabilities," he said, "but it is possible the rocks were arranged by visitors."

She took a step closer, eyes widening. "Visitors?"

The movement drew his attention to her gown, and for the first time he took in the whole picture. The green wool was tight under her slender bosom and puffed out about her hips. If she hadn't been wearing boots, the skirt would have been cut scandalously short.

"Yes," he managed. "Visitors. Forgive me. What are you wearing?"

She glanced down at the strange gown as if she'd forgotten she'd put it on. "My hunting clothes."

He blinked. "You hunt?"

She met his gaze, her own becoming frostier. "Not the sort of hunting you might expect, my lord. I assisted my uncle in collecting fossils and other curiosities from the shore and along cuts through the hillsides. Certain concessions had to be made in fashion to accomplish our goal."

A fossil hunter. He would never have imagined. A million questions came to mind, but he would have to find another time. For now, what mattered was making her understand why strangers might be using the caverns.

"A worthy pastime, I'm sure," he said. "As to our visitors, I believe you know our local privateer."

She started, then resumed her usual professional demeanor, back straight, head high and proud. "Everyone knows Captain St. Claire."

"Indeed," Drake said, watching her. "He asked permission to use the caverns to land the goods he trades. I agreed. This isn't common knowledge, so I would appreciate you keeping the matter to yourself."

Her mouth twitched. "A dram for the mayor, a dram for the lord."

He'd heard the old rhyme about smugglers transporting alcohol without paying the tax and bribing those in authority to look the other way. Drake's face felt hot even though he'd done nothing wrong. "Spirits, of any kind, were not mentioned. He attempts to appear the gentleman."

That smile was wry. "Not often enough, but all the more reason to avoid the caves with Miranda."

"I don't expect their paths to cross. He is to come in only late at night, when the tides are right."

A frown gathered on her brow. "He has access to the castle, then?"

"He will take his goods through the kitchen. I'm assured we won't even be aware of his passage."

Her face hardened. "You place a great deal of trust in him."

Drake cocked his head. "Do you know a reason why I shouldn't?"

She opened her mouth, then shut it again and shook her head.

He could not leave it at that. "Has Captain St. Claire done something to make you take him in dislike?"

"How could he?" she asked, each word incised with precision. "Captain St. Claire had a distinguished naval career and was wounded in service to his country. He is highly regarded in the area. Every unmarried lady has set her cap at him."

Had she? He had no right to ask, even as her employer. He wasn't sure why he wanted so badly to know.

"I'm glad to hear you think well of him," he made himself say. "I had some concerns about allowing him such access to our home."

Her eyes narrowed. "And well you should. Everyone's heard the tale of the French sneaking through Castle How when it was empty, leaving messages to be picked up by those following from across the Channel. You cannot want trouble brought to your door again."

"And you think Captain St. Claire will bring it?"

"Possibly. Probably. He cares for no one but himself."

Not according to James. The captain cared for one thing only, it was true, but that was preventing France from winning the war. If he cultivated a carefree attitude, it was only to mask his intentions.

"I will take that under advisement," Drake promised. "Allow me to finish my breakfast, and we'll go down together. I know how Miranda can be when she loses interest."

"And she loses interest easily," she agreed. "Thank you for understanding about this morning, my lord. It won't happen again."

She curtsied and left before he could decide which she meant to avoid in future—her trip to the caves without him or her candidness about Quillan St. Claire.

CHAPTER SEVEN

THE NEXT TWO DAYS FLEW by. Rosemary kept Miranda's agile mind and body engaged, with no more trips to the cavern except with his lordship on Monday. He'd explained the probabilities of the rock placement being natural to his daughter, then explored along the edges of the vast space with them. He was so patient with Miranda that Rosemary could almost forget his questioning in the breakfast room. But he'd been watching her then, as if he'd expected her to tell him all about her previous fascination with Captain St. Claire. She wasn't about to confide. She hadn't even confessed her failings to her mother!

But she almost had to confess those failings in public, because the captain showed up at the assembly that Wednesday evening.

Hester had come to fetch her from the castle, and Rosemary had wrung a pledge from Miranda that the girl would stay in her room or with her father when Rosemary was away. Warren would remain nearby, just in case, and the washbasin was in position. But Rosemary couldn't help glancing back at the castle as Hester turned the gig on the drive.

"Worried about your little charge already?" her sister asked with a fond smile. Her silk-lined grey cloak was open enough for Rosemary to spy her deep red silk ballgown with the braid along the hem and modest neck.

"Worried for the others, more like," Rosemary said, facing forward and adjusting her own cloak about her. "Lady Miranda can be…challenging."

"Surely not for you," Hester said, sounding affronted anyone would suggest otherwise.

"No, not for me," Rosemary admitted. "Well, perhaps occasionally. But it's nothing I cannot handle."

Her sister sent her a look. "And the earl? Does he support you in your work, or is he proving challenging too?"

Not nearly as challenging as she'd expected. At times, he was rather pleasant to converse with, making her think, keeping her focused. And he was always rather pleasant to look upon.

Not that she'd confess as much to anyone, even her sister.

"He is a conscientious father," she said.

Hester laughed. "Oh, such high praise. I can see he's made an impression."

He certainly had. So much so, that she caught herself glancing back twice more before Hester turned the horse onto the road to the village.

They had arranged to leave the gig at Shell Cottage, where they freshened up before walking the short distance to the assembly rooms. Jesslyn was already there, being the hostess of the assembly as well as the spa. Others from the village were also making the trek. Torches outside the stately building up the hill glowed against the creamy stone. A briny sea breeze ruffled Rosemary's hair as she followed her sister inside.

"Excellent attendance tonight," Hester remarked, glancing around the high-ceilinged room with its ocean blue walls. Spa guests in velvet and silk condescended to chat with the members of the spa corporation council and their families. Prominent citizens from Upper Grace rubbed elbows with the stalwart officers from the encampment at West Creech. Voices buzzed as the quartet began taking its place in the alcove at the back of the rooms.

"Look," Hester said with a nod, "there's Mother."

Her voice trailed off, and Rosemary could see why. Her stomach dropped to the toes of her kid leather dancing slippers.

"Perhaps we could pretend we don't see them," Hester offered, turning away from where their mother was conversing with Captain St. Claire, resplendent in his evening black.

Rosemary raised her chin. "No. I refuse to allow him to ruin another evening. Come along." She started around the floor. Hester hesitated only a moment before joining her.

Captain St. Claire bowed as they approached. "Ladies."

"I believe you know my daughters, Mrs. Todd and Miss Denby," her mother said smoothly.

"Always a pleasure," he said.

"Captain St. Claire," Hester said. "It isn't often we have your company at the assembly."

He lay a hand on the chest of his pristine white waistcoat. "Mrs. Todd, I am touched that you'd notice. But how could I stay away from such beauty? Besides, with all the excitement recently, it seemed a good time to make sure my fellow citizens know that I remain interested in the welfare of the village."

"And the perfect time to ask our mother for the first dance," Rosemary said, hoping her smile wasn't as brittle as it felt. "What a gallant."

The tightness around her mother's eyes said she knew exactly what Rosemary was about. "You needn't feel obligated by that statement, Captain."

His smile never wavered. "Nonsense, madam. I would count myself fortunate indeed." He offered her his arm. "And perhaps your charming daughters will reserve a dance for me later."

Rosemary and Hester dipped curtseys, but neither commented as he led their mother out on the floor.

Rosemary dropped her voice an octave and oiled it well. "'I fear I don't dance, Miss Denby. Bum knee, you know.' Do you know how often he said that to me? What rubbish."

"Perhaps he's recuperated sufficiently that dancing no longer pains him," Hester, ever the kind-hearted, suggested.

"Perhaps he finds it a handy excuse to suit himself," Rosemary countered. She shook out her lace overskirt, wishing she could shake off her feelings as easily. "Forgive me, Hester. I only wanted us to enjoy ourselves tonight. Let's find partners."

That proved an easy task for her sister. Lord Featherstone, one of the spa Regulars, claimed Hester, silver-head high and steps elegant. It was said the older baron had come to Grace-by-the-Sea in search of a wealthy widow to wed, but so far his generous nature had prevented him from pressing his case with any of the ladies he had pursued. And he must know her sister, though a widow, was hardly wealthy.

Now, to find her own partner. Fingers twirling her lorgnette by its ribbon, she cast about and spied a handsome fellow making his way toward her. The light from the massive crystal chandelier overhead glinted on his short-cut blond hair. Her heart jumped into her throat. What was it about her anatomy tonight! First her stomach and now her heart!

"My lord," she said, curtseying, as the earl strolled up to her.

"Miss Denby," he greeted, inclining his head. "Has no one claimed you for a dance?"

"I hadn't decided on a partner," Rosemary told him. Better to correct the impression that she was in any way lacking.

"Then might I request the honor?"

Rosemary blinked. "You want to dance. With me?"

His blue eyes twinkled. "As a wise woman once commented, I distinctly said as much. Have you a difficulty with hearing or recall?"

She chuckled to find her words on his lips. "Neither. I would be delighted, my lord."

She allowed him to lead her out.

It was a simple country dance, with a great deal of skipping and turning and threading among the other couples. She didn't think it particularly new. Jesslyn generally maintained a smaller, familiar repertoire so as to encourage Newcomers to join in. Yet the earl went left when he should have gone right and missed taking her hand twice in the first segment of the dance until he settled into the pattern.

"Forgive me," he said when it came their turn to stand out at the end of the line. "It has been some time since I danced. I seem to have forgotten a great deal."

"The spa keeps a dance master on retainer," Rosemary said. "Perhaps you should request a few lessons to reacquaint yourself."

"Ever encouraging learning?" he teased her.

"Always," she told him. "Now, take my hands. We are about to rejoin the fray."

She was ready for his mistakes now, tilting her head in the direction they were to go, holding out her hands just a beat sooner than needed so he'd know to take them. They finished the set in style, and Rosemary curtsied to his bow.

"Thank you, Miss Denby, for a most edifying dance," he said, straightening. "Enjoy your evening off."

"I will, my lord," she answered and realized her spirits were just high enough to make that possible. Funny how one dance, one conversation, could change her outlook.

She sailed off the dancefloor to find Abigail waiting. The blue of her gown complemented her red hair. Rosemary had noticed her dancing with her physician husband down the line from her and the earl.

"We have a dozen women interested in joining the Women's Militia," her friend told her now, as others scurried around them to secure partners for the next set. "But Jess was right. More than one has expressed concerns about practicing openly."

"Censure?" Rosemary suggested. "Ridicule? Is that what they fear?"

Abigail nodded. "And I can't bring myself to argue otherwise. The painter, taking up arms? The woman who dispatches servants to visiting aristocrats, capable of knocking heads? Some of us could jeopardize our vocations by being seen as militant. Not that that deters me."

It wouldn't. Abigail had ever been the crusader in the village. But others might find it hard to explain themselves.

"We need a sponsor, someone the other villagers look up to. I don't suppose Mrs. Greer would join us."

Abigail shuddered. "I didn't ask. I'm not fond of her tongue-lashings. You know our spa corporation president's wife is nothing if not a stickler for propriety. You see her there by the countess? She's positively salivating to make the lady's acquaintance, but she would never presume to attempt an introduction."

Rosemary could see the lady in question. The angular Mrs. Greer was dressed in white silk tonight, with rosebuds embroidered along the neck and hem of her gown. With her ostrich plumes waving, she looked every inch the countess's equal.

But Lady Howland sat on a chair against the back wall, with her former companion, Mrs. Marjorie Howland, at her side, as if determined to keep her distance from the entire company.

"There's nothing for it," Abigail said. "We'll have to find somewhere on the edge of the village to practice, away from prying eyes, preferably with walls and a floor impervious to our actions."

Rosemary started. "I believe I know just the place. I'll tell you if it's possible on Sunday. If all goes well, be prepared to start instruction on Monday morning."

Drake sat with his mother and aunt along the wall of the crowded assembly room. He'd told James he'd keep an eye on the Newcomers, but it was almost impossible to spy them among the guests.

"So many lovely ladies in attendance and not an heiress among them," his mother lamented.

Drake frowned. "I understand heiresses occasionally visit the spa, Mother. I recall meeting a Mrs. Harding recently, a wealthy widow I believe, though Eva confided she has returned home for the winter. Were you expecting her company?"

His mother patted his hand as if to console him. "No, dear. I'm looking for a bride for you."

He had the sudden urge to leap to his feet and flee. "I have no plans to wed."

"Nonsense." She drew back her hand. "Your marriage to a young lady of considerable fortune will allow us to remove ourselves from this depressing little backwater."

"Now, dear," his aunt Marjorie put in, as warm and welcoming in her sunny yellow silk as his mother was commanding in her black, "you know Grace-by-the-Sea is far from a backwater. The spa brings in good company from all over. Look how many are attending the assembly tonight. It's as great a crush as any of your London balls."

His mother sighed. "And still an utter dearth of eligible

females."

For some reason, his gaze was drawn to Rosemary Denby. After their dance, which he'd survived only because of her help, she'd spent time talking with Mrs. Bennett, her sister and mother, Eva, and her sister-in-law while the dancing continued. Now the partners were changing again. He hadn't considered attempting the floor after his trouble in the first dance. Dare he ask her for a second?

No. A gentleman only requested a second dance if he was considering courting the lady. He wasn't courting. He would likely have to marry again one day to beget an heir, but he certainly wasn't about to wed an heiress he barely knew. Once had been enough.

But even as his gaze lingered on Miss Denby, he spied Captain St. Claire approaching her. Her eyes narrowed, and she turned and hurried in the opposite direction. The redoubtable Miss Denby, running away? Surely not.

St. Claire must have realized he'd missed his opportunity, for he drew himself up short. Drake could almost see the calculations spinning through his mind. Should he pursue? Find a more willing lady?

Apparently, his consequence was elevated enough that defeat was not an option. The fellow dodged across the ballroom, narrowly missed colliding with others, and raised more than one eyebrow in the process. Then he put himself directly in her path just a few feet away from Drake and his family. It was all too easy to overhear the conversation.

"I believe you owe me a dance, Miss Denby," St. Claire said.

"I believe I owe you nothing, Captain," she returned. She started forward again, and he caught her arm.

"Come now. We've had our differences, you and I, but surely you haven't decided to take me in dislike." The puffed-up privateer made it sound a sacrilege!

Drake pushed to his feet, setting his mother to frowning.

"Perhaps it is merely a change in vision," Miss Denby was saying as Drake approached the pair from behind. "I thought I saw a gentleman worthy of my admiration. You thoroughly disabused me of that notion."

St. Claire's hand pressed against his cravat. "And here I thought you, as a new governess, would value honesty."

"I will *not* have this conversation with you, sir." She spun on her heel and froze, gaze hitting Drake's. Were those tears in her eyes?

"Ah, Miss Denby," he said brightly. "We'll be leaving shortly. Would you care for escort back to the castle?"

She latched onto his arm as if it were a rope securing her to the side of a cliff. "That would be delightful, my lord. I've had quite enough frivolity for one night."

Without a nod to St. Claire, he led her away.

"The countess?" she asked.

"I'll fetch her," Drake promised. "Right now, I think a strategic retreat in order." He led her into the short corridor between the assembly rooms and the main door.

"Thank you, my lord," she murmured, stepping deeper into the shadows. "I feel as if I owe you an explanation for what you witnessed."

"I believe you owe me nothing, Miss Denby," he said with a gentle smile.

She shook her head. "I can see I must watch my words more closely if you intend to repeat them to me."

"And I fear I am doomed to repeat them because they fit situations so well."

He was rewarded with a ghost of a smile. "Nevertheless, you are my employer, and you have an arrangement with Captain St. Claire, so you should know why I hold him in such antipathy."

She drew in a breath as if summoning her courage, and Drake nodded for her to continue. Indeed, he would not have stopped her for the world.

"I am a bluestocking," she announced, "and a thoroughly unrepentant one. That fact seems particularly concerning to the gentlemen who have attempted better acquaintance with me."

"The more fool them, then," Drake said. "An intelligent wife is priceless."

She peered closer in the dim light as music from the quartet trickled down the corridor. "You truly believe that. How extraordinary."

He had obviously gone up in her estimation. He refused to preen. "I take it Captain St. Claire was one of those fools."

"Worse." She dropped her gaze, fingers wrapping about her lorgnette. "I did the very thing I despise in a courtship. I saw a particularly pleasing exterior and assumed the interior must match. I decided he was the only man for me, and I threw myself at his head. He let me know he has no interest in furthering an acquaintance with a lady. Yet he is perfectly happy to dance and flirt with any number of ladies as if wishing to further *their* acquaintance. It was me he found abhorrent."

The man was worse than a fool—raising expectations only to dash them. Even now, he could feel her trembling. In mortification? In anger? Oh, how he knew those feelings.

"Thank you for telling me," he said. "I don't know whether it helps, but you are not alone in this."

She eyed him as if she highly doubted that.

"It's true," he insisted. Perhaps it was the darkness, perhaps her presence, but confidences were easy to share.

"I adored my late wife, Felicity," he started. "She was everything I had ever dreamed of in a bride. Dozens of men, including my cousin James, vied for her hand, and she picked me. I had never been prouder. But I learned later that she chose me under duress. Her family was on tenuous standing socially. Her heart belonged to James, but, out of duty, she chose the son of an earl rather than the son of a land steward. She was always kind, always caring, and never really mine."

Her face sagged, as if her heart hurt along with his. "I am so sorry, my lord. We both deserve to be loved for who we are, what we have to offer a partner."

He'd never thought of marriage that way before. "A partnership. That's it exactly—two people committing to the same future, the same life."

"Two hearts beating as one," she murmured. "That's what I've always believed as well."

"Then do not give up, Miss Denby," he said. "The captain may be oblivious to your qualities, but other gentlemen will surely prize them. You have only to keep your eyes open."

"I think it wiser that I attend to my duties, my lord," she replied. "I may not make the perfect wife, but I can be a superlative governess. Thank you for giving me that opportunity."

He inclined his head, but he couldn't help thinking that she would excel at whatever she undertook, even the role of bride.

CHAPTER EIGHT

WHO WOULD HAVE THOUGHT THE earl would love in vain?

Seated with her back to the coachman, Rosemary watched him as the carriage returned them to the castle. The lanterns on the outside of the coach cast wavering shadows across his lean face. It wasn't just the death of his wife that made him seem lost. It was the loss of an ideal, a dream.

True love.

She knew the allure of it. To be truly valued, adored, for herself. What more could anyone want? She wasn't sure why she had thought Quillan St. Claire might offer her that. Perhaps it was because he too was alone—a man known only to himself. Perhaps it was that he had seen so much more of the world. Surely a well-traveled individual would appreciate variety, the differences among people. But he hadn't seen anything worth loving in her. Easy enough to feel a bit melancholy at that.

But she could not allow herself to fall into such a state over Quillan St. Claire, for all he could be dashing and audacious and in all ways a man.

Oh! She was impossible!

She was merely glad to find that Miranda had been true to her word, or at least Rosemary found her asleep in her own bed when she checked before retiring. The fact that her charge slept until seven the next morning made her suspect the girl had been up late.

"And how did you spend your evening?" she asked as they breakfasted together in the schoolroom.

"I couldn't sleep," Miranda confessed, silver spoon dripping porridge back into the porcelain bowl. Rosemary had spoken to Mrs. Hillers, and the food was plentiful.

"Someone left a washbasin in the corridor," Miranda explained. "I tripped over it, and it made such a noise! But Warren agreed to come with me on a ramble. Did you know there are three suits of armor on the third story of the west wing? One's my size. I measured the arm. Warren said I should ask you before trying it on."

"We should ask your father if it has particular historic value," Rosemary cautioned, reaching for a piece of toast. "If not, we can take it apart to see how it's constructed, determine why someone your age might need armor, and decipher how it was used. And *then* you may try it on."

Miranda slid off her chair. "There was a mace too, a great silver ball with spikes. I want to see if it will smash a pot."

It could probably smash a head! "That may have to wait until we practice a bit."

Her eyes lit. "You'll let me practice with a mace?"

"No," Rosemary said firmly. "You may practice with a blunt-edged wooden staff. When you have proven you can control it without doing yourself or anyone else harm, we can discuss moving on to more lethal weapons."

"Is that what Grandmother meant when she said you would give me an unconventional education?"

Miranda sounded thoroughly entranced with the idea. The countess would not have been as enthusiastic.

"I cannot presume to know what the countess meant," Rosemary said. "I promised your father and grandmother

I would equip you to understand what you might accomplish in this world. To do that, we must try many things."

"Many, many things," Miranda agreed happily. She grabbed Rosemary's free hand and tugged. "Hurry and finish, Miss Denby. I want to ask Father about the armor."

Rosemary had something else she wanted to ask him in any regard, so she quickly finished her breakfast and allowed Miranda to tow her out of the schoolroom and down the corridor for the stairs.

They once more found the earl in the breakfast room, attended by the footman Rosemary had learned was named Giles. His lordship stood as they entered, and Miranda swung herself up onto a chair beside him as if fully intending to help herself to a second course. "Good morning, Father. That looks good."

"I'd be delighted to share." He nodded toward Giles, who headed for the kitchen. "And good morning to you as well, Miss Denby."

"My lord." She sat beside Miranda as the earl resumed his seat.

"Miss Denby says I may use a mace," Miranda announced.

Cup at his lips, he choked on his tea and lowered his hand carefully. "A mace," he said when he could find breath.

"Lady Miranda discovered a suit of armor in the west wing that intrigues her," Rosemary explained as he wiped tea off his hand, where it had spilled. "I haven't seen it yet, but she tells me it is close to her size. I offered to let her study it, if you agreed."

He frowned as he set down the napkin. "I believe I know the one she means. It was ceremonial armor, used when her great-great-great-grandfather was knighted at the age of thirteen. You may study it so long as you can put it back exactly the way you found it."

"Thank you, Father." Miranda sat up taller as Giles

returned with a gold-rimmed plate loaded with salmon and scrambled eggs. As he set it down before her, he looked to Rosemary, brow up as if to ask whether she wanted any. She shook her head.

"My lord," she said as Giles returned to his place along the wall and the earl and his daughter tucked into their food, "I had another request for you."

He looked up. "Oh?"

"Yes. Would it be permissible for Lady Miranda and me to host a group of women from the village once a week?"

Miranda frowned at her. Her father nodded. "Certainly. Excellent idea. It would give Miranda practice in the social niceties."

And drilling and defending the village, but she saw no need to concern him with the specifics. "Thank you. Until Lady Miranda grows more proficient, perhaps we could forego attendance by the countess."

That was the trickiest part, and she thought he might protest. After all, this was Lady Howland's home. She would generally be the hostess for any visitor. Mrs. Greer's adulation proved how much the women of the village longed to associate with her.

But he nodded. "Very wise. My mother's expectations tend to be rather high. Perhaps the ladies can greet her separately."

"Leave it to me," Rosemary said.

She ought to be pleased he trusted her enough to agree. Instead, guilt jangled like a badly played harpsichord. He seemed far more reasonable than most men, but she'd been disappointed enough that she didn't dare share the truth with him just yet. Too many people might be hurt.

So, she sat quietly and let the two of them talk, only interrupting when Miranda spoke with her mouth full or forgot to use her napkin. Finally, Miranda ate the last bite, slipped off her chair, gave her father a credible curtsey, and scampered from the room.

"Armor," her father said with a shake of his head as Rosemary rose to follow. "Don't let her use the mace."

"Not today," Rosemary promised.

They were still studying the armor Friday morning when Warren appeared in the schoolroom doorway.

"Begging your pardon, Miss Denby," she said. "But Davis says Lady Miranda and you are expected to go with the countess to the spa today. We need to get her changed."

As her chest was currently wrapped in the shiny cuirass, with a jointed pauldron weighing down one shoulder, very likely. Between Rosemary and Warren, they managed to dress the girl in a frilly muslin frock with a blue satin ribbon and have her ready when her grandmother called for her at half past eleven. Rosemary had already been suitably dressed in a blue wool gown that tied under her chest. Of course, the countess put them all in the shade in her white muslin gown covered by a grey wool overdress lined in lavender, with a lavender collar and ribbon around her chest and a lavender turban on her head.

As they descended the stairs in her wake, Rosemary was surprised to see the earl waiting at the bottom.

"I thought to accompany my ladies," he said with a smile at his mother and daughter.

"Then this might not be an utter waste of time after all," the countess said, sweeping past him for the door.

Rosemary had visited the spa many times over the years. Jesslyn had had it redecorated like the conservatory of a great house, with white columns, potted palms along the pale blue walls, pastoral scenes on the arched ceiling, and wicker chairs here and there to encourage conviviality. It was difficult for Rosemary to look at the creamy stone fountain in the corner across from the white lacquered harpsichord without hearing her uncle's voice.

"Sulphur, soda ash, magnesium, and iron," he'd say,

pointing to the faint chalky deposit on the inside of the fluted bowl. "They call it mineral water for a reason."

She'd never been particularly fond of the slightly fizzy water, but Miranda shuddered after one sip.

The earl drained his glass.

Jesslyn's elderly aunt, the diminutive Mrs. Maudlyn Tully, crept closer, tight grey curls trembling on either side of her round face. Rosemary had become acquainted with Maudie and her eccentricities. The widow always dressed in black and frequently foretold doom.

"Feeling bilious?" she asked Lord Howland.

"Not in the slightest," he assured her.

She looked disappointed.

"Highly efficacious," the countess pronounced, holding her glass delicately. "Perhaps another."

"Allow me, dear lady." Lord Featherstone stepped in with a bow. He looked quite the gentleman in his navy coat and buff breeches. Taking the glass from her hand, his fingers brushed hers. The countess turned pink.

"How delightful to see you all today," he said as he caught the splashing liquid from the fountain in the crystal glass. Maudie watched his every move as if determined to find fault. "You left the assembly so early the other night many of us were concerned." He handed the countess her glass with a bow. "I hope all is well."

"Perfectly fine," she said. "Forgive us for worrying you, my lord. We thought it best to return home to dear Miranda."

He glanced over at the earl's daughter. Miranda gazed back at him.

"Do you drink the water?" she asked.

"At least two glasses every day," he told her.

"Do you like it?" she demanded.

"Miranda," the countess scolded, but the silver-haired lord bent to put his gaze on a level with the girl's.

"I like knowing I am contributing to my health. At

my age, that's important enough I can overlook inconveniences."

"You are not so very old," the countess simpered as he straightened. "A fine wine improves with age."

He smiled. "You are too kind, Countess."

Rosemary glanced between them. Was a romance brewing? She met the earl's gaze and knew by his smile he thought so too. He took Miranda's hand and led her away from the pair as if to give them some privacy.

Jesslyn beckoned Rosemary closer just then, and she hurried over before Miranda might need her. Her sister-in-law still resembled a dewy miss with her blond curls and slender curves, but those big blue eyes held an intelligence Rosemary respected.

"Abigail says you may know where our militia can practice," Jesslyn told her.

"The caves under Castle How," she explained. "They're large enough to hold us, and no one will overhear us or watch what we do."

"Perfect!" Her smile faded as she glanced toward the earl. "But will he allow it?"

"He already granted his permission. I told him you all would come visit Lady Miranda. I'd like her to join us."

"He may not approve when he learns the full of it," Jesslyn warned. "You could lose your position."

"Let me worry about that," Rosemary said. "This Women's Militia is far more important to everyone's safety." She glanced around and lowered her voice. "I only want to know one thing—are we certain the French have left?"

"No," her sister-in-law admitted, "though I try not to discuss the matter in front of the guests. We've had a half dozen gentlemen arrive since the regatta, and one, Mr. Donner, who has long overstayed his time." She nodded to where a tall brunette fellow in a bottle-green coat and chamois breeches was bowing to the countess. "Any could be a spy or exactly what they seem—English gentlemen enjoying the spa."

"At least the spa is busy," Rosemary commiserated. "I recall when the spa corporation thought this impending invasion would frighten everyone away."

"Not yet," Jesslyn said. "And I believe the countess's attendance will do us even more good. There has been a decided hole in our society since Mrs. Harding and Mr. Crabapple left last week. The countess will attract interest. So will the earl. I can imagine any number of ladies posturing to catch his eye."

Why was her spine stiffening? "He needs no help in finding a bride," Rosemary warned her, thinking of her conversation with the earl the night of the assembly. "He still mourns his wife."

Jesslyn's smile dipped. "Poor man. Then I'll simply have to turn my matchmaking eye in your direction instead."

"You will not," Rosemary told her sternly. "I am doing exactly as I please."

Her sister-in-law winked at her. "So I see. Carry on, my dear."

As Miranda dragged him about the spa, from the chess board on a table under the bronze wall clock to the wide windows overlooking the cove, Drake kept an eye on the gentlemen. It wasn't lost on him that the number of visitors was swelling. If it was in anticipation of this upcoming Harvest Fair, Mrs. Denby certainly knew how to attract interest. He recognized Admiral Walsey with his booming voice and impressive gut, but the others were new to him. Were any of them French agents?

And did they have to keep ogling Rosemary?

She was animated in her conversation with the spa

hostess. And she looked rather fine today in that blue gown tied under her bosom and falling to her toes. The color made her eyes sparkle and brought out the rose in her cheeks.

Or perhaps his study of her was doing that. And when had he decided to think of her as Rosemary?

Miranda twitched her own frilly white skirts from side to side. "Can we go now?"

"Have patience," he said. "Your grandmother is enjoying herself for once."

Miranda pouted. "I'm not enjoying myself. There's nothing to do here. Everyone is old."

Her voice was sufficiently loud and whining that several heads turned their way. Mrs. Tully moved in beside them with a rustle of her black skirts.

"Have you heard the hound yet?" she asked Miranda.

His daughter brightened. "The spa has a dog?"

"No, worse luck," she said. "We might be able to catch Napoleon sneaking into the village if we did. I speak of the Hound of the Headland, a great white beast with glowing red eyes."

Drake began to question the conversation, but at least Miranda was being attentive. Across the room, his mother trilled a laugh at something Lord Featherstone had said.

"Where does the Hound of the Headland live?" his daughter asked breathlessly.

Mrs. Tully looked both ways as if expecting someone to dash up and stop her from confiding all. Then she leaned closer. She was a small enough woman that she was nearly eye to eye with Miranda, who was tall for her age.

"Some say the Downs above the village. Others say the caves under Castle How."

He should not be surprised she knew about the caves. James claimed most youths in the village grew up passing the tale.

"Not the caves," Miranda told her. "I've looked."

"Still, you must beware," she insisted, voice low and haunting. "And there's always the Lady of the Tower, pining for her lost love, alone in the castle."

That was enough. "Very kind of you to think of us," he said to Mrs. Tully. "We should not detain you further. Miranda, go see if Miss Denby is ready to leave."

His daughter hurried off. He turned to see to his mother, and Mrs. Tully grabbed his arm.

"They're coming through the castle, you know."

Drake paused. James had related the stories told of this woman. She'd lost her sailor husband early and retreated to fantasy in her grief. She'd been prophesying doom and gloom ever since, always dressing in black, telling tall tales. But James's wife Eva doted on the lady. Shouldn't he at least attempt to hear her out?

"Who's coming through the castle, madam?" he asked gently.

She squeezed his arm. "The French!"

Drake nodded. "So I've heard. Would you know which of these fine gentlemen might be associated with them?"

Her gaze darted around, as if she saw danger everywhere. "All of them. Or none. They're tricky that way. But I've seen Napoleon himself on the headland."

Perhaps riding a hound with glowing red eyes. He lay his hand over hers, trying not to show his disappointment. "I'll be watchful."

She snatched back her fingers as if he'd burned her. "You'd better do more than watch! There's only so much the mermaids can do, and there's no trusting the trolls, fickle things that they are."

"Yes, of course," Drake managed. "I'm surprised I didn't see that myself. Thank you for your counsel."

"Oh, you don't believe me any more than the rest of them," she complained, and she turned and stomped off.

He was staring after her when Miranda skipped back

to him, bringing Rosemary with her. "We're going back to practice with the mace."

"Study the armor," Rosemary corrected her.

"And Tuesday, Miss Denby says we can visit the shore to collect specimens."

"If the weather holds," Rosemary amended.

The shore? Near where the caves opened, and Captain St. Claire and the French entered? Where mermaids gathered, and trolls marched? Under the headland inhabited by Napoleon, the Lady of the Tower, and a hound with glowing red eyes?

"That sounds delightful," Drake said. "I'll join you."

CHAPTER NINE

ROSEMARY WAITED ONLY UNTIL THE earl, countess, and Miranda were seated in the carriage to return to the castle before asking what was foremost on her mind. "Pardon me, my lord, but is there a reason for concern about Lady Miranda and me visiting the shore on Tuesday?"

The countess frowned, but the earl leaned back against the squabs. "No."

Then why insist on accompanying them? She could not push her case too far lest she sound insubordinate. Such a difficult line to walk!

"I know the tides," she ventured, trying to think of possible objections. "They are published daily in the *Upper Grace Gazette* and annually in Mr. Smythe's almanac. We have a copy in the schoolroom."

"Then you can choose an appropriate time when the beach is clear," he acknowledged.

What else troubled him? "I am well aware of potential hazards," she tried. "I've walked the shore and scaled the cliffs with my uncle since I was a girl."

"I'm certain Miranda couldn't be in better hands," he said.

His daughter was busy gazing out the window as they left the village and started out onto the headland. She gave no indication she even heard what was being said.

The countess, however, glanced between Rosemary and her son.

"I don't understand. Is there some issue with Miranda going down to the shore?"

"No," the earl repeated. "I think it a fine idea. That's why I'd like to accompany her."

Perhaps.

But he hovered when they returned to the castle, joining them in the schoolroom and listening while Miranda told him everything she'd learned about the armor.

"And this is the helm," she said, shoving the helmet down over her head. Her next words boomed out through the grill. "I can see you through the slits. Can you see me?"

"No indeed," her father said from his place on one of the chairs. "Can you breathe?"

She sucked air in and out noisily. "Yes. But it's hot."

"Imagine fighting in such a thing," Rosemary said, helping her lift it off. "In the sun on a warm summer day for hours."

"You'd cook," Miranda said. "Like a lobster in a pot. Cook was boiling one once when I went to the kitchen. May I try the mace now?"

It took the combined refusal of Rosemary and the earl to dissuade her.

Rosemary half expected to find him in the schoolroom when she and Miranda entered on Saturday. Had she shaken his faith in her that he felt the need to watch over his daughter? What had she done wrong?

Especially since having him there with them felt so right.

She could not understand why. He was attentive—asking her questions and answering some from Miranda, and she envied him his easy camaraderie with his daughter that she had never achieved with her mother. But, working beside him to teach Miranda almost made them feel like a family, and she must remember she was only a member of his staff.

She didn't know whether to be relieved or disappointed when he did not join them on Saturday. Warren related the reason as she brought them tea later in the day.

"He went down to that spa again. Davis says the countess ordered him to look for an heiress to wed so we can all go back to London."

Rosemary frowned at her as she poured tea for herself and Miranda in the dainty violet-patterned cups.

"He has to marry an heiress because we're penniless," Miranda supplied, sloshing her cup sufficiently to splatter tea on her muslin day dress. "I heard Grandmother say so."

Hardly penniless if he could afford to maintain a staff. Or would they all have to forego wages this quarter? She'd heard from Jesslyn that Mrs. Catchpole, who found temporary staff for visitors, had little patience with those who didn't pay their servants.

But, having loved in vain, surely he would not marry for money alone, even if he must marry again at some point. She knew the rules of inheritance. He needed a son to become the next earl, or his estates would go to some distant relative who might not care about Miranda's welfare. It must be concern for her charge that made the idea of him marrying at all so unpalatable to her.

She and Miranda attended church services with the earl and countess on Sunday, and she fancied the earl looked just a bit saddened when she excused herself to start her half day off. Very likely it was because Miranda was already tugging at him to look at the gravestones. Rosemary turned her back on them and went to meet with Abigail and Jesslyn to tell them the plan for the Women's Militia.

"Miranda and I will meet you in the great hall at eight and offer to take you on a tour of the castle," she explained as they stood at the edge of the churchyard, sea breeze setting their bonnet ribbons to fluttering. "We'll finish in the kitchens and go down to the caves, where we can practice."

"I may not be able to join you for a few weeks," Jesslyn warned. "I haven't been able to find anyone else to watch the spa. Everyone I'd normally ask will be at the meeting."

They were indeed. More than a dozen women showed up at the front door of Castle How Monday morning. Besides her friend Eva, Rosemary recognized the blond-haired Mrs. Catchpole, the employment agency owner; slender Mrs. Ellison, wife of their baker; Abigail's mother, Mrs. Archer; and both the Misses Pierce, owners of the linens and trimmings shop. Jesslyn hadn't come, but her aunt, Maudie, strolled in, gaze going longingly toward the statues flanking the hearth as if hoping they had stories to tell.

Mr. Jonas raised his black brows as the knocker continued sounding, but at the unfashionable hour or the number of visitors, Rosemary wasn't sure. She had let the butler know she and Miranda would be hosting some ladies with the earl's approval and managed to dissuade him from waking the countess now. She and Miranda had also slipped down to the caverns earlier and lighted lanterns, leaving them safely burning on a stretch of sand.

It was half-past eight when they all ventured into the kitchen.

"And Lady Miranda is certain the rocks contain valuable minerals," Rosemary said loudly as they entered. "Come this way, and I think you'll see what I mean."

Mrs. Hiller and the pot boy stopped work to watch them. Her assistant waved at Mrs. Ellison, who was apparently her mother.

Miranda led their comrades down the stairs. Rosemary remained in the kitchen until the last lady had passed, then shut the door firmly behind her.

Once down on the rock-strewn shore, the ladies glanced around at the cavern. Their hushed voices still echoed, until it sounded as if a hundred women prowled the shadows. Abigail went to the edge of the receding tide, beside the abandoned boat, and turned to face them.

"Thank you all for coming," she said as they gathered in a half circle around her. "I'm glad so many believe in the need to protect our village."

"Well, the men can't do it all, can they?" Miss Pierce the elder asked with a shake of her grey head.

"They proved that when the French showed up on the waves," her younger sister agreed.

The others nodded.

"And we cannot rely on the mermaids," Maudie put in sadly.

"No indeed," Abigail said. "We must learn to rely on ourselves. That said, there may be times when we must act as one. So, we'll start with some marching drills. You've all seen the Men's Militia, I trust."

Heads nodded again, and more than one laugh floated up. Their magistrate had chartered the militia as a way to protect the men when the army had threatened service overseas. But the men of Grace-by-the-Sea had shown a noted difficulty in obeying orders, even from their own magistrate.

"Right," Abigail said, rubbing her hands together. "Line up arm's length apart in a row. Very good. A little closer, Maudie. Mrs. Ellison will not bite."

"I might," Maudie said. "She smells like cinnamon buns."

Before Rosemary could catch her, Miranda wiggled in between them and sniffed. "You do!"

Mrs. Ellison smiled at them. "The dangers of being married to a baker, I fear."

"Focus, if you please," Abigail admonished. "Stand at

attention, heads high, eyes forward."

Rosemary straightened her spine and was pleased to see Miranda doing likewise as she returned to her side.

Abigail's gaze traveled the line of women. "Very good. Ready? Right face."

Everyone swiveled to the right.

"Well, will you look at that," Mrs. Archer marveled.

"I'd brag to my Freddy, if I could tell him about this," Mrs. Catchpole added. "He didn't do so well his first outing."

Abigail was undeterred. "Forward, march!" she ordered, and they stomped across the cave, the swish of their skirts sounding like a rising wind. "Right face! March!"

They spun and headed for the back of the cavern.

Miranda broke rank. Rosemary started after her, but the other women frowned Rosemary back into place. Still, they all looked back to see how their leader would react to this insubordination.

"Halt!" Abigail told the others before catching Miranda as the girl reached her side. "What is it, your ladyship?"

"I want to order them," she said. "Please."

Several of the women exchanged glances, but Abigail inclined her head. "Of course, your ladyship. You are our hostess, after all." Still, she bent and whispered something in the girl's ear. Miranda nodded as Abigail straightened.

"About face!" she cried.

The women spun to fully face her. Miranda beamed. "Forward, march!"

They clomped toward her.

"Halt!"

They stopped, waiting.

"That was excellent," Abigail cheered. "A round of applause for our hostess."

The sound echoed and re-echoed in the cave. Somewhere beyond the light, a rock fell with a splash. Sound snuffed out, and the women crowded closer, gazes bouncing around.

"What was that?" someone cried.

"The French are coming!" another put in.

"That was no Frenchman," Rosemary assured them. "In future, perhaps we could find another method of acknowledgment. As you can see by the cave floor, rocks do fall on occasion. We wouldn't want to hasten that."

Everyone quieted down, and Abigail beckoned them closer. She had Eva come up and go over the changes to the evacuation plans and the roles the women might play to see that their families and friends made it safely out of the village in case of an invasion.

"I know you have work awaiting you," Abigail said when Eva finished. "We won't practice any more today. Next week, Mrs. Catchpole is going to discuss hand-to-hand combat."

A few of them brightened at that, then they all began moving for the stairs. Rosemary breathed a sigh of relief when the last lady went through the main castle door.

"An unusual gathering," Mr. Jonas remarked. "Perhaps we might offer refreshment and a more suitable time of day next week."

"Perhaps," Rosemary said. "Come along, Miranda. We have geology to study if we are to be ready for our trip to the shore tomorrow."

In hopes of having something to offer his cousin, Drake had spent much of Saturday at the spa. Newcomers, Irregulars, and Regulars came and went, and many were keen to be introduced to the head of the leading family in the area. Mrs. Denby was very good about bringing him to their notice. After all, he'd never had his father's commanding presence or austere demeanor. In the navy coat and chamois breeches he'd convinced Pierson to allow him to wear, he probably looked no different than most of the men strolling about the spa, taking the waters, and conversing with acquaintances.

But James was right, and being the earl had benefits. He could ask questions of anyone introduced to him, even to the point of rudeness, and it was viewed as his right as the major landowner in the area.

After questioning nearly every attendee, four men stood out as possible French agents. Mr. Donner, a tall, dark-haired fellow, had long overstayed his welcome. Normally, that might qualify him to become a Regular, but the other Regulars had not embraced him.

"Nosy," the Admiral said when Drake struck up a conversation with the portly retired Navy man. "Always asking questions. And I'd say the same of Mr. Cushman there. He's been here all of a week and thinks he is entitled to know everything."

Cushman proved to be a curly-haired blond who seemed compelled to fill any moment of silence with talk. But Drake could find nothing untoward in his conversation.

"The other two, Fenton and Nash, keep to themselves mostly," Drake had reported to James after his cousin, wife, and mother had joined them at the castle for Sunday dinner. The ladies were taking turns playing at the harpsichord while he and James talked in the withdrawing room, and he knew exactly when Miranda took her seat at the instrument. He tried not to wince at the noise.

"That's surprising enough at the spa," James commented. If he heard the bangs and twangs emanating from the other room, he gave no sign. "Most people come for the company."

"Not all," Drake argued. "Invalids sometimes prefer to be left alone."

"Do they strike you as invalids?" James asked. "Have

they availed themselves of our good physician?"

"No," Drake admitted. "It's almost as if they're watching."

"Waiting," James surmised. "For what?"

The banging in the room next door stopped, and he thought his cousin sighed in relief.

Aunt Marjorie's voice drifted out. "I do believe you are improving, Miranda."

"And with more practice, you'll be even better," his mother insisted.

"In any event," Drake said, knowing the ladies would join them any moment, "I think we may have to look elsewhere for our French agents. I'll make one more pass on Monday, just to be sure."

James nodded, rising as the countess led the other women into the withdrawing room. Drake stood and made room for Miranda on the sofa beside him.

"Did you hear me, Father?" she asked.

"I did," he admitted. "And I heard you are improving." Even if he saw little sign of it.

She wrinkled her nose. "I don't like the harpsichord. Miss Denby read me a book where the people had drums to beat upon. I think I'd like a drum."

None of them would ever know peace again.

His mother sniffed. "Ladies do not bang drums, Miranda. Whoever heard of such a thing?"

"I don't know," Eva said, sitting beside her husband. James's doting smile proved how much he admired his wild-haired bride. "I think it sounds like a fine instrument. Very good for expressing your feelings. All that banging." She smiled at Miranda.

"A Howland plays a harp or a harpsichord," his mother insisted.

"Harps are tiresome," Miranda said, leaning back against Drake. "Will you buy me a drum, Father?"

"I'll take that under advisement," he said, and his

daughter snuggled closer with a happy sigh.

"You're spoiling her," his mother accused later, after James, Eva, and Aunt Marjorie had taken their leave and Warren had come to see Miranda to bed.

"I wasn't the one who bought her a pony in London," Drake pointed out, "then a second when she declared she would only ride a grey beast."

She raised her chin, but her fond smile spoiled the haughty look. "Well, she did look better on the grey. But a drum? And this business of armor. Davis tells me she is trying it on like some sort of knight of old."

"And learning her family history, her nation's history, and metallurgy at the same time," Drake pointed out.

"I grant you history is important, but metallurgy? She is not the daughter of a blacksmith."

"But there is a blacksmith in the village," Drake countered. "On lands her family owns. I see no reason why she shouldn't appreciate his art."

His mother shook her silver head. "You will persist in indulging her. I'd hoped that would stop with this new governess, but I'm not so sure she is good for the girl."

Drake was. Even his mother had to notice that Miranda sat properly when Rosemary was at her side for Monday dinner. She cut up her veal with her knife and fork, chewed quietly, and requested a second helping without interrupting the conversation.

"I see you're learning more about manners," Drake commented, determined to make his mother notice the improvement. "I'm very pleased to see Miss Denby's lessons bearing fruit."

Rosemary smiled at his daughter.

"We're going to practice hand-to-hand next week," Miranda announced.

Rosemary's fork paused on the way to her rosy lips.

"A new style of embroidery?" Drake asked.

"A very important art," Rosemary said, setting down

her fork, potatoes uneaten. "Did you care for more veal, Lady Miranda?" She signaled to Giles, who brought forth the platter.

"I hope you'll be ready early for our trip to the shore tomorrow, Father," Miranda said as the footman loaded her plate again. "You get up entirely too late."

"Miranda," his mother scolded. "It is not your place to question your father."

"But I don't want to miss the fossils," his daughter protested.

"Any fossil we find has been waiting for you for thousands of years," Rosemary told her. "A few more hours won't hurt."

Miranda sighed, then dug into her veal.

"I've strolled the shore many times over the years," Drake told Rosemary. "I don't recall finding fossils. Is that likely?"

"Extremely," Rosemary told him. "This part of Dorset is particularly rich. When I collected specimens with my uncle, we found shells, leaves, even a bone or two."

"I want to find a bone," Miranda said dreamily.

"That's quite enough talk of bones at the dinner table," the countess put in. "Let us speak of more congenial subjects. I understand you visited the spa again today, Drake. Did you meet anyone interesting?"

"Not particularly, Mother," he said, hoping to ward off any talk of heiresses and matrimony. Goodness knows he hadn't located the French agents.

And he doubted his mother would want to hear that the most interesting person he'd met recently was his daughter's governess, Rosemary Denby.

CHAPTER TEN

ROSEMARY WENT TO BED THAT night feeling both relieved and guilty. She was heartily glad the earl hadn't realized the meaning behind Miranda's comment at dinner, but she couldn't help thinking she ought to tell him the truth about what they were doing in his caverns. She finally consoled herself with the vow to tell him everything when the Women's Militia was a little farther along.

Her charge must have also been finding sleep challenging, for she popped up at Rosemary's bedside at half past four. This time, Rosemary insisted that she return to her room. She reappeared at five, half past, and a quarter to six.

"It seems we must have a lesson in telling time after all," Rosemary said, giving up and throwing back the covers to rise.

"I know how to tell time," Miranda insisted. "I just want it to move faster."

"Alas," Rosemary said, slipping an arm into her dressing gown, "time is one of the things we can't control. Look out the window and tell me another thing outside our control."

Frowning, Miranda went to pull aside the drapes and stare out into the darkness. She glanced back at Rosemary. "I can't see anything."

"Precisely. We also can't control the rising and setting of the sun. It won't be up for another hour yet, and neither will your father."

She puffed out a sigh.

Rosemary kept her busy studying tide cycles until Warren came to help them dress.

"Determine the best time to access the shore today and every day for the next fortnight," she told the girl. "I expect you to be able to justify your recommendations with more than 'I want it that way.'"

Miranda bent over the tide tables.

"What time was it this morning?" Warren asked as she accompanied Rosemary across the corridor to her room.

Rosemary yawned. "Far too early. I laid out my clothes and hers. They may look dowdy, but they are the best choices for where we're going. Don't let her convince you otherwise."

Warren helped her dress, raising her brows a little at the sight of the voluminous green gown again.

"Noon today," Miranda declared when Rosemary returned to the schoolroom a short time later.

"Because?" Rosemary asked.

Miranda sat back in her chair. "The tide's coming in now and will be at its highest at half past nine. It will be at its lowest at a quarter past one, so if we arrive at noon, we will have the greatest amount of time with the largest amount of beach."

"Nicely reasoned," Rosemary said.

Miranda slumped, face puckering. "Whatever are we to do until noon?"

Rosemary went to the bookshelf, where she'd stored her uncle's books. "First, Warren will change you into a suitable outfit. Then, we can discuss what we might find on the shore, so we'll be able to identify it. And we can ask Mrs. Hillers to pack us sustenance, so we won't have to leave because of hunger. Warren, after you help Lady

Miranda dress, would you carry word to his lordship on the change in schedule?"

"Yes, Miss Denby." The maid held out her hand, and Miranda slid off her chair and joined her. The two hurried out.

Rosemary went to pull down one of her uncle's journals, where he'd sketched the specimens they had found along the shore. Every time she descended to the beach was another opportunity to add to the record, expand upon what they had learned previously. Would the earl find the process as fascinating as she did, or would he too see it as nothing but an odd hobby?

Noon did seem a very long time to wait.

He met them in the great hall at a quarter to the hour. She'd been concerned he'd comment on her attire, but she had to press her lips together to keep from commenting on his. Surely he hadn't chosen the black velvet tailcoat. But what valet would suggest he visit the shore in eveningwear? At least his chamois breeches and top boots were sensible.

"Ready to go, I see," he said, looking her up and down.

Her cheeks felt warm. "Indeed."

"Since before the sun was up," Miranda informed him. "We had to wait for the tide."

"Very wise," her father said with a nod. "I take it the tide is in our favor at the moment?"

"Yes," Miranda said, foot starting to tap under the blue wool gown Rosemary had found for her to wear. "Now."

"I have generally descended through the village or on the foot path by Durdle Door," Rosemary put in. "Is there an easier way from the castle?"

"Through the caves?" Miranda guessed, perking up.

"Not necessarily," he told her. "There's groundwater seepage in the caves, so there's always some water in the channel out to the sea. If the tide has receded far enough, you could walk out, or in, but there's a chance you'll be stopped by rising water along the way."

"The tide," Miranda announced, nose in the air, "will be outgoing for the next hour and a half."

"I'd prefer to follow the cliff path regardless," he said. "It opens behind the stables. I used it often as a boy. Allow me to be your guide."

In the end, one of the footmen, the burly, black-haired Dawson, accompanied them as well to carry the hamper from the cook and a blanket his lordship suggested. They crossed the emerald lawns and circled the stables to where a path opened at the very edge of the cliff.

Miranda darted forward, but the earl caught her arm. "Easy. I doubt it's been used since the regatta, and the cliffs slump frequently. Let me go first."

It was narrow enough that they had to walk single file. Miranda followed her father, who picked his way down the steps, where grass jutted up among the rocks. Rosemary and Dawson came behind. The sandy soil was eroding, leaving steep drop-offs on their left. Bushes, turning brittle with autumn, reached skeletal fingers at her skirts from the right. Rosemary was thankful for her stout boots. Though Miranda crowded her father as if she found his pace too slow, they reached the beach safely.

The last few yards cut through a stony draw to allow them access to the shingled shore. White slabs, pink-tinged sand, and golden rocks combined to paint a tapestry across the beach to where the blue-grey waters of the Channel stretched into the distance, waves choppy in the breeze.

"I can see all the way to France," Miranda said as they walked out toward the water.

"Perhaps not quite that far," her father said with a smile.

"I believe that land on the horizon is the Isle of Portland."

Miranda glanced over at Rosemary. "Has anyone ever swam across to France?"

"No," Rosemary told her. "It's more than forty miles from here."

Miranda nodded. "I'll be the first, then."

"A noble goal," the earl said. "Perhaps we can start next summer, when it's warmer, by teaching you to swim."

They were at the tideline now, the waves lapping with soft sighs. Miranda picked up a rock and hurled it to splash in the sea. Then she turned to Rosemary. "Where are the *elephas* buried?"

"My uncle believed the best location to find them was closer to Lyme Regis," Rosemary said. "But, as we saw in his journals this morning, we should be able to locate evidence of ancient life closer to hand. Come with me."

Miranda abandoned the water to follow Rosemary up the beach toward the west. The earl followed after directing Dawson to make camp on a drier stretch of sand closer to the cliff.

The incoming tide had washed against the cliff sufficiently to eat away the soil, leaving the arching stratigraphy evident. Rosemary led her charge closer, where the land was seamed in cracks and gullies. Then she bent and picked up a greenish-colored rock.

"This is greensand," she explained. "You can find specimens in it, but they're more often found in grey or white chalk or grey limestone, so look for rocks that color, closer to the cliffs."

With an eager nod, Miranda scampered down the beach, head bowed as she studied the stones.

The earl had come up beside Rosemary. Already that black velvet was flecked with dust. The color still made his eyes look bluer than the waves.

"Fascinating," he said. "Something you learned from

your uncle?"

Was that amusement under his tone? "Did you think I invented him?" Rosemary challenged. "I've followed him about since I was nine. I have all his journals. I can show you, if you'd like."

He held up a hand. "No need. I do not doubt you. I'm merely surprised he involved a child in his activities."

"Children are perfect for the task," she argued. "They are eager to learn, in some cases just as eager to please. My uncle never complained about my assistance. Indeed, he grew to rely on it as he aged."

He nodded. "I'm sure he counted himself fortunate to have you as a niece."

Was he still questioning her? Rosemary frowned at him. No, that didn't appear to be sarcasm. His lips held no sneer, his brows didn't quirk. In fact, she might think that look on his handsome face to be admiration.

What was she to make of that?

She was frowning at him, as if he were some unusual specimen of sea creature she couldn't place. Perhaps he had been too obvious in his admiration. She was his employee, after all. He wasn't supposed to notice her any more than the other staff, certainly not comment on her upbringing. But having spent a good amount of time in her company recently, he found it difficult not to compliment her. No one, with the possibility of Felicity, handled Miranda's high spirits so well, and even his wife had grown exasperated at times.

"I found something!"

Miranda's cry had him and Rosemary turning to look down the beach. His daughter's governess moved surprisingly fast in the blue-green leather boots her skirts barely covered. He'd always thought it an unusual gown, but he could see the practicality of it, especially if she did scale cliffs on occasion.

When he joined them, Miranda and Rosemary were examining a flat segment of rock that had fallen from the cliff.

"See here?" Rosemary said, finger tracing the indentation in the rock. "All those delicate brown branches etched in the limestone? That's horsetail. You can still find it in marshy areas now, but it grew much larger hundreds of years ago."

"Was it poisonous?" Miranda asked, fairly wiggling beside her.

"Likely not," Rosemary allowed. "But it's possible we might find evidence of larger trees nearby. Look closely."

Miranda bent to continue down the beach. Ahead, the twin boulders guarding the entrance to the caves stuck up like giant teeth. There was a reason the area was called the Dragon's Maw.

"Is it particularly valuable?" he asked as she slipped the stone into the side of her gown. What, did she have pockets in that thing?

"No," she allowed, starting after Miranda. "It's some of the easiest to find. But every bit is a treasure. Where else can you touch something so old?"

There was that. "Miranda certainly is getting into the spirit of the chase," he said, watching as his agile daughter clambered up on a smaller boulder to study the cliff. "Thank you for allowing her to roam like this. She has such a scope of interest."

"Thank you for allowing her to explore that scope," Rosemary said as they began to close the distance. "You may find yourself criticized for it as she grows older. Some will counsel you to enroll her in a stern finishing school, where they will mold her into the perfect, proper lady."

Her tone had turned bitter. "Was that what happened to you?" he asked.

"No," she admitted. She put a hand on his arm to stop him, her face pinched. "I'm the daughter of gentry, and few dared question my uncle. Lady Miranda is the daughter of an earl. More will be expected of her. You must protect her."

His mother's harping came to mind. "I'll do all I can. But I have already been accused of being overindulgent."

"You love your daughter. That much is evident. Still, there are times when every child must be told no."

He grinned at her. "Fortunately, I rarely have to say no."

She smiled back. "So I've noticed. I have tried not to say that word myself." She glanced to where Miranda was nearing the Dragon's Maw. "The countess and others may question the things I teach her. I hope you won't."

"I can find teachers to instruct her in being the proper lady, if necessary," Drake said. "I doubt I could find a better teacher to help her be herself."

Once more she frowned at him, then, as if she noticed his sincerity at last, she dropped her gaze, and her fingers closed around her lorgnette. "Thank you, my lord."

Her lashes were the color of cinnamon, and they swept her cheeks like spice on a bun. Easy enough to lean closer, bend his head to hers…

Another cry down the beach raised his head in time to spy Miranda tumbling backward off a boulder. Blood congealing, he threw himself down the shore. Rosemary paced him.

Miranda was sitting up, rubbing her hip, when they reached her.

"Are you hurt?" Drake asked, crouching beside her.

"A little," she admitted, face bunching. "I slipped."

Rosemary put an arm around her and helped her to rise. "Can you walk?"

Miranda took a step and nodded. "Yes. But I was reaching for a shell. It's shiny brown, just like what your uncle described in the book you showed me. It's just there." She pointed higher on the cliff beside her. "See?"

Rosemary straightened and peered up at the pointed fragment sticking out of the cliff.

"That's a shell?" Drake asked, standing and keeping his eye on Miranda as she took a few hesitant steps.

"It's called Ammon's horn, Father," Miranda insisted, glancing back at him with a frown.

"No, it's not." Rosemary sounded so breathless he had to look at her. Her color was high, her gaze intent.

"That," she said, pointing, "is a bone, part of a skeleton. I do believe your daughter has discovered an ancient creature."

CHAPTER ELEVEN

ROSEMARY COULD HARDLY STAND STILL for the enormity of it. There, on the cliff, a bronze-colored, foot-long piece jutted out from the limestone. Could that be a femur? The cliff closed in on the other end and above and below, so she couldn't be certain. Was there more? Had they found an intact skeleton?

"Let's fetch it down," Miranda said, bouncing on her booted feet.

Rosemary put out a hand to stop her from scaling the cliff. "We must be very careful. We'll need to document each piece, sketch it as it is in the stone and after we remove it."

"And prevent a further cave in," the earl suggested.

She forced her gaze away from the treasure. His smile was proud, but he nodded toward the cliff closer to the Dragon's Maw. He was right. The reason the bone was so easy to spot was that the land was slumping so near the cave entrance, as if the Dragon's Maw was taking a further bite into the rocky cliffside.

"A wise idea, my lord," she said. Still, the tantalizing sight above her pulled her gaze back to it. She slipped an arm about her charge's shoulders.

"Look what you found, Lady Miranda, merely by keeping your eyes open and your wits about you. We won't know the age or species until we uncover more of it, but if it's an otherwise unknown specimen, it might be named after you."

She scrunched up her face. "Who'd want to call an old creature Miranda?"

"*Hippopotamus mirandi*," Rosemary extemporized. "*Elephas Howlandia*. Either has a fine ring to it."

The earl chuckled. "Perhaps we should remove the beast before we name it."

How could he stand there so calmly? Did he not comprehend what lay before them?

"Your daughter has made a significant scientific discovery, my lord," she informed him, removing her arm from around Miranda. "We should alert the Royal Society, the British Museum. My uncle had a network of colleagues who would be thrilled to learn of this."

He glanced up at the bone. "All that, for what may be a tree root?"

"It's no root," Rosemary promised. "You'll see when we can get closer."

Miranda was back to dancing on her feet. "When can we start digging it out?"

"I'll request Uncle James to round up a few men," he said.

Rosemary whirled to face him. "That won't do at all! They'll rip through it with shovels, hack at it with pickaxes. This must be done slowly, carefully, by people who know what they are about."

He raised a brow. "Who did you have in mind?"

She lifted her chin. "Miranda and I will attempt it."

He peered at her. "You've been with us a little more than a week now, Miss Denby. Have you ever seen my daughter do anything slowly and carefully?"

"She can learn." She turned to Miranda, who was eyeing the cliff as if trying to determine the best way to clamber higher. "Our first task is to see if anything has already fallen to the beach. Start at the cliff and move toward the waves, Lady Miranda. I'm counting on your sharp gaze to miss nothing."

"I'll find it," Miranda vowed, head down and feet moving.

Rosemary looked to the earl, who was watching his daughter scamper along the cliff. "If you would ask Dawson to return to the castle and bring back my sketchbook and pencils, my lord. They're in my trunk. Warren will know where to find it."

He glanced at the cliff, then at her. "Very well, but please tell me you don't intend to climb up there."

"Not at the moment," Rosemary hedged.

Still he studied her, as if he didn't trust to look away. Then he nodded and strode down the beach, calling Dawson's name.

Miranda was crossing and recrossing the shore a few yards out from the cliff now.

"Nothing so far," she reported, bonnet slipping down over her forehead.

"Keep looking," Rosemary advised, then she trained her gaze up the cliff.

Excitement arrowed into her, striking to the heart. Oh, how Uncle Montgomery would have loved to see this! Could it be an ancient *elephas*, his dream? No, that femur looked much too narrow and rather short. A *hippopotamus*? Some suggested crocodiles were possible. If only she could get a better look!

She glanced to Miranda, who was partway to the waves now, then narrowed her gaze on the cliff again. Thicker clumps of rock stuck out here and there. Easy enough to secure her boots, set her hands. She began climbing, cautiously, edging herself higher with each movement. Yes! She could make out cracks in the bone now, and was that the mark of an ancient tooth? Had their find been a victim of some greater monster of the deep?

Just a little higher and she might know for certain.

"Nothing," Miranda called from below. "I'll climb up with you."

"No, don't," Rosemary started, then she felt her hand slipping. Before she could reposition it, her balance canted. She struggled for purchase on the crumbling soil, and suddenly she was tumbling backward.

To land cradled in the earl's arms.

She blinked, struggled to find breath, and not just because of the fall. His eyes, wide in surprise, were clearer than the summer sky. Lines fanned out from the edges. Had they been put there by sorrow? Joy?

"I believe," he said, "you promised me you wouldn't climb that cliff."

Cerulean blue. That was the color of her eyes. And she had the faintest cleft between her nose and rosy lips, making her look a bit like a startled rabbit. Her cheeks were probably softer than rabbit's fur too.

"And I believe," she said, "you should put me down."

He should. He knew that. But, for so formidable a lady, she felt light in his arms, as if they had been formed for just this purpose. He could have held her like this all day.

"Father?" Miranda tugged on the black velvet evening coat Pierson had been determined that he wear on an outing, of all things. "I don't think Miss Denby meant to disobey you."

"It was not a question of disobedience, Lady Miranda, but of expedience," Rosemary told her. "My lord, I must insist. I'm fine. Release me."

He set her on her feet, feeling the cool of the sea breeze as her warmth moved away.

"Your sketchbook should be here shortly," he told her. "But I see you can be as impatient as Miranda."

"Scholarly curiosity only. I was trying to determine whether there's a full skeleton or merely a misplaced bone."

Drake glanced up at the cliff. "How does the bone of an elephant become misplaced?"

"We do not know if it's a member of the genus *elephas*," she cautioned. "That bone seems too small to me."

"Maybe it's a baby," Miranda said dreamily. "My own baby *elephas*."

"Perhaps," Rosemary allowed. "But we may never know for certain. A skeleton may be impressed in stone out at sea, and wave action washed it in at some later date, breaking it apart so that only one of the bones is found. Or some predator attacked the creature and carried off most of the bones, leaving this one behind."

"That sounds horrid," Miranda said. "I want my *elephas* all in one piece."

"We'll only know when we can release the bones from the cliff," Rosemary said. "For today, we'll sketch the site from various angles for thorough documentation."

"That's not very interesting," Miranda pronounced, and Drake found himself in agreement with his daughter.

"Then return tomorrow at low tide with hammers," Rosemary continued.

His daughter grinned at that.

He could see any number of issues with that plan. "I must insist on safeguards," he said. "Scaffolding to support you on the cliff. Workers to move rock and carry heavy items."

He thought Rosemary might protest. Certainly her face tightened.

But she nodded. "Very well. That sort of help would be appreciated, my lord."

He'd been a lord all his life, using his father's lesser title, Viscount Thorgood, until his father had passed. But he could not like the title on her lips.

"Perhaps," he said, "we could dispense with calling me my lord."

She nodded again. "Howland, then, if you prefer."

Howland had been a proud name for generations and never more so than when his father had worn it. It wasn't a name that suited him. But propriety demanded he could give her no other.

"Would you allow me the honor of using your first name, then, Rosemary?" he asked. After all, he already thought of her as Rosemary.

Once more, the color climbed in her cheeks. "If it pleases you."

"I'll call you Rosemary too," Miranda volunteered.

She put a hand on his daughter's shoulder. "Perhaps we should keep to Miss Denby for now. Calling me Rosemary might encourage you to disobey."

"But you said expedience was better than obedience," Miranda protested.

"Did I? Let's review that sentence, shall we?" She drew his daughter a little farther down the beach.

Drake glanced at the bone protruding from the cliff face. It still looked more like a tree root to him than a piece of some ancient creature. But it had certainly excited Rosemary.

He wasn't surprised to discover that excitement was very attractive on her.

They spent the rest of the afternoon on the shore, until the waves crept too close for comfort. Rosemary showed Miranda how to sketch their discovery, and his daughter actually sat still long enough to complete one page before beginning to fidget.

He had never seen anyone as inventive as Rosemary.

She asked Miranda to find shells and categorize them by size and shape, had her draw what she thought might live in the largest and smallest, timed her run to a point along the shore and back, then challenged her to beat her time. Where sand had been exposed, she had her construct a fortress and people it with flotsam and jetsam she found along the shore. Miranda then drew her creation to preserve it for posterity. All the while, Rosemary sketched the cliff and her prize.

He convinced them both to stop and eat what Cook had sent—yellow hard cheddar with a tang to it and slices of freshly baked bread, washed down with the first apple cider from this year's pressing.

"I want to use the hammer tomorrow," Miranda said between bites. Her bonnet had fallen back, and the tip of her nose was turning red. Drake set the satin-lined wicker back into place.

"After we discuss the finer points, and you show proficiency," Rosemary said. "Tonight, we'll go through my uncle's journals and see if we can locate anything related to our find. We never identified any mammals or larger reptiles when I was at his side, but he may have discovered one before I joined him."

"My *elephas* will be larger than anything ever found," Miranda bragged.

"We'll see more tomorrow," Drake predicted. "In the meantime, I would enjoy learning about your uncle's work as well, Rosemary. Perhaps I can join you this evening after dinner."

"We would be delighted, my... Howland," she answered.

There was something sweet about saying her name and the way she dropped her gaze shyly when he did so. It had been a long time since he'd enjoyed a lady's company so much. It was almost like courting.

Courting?

He surged to his feet, scattering cheese rind and bread

crusts, and both Rosemary and Miranda looked up in surprise.

"I believe I left something near the cave opening," he said. "Excuse me a moment." He strode down the beach, leaving Dawson to clean up after him.

Why had courting even popped into his mind? He wasn't courting Rosemary. He wasn't courting anyone. His mother might be determined to find him a wealthy bride, but he had every intention of waiting before considering another marriage. He was healthy. Plenty of time to find a wife and sire an heir to the title once their finances had recovered a little.

Yet his own actions the last few days called him liar. He'd singled Rosemary out at the assembly. He'd used any excuse to spend time with her. He'd held her in his arms far longer than had been necessary when she'd slipped from the cliff. He'd asked for the intimacy of using her first name.

If her uncle had been alive to witness all that, he'd have demanded to know Drake's intentions.

Did he have intentions?

He'd reached the trickle of water out of the Dragon's Maw, splashing now as it met the incoming tide. Just to one side, Miranda's bone stuck out of the cliff as if waving at him. More real was the memory of holding Rosemary close, watching the surprise on her face warm into something more.

Something that called to him. Made him feel as if he might be the sort of man who would make a better Earl of Howland than his father, a man who protected and cherished those who had been given to him—Miranda, his mother, the people who lived on his lands.

Rosemary.

No, he didn't have intentions. These feelings were too nebulous, too new. But he began to wonder what other role his daughter's intriguing, delightful governess might play in his life.

And his heart.

CHAPTER TWELVE

ROSEMARY BARELY SLEPT THAT NIGHT, thinking about what might be waiting on the shore. She, Miranda, and Howland had pored over her uncle's journals in the schoolroom, but nothing had seemed to match their bone. Had they found something that had eluded him, or an entirely new species?

But just as engrossing were Howland's reactions. The way he'd listened to her explanations, so focused, so engaged. The way he'd held her when she'd fallen, as if she were important to him, precious. The way he'd requested to use her first name, as if they were becoming friends.

Or more than friends.

Was that possible? She shouldn't hope. He seemed undaunted by her bluestocking tendencies, even encouraged them in his daughter, but Rosemary was hardly his social equal. Then there was his late wife. He'd said many men had vied for her hand, so she must have been a great beauty. Wouldn't he expect as much in his second wife?

She knew her assets, and great external beauty wasn't one of them. Oh, her hair was a rich brown and particularly lustrous after it had been freshly washed. Her features and figure were not unpleasant. But she had never taken much time to accentuate them. She would rather be known for her intellect than her looks.

It seemed best to remember why she'd come to Castle How—to share her knowledge with Miranda, help the girl grow into a confident, accomplished young lady. She could not afford to think about more than that right now.

Even if she couldn't stop thinking.

She wasn't surprised when Miranda showed up at her bedside shortly after the hall clock had chimed four.

"Can we go now?" she begged.

"Alas, no," Rosemary told her. "It's dark again, and the tide won't be far enough out. Why don't you climb in with me and we'll keep each other company?"

She managed to shelter Miranda upstairs until Warren appeared at a quarter past six.

"His lordship is at the breakfast table already," she said, sounding faintly accusatory.

"Then we will join him," Rosemary said.

She and Miranda dressed in their sensible clothes again, but Howland was wearing an even more surprising outfit—a cream-colored tailcoat, thoroughly mangled cravat, and bark-colored breeches with gold buttons. Either his valet also struggled to wake up so early or the earl had decided to throw on whatever was handy himself.

"Ready to go, I see," he said with a smile as Miranda plunked herself down on the chair next to his.

"Yes, Father," she said primly. "As soon as you finish eating."

"As soon as the sun rises and the tide turns," Rosemary reminded her, sitting on her other side. "So you might as well enjoy your meal, Lady Miranda."

"And it will take a while for the scaffolding to be erected," he cautioned his daughter. "I sent word to the village before I retired last night, but work won't start until the sun is up. I'd prefer you remain in the castle until we hear all is ready."

Miranda scowled at the coddled eggs and toast Giles brought her.

Rosemary was in full sympathy. She positively itched to start removing their discovery from the cliff.

"Could we at least go down and *watch* them erect the scaffolding?" Miranda asked her father.

"It would provide an opportunity to calculate angles and the ratio of surface area to weight," Rosemary suggested helpfully, hoping she didn't sound overly eager. "Or the history of how the great cathedrals were constructed."

His mouth quirked. "If the two of you can sit still long enough to learn all that, I'll be surprised."

"Who said anything about sitting still?" Rosemary asked.

He smiled.

Miranda clapped her hands. "Oh, thank you, Father." She applied herself to her eggs.

After breakfast, they gathered the supplies they'd need for both the study and the removal of the fossil. Dawson had dragged her trunk into the schoolroom, so it was easy enough to put her tools into a sturdy, lidded, wooden basket Warren had provided.

"Lorgnette," Rosemary said, draping the glasses about her neck on their satin ribbon. "For peering closely at the object. Brush, for removing dust. Tweezers, for plucking away tiny bits of rock or debris."

Miranda picked up the silver tweezers and pinched at the air. "I like these."

"At least she didn't pick up the hammer or chisel first," Howland said, taking the two implements from Rosemary and depositing them in the basket. "What else will you need?"

Enough that he had to bring both footmen with them, one carrying the basket and the other the hamper of food and blanket. They made quite the parade following the cliff path down to the shore later that morning. The sun was hidden behind a wall of clouds, but bits of blue speckled the sky, giving Rosemary hope any rain would wait.

The men from the village must have started work as soon as the tide had begun to recede, for the first course had been laid against the cliff face right next to the Dragon's Maw, and four men were working at erecting the second platform. Rosemary was surprised to see Alex Chance, Jesslyn's brother, among them. Unlike his forefather's, the young tawny-haired blonde had decided against a career as a physician, but she had never heard he was particularly good at building anything. Or was there another reason he had decided to come to the cliff this morning?

She had no opportunity to ask. Miranda was even more mobile than usual. Though the earl had Dawson lay out the blanket and hamper of food in the shade of a boulder farther along the beach, Miranda was hardly content to stay there. Rosemary had to watch her every moment to prevent her from pelting down the beach to question the workers. She tried sums, stories, feats of agility, and still the girl fretted.

The earl seemed just as restless, but Rosemary could hardly stop him from going down to watch the workers. He must have realized her difficulty, however, for he came back to join them on the blanket.

"Miranda," he said, "I need your help."

She perked up. "Yes, Father? Do you have difficulty calculating angles too?"

"No," he admitted. "I have a much greater failing, one that threatens my reputation as a gentleman."

Rosemary frowned. For all he chose the oddest combinations of coat, waistcoat, and breeches, she thought him in every way a gentleman.

Miranda leaned on his arm and gazed up at him. "Really? What did you do?"

He lowered his voice as he bent closer to her. "I have

forgotten how to dance."

She straightened with a giggle. "Oh, that's easy. Watch." She hopped up and began skipping about on the sand, arms flailing.

"I fear that's not the sort of dance your father has in mind," Rosemary said. "At assemblies, a gentleman is expected to be able to partner a lady."

Howland nodded. "And there's an assembly tonight. You'll meet the same expectation when you grow older, Miranda. Perhaps you're too young to learn yet…"

Oh, he had her now.

"I'm old enough," Miranda insisted, coming back to them. "Show me."

"That's just it," he said, rising. "I can't. But if Rosemary will teach me, perhaps we can both learn."

Her heart started beating faster as she stood to join him. "That might be challenging. We have no music."

"The waves make music," Miranda offered. "Shush, shush. Hear it?"

There was a kind of cadence to the movement of the tide. She forced herself to look away from his gaze and meet Miranda's eager one. "Watch us closely, then. I'll practice with your father first. Afterward, he can practice with you."

She nodded, gaze on her father.

"Perhaps if you were to take my hands," Rosemary suggested, holding them out.

He clasped them in his own, and warmth flowed from his touch.

"Good," she managed. "Miranda, only certain figures of the dance require you to hold hands, but since I'm attempting to teach your father, we'll remain mostly in hold."

Out of the corners of her eyes, she saw Miranda nod.

"Each dance comprises a number of repeated figures," Rosemary explained. "Each figure takes from two to eight beats to accomplish. A dance generally starts with the couple saluting each other—the lady curtsies and the gentleman bows. We'll dispense with that for now."

"A shame," Howland said. "It's always a pleasure bowing to such an accomplished lady."

Was he flirting? She should not acknowledge it even if something fluttered inside her.

"One of the most common steps is the set," she continued, keeping her voice level. "It's a little step to the right, and then to the left. Like this." She went right and left, boots feeling heavy on the sand after dancing in her slippers.

"Ah, yes," he said, and he eased his hold so he could mimic her.

"Let's do two," Rosemary said. Her heart was pounding loud enough to call the beat, but she focused on the waves and announced the words aloud anyway. "One, two, three, four, five, six, seven, eight. Nicely done, sir."

"That's it?" Miranda asked. "I could do that."

"That is only one figure," Rosemary warned her. "Here's another one. The gentleman and lady entwine arms and circle, like this."

Now he was even closer, his shoulder brushing her as they turned. Breathing became difficult.

"Then we release and cast off, turning behind another couple to come back into place. Follow my lead. One, two, three…"

As she counted, they turned and flowed back to each other. But as she reached him, her foot caught on a stone. His hand landed on her waist, steadying her.

For a moment, she stood in his embrace. She couldn't think. Couldn't think! And her a bluestocking. All she could do was gaze up at him in wonder.

It was the second time Drake had held Rosemary, and the feat was no less thrilling. His heart was beating a rapid tattoo, and she looked up at him as if he were equal parts amazing and heroic. He didn't want to let go.

"I have it," Miranda declared, striding up to them. "I'll show you, Father."

Rosemary dropped her gaze and stepped out of his reach. "Yes, perhaps that would be wise."

It might be wise, but he felt a protest building inside. What, was he turning into his daughter now, stomping his feet until he achieved his ends? Nonsense. He made himself turn to Miranda.

"Be patient with me," he told her. "I fear I don't learn as quickly as you do."

His daughter was very understanding as they set back and forth. He was more aware of Rosemary watching, cheeks still a warm rose.

"Turn your toes out more, Father," Miranda advised. "Miss Denby did it like this."

His daughter was an excellent student. She circled away from him and back to Rosemary's count.

"Very nice," Rosemary said as he bowed and Miranda curtsied. "We can practice taking hands all around another time. I believe your fossil awaits, Lady Miranda."

Miranda squealed and darted toward the cliff, where scaffolding now rose to within easy reach of the bone.

"Stay on the ground until I'm with you," Drake ordered her as he and Rosemary followed.

The workers stepped back as they approached. Miranda had waited as he'd asked, hopping from foot to foot as if every moment was torture.

"Quite a find, Rosemary," a young man said, nodding to the bone.

Drake frowned at the upstart, but Rosemary smiled.

"Lady Miranda, Lord Howland, allow me to present

Alexander Chance. He's the younger brother of my sister-in-law, Mrs. Jesslyn Denby, who you met at the spa."

Ah, family of a sort. Drake nodded as Mr. Chance bowed. "Your ladyship, my lord, a pleasure."

"You were on the *Siren's Call*," Miranda said. "I heard your name at the regatta."

His brows rose as he straightened, as if he were surprised that she'd remember. "That's right. It's my honor to sail with Captain St. Claire."

Drake frowned. Interesting. Brother to a noted local family, skilled sailor. Chance could very well be part of the crew St. Claire was using on his trips to France. None of that qualified him to help erect scaffolding.

But it did qualify him to protect the cliff that held the Dragon's Maw.

Rosemary might have had the same thought, for her gaze darted the short distance to where the two massive boulders jutted out of the sand, water flowing between them.

"You came in second," Miranda reminded Mr. Chance. His smile deepened. "Alas. Perhaps we'll do better next time."

Rosemary's gaze had returned to the scaffolding, as if Mr. Chance could never be so fascinating as what lay waiting above. Drake wasn't sure why that pleased him.

"I see you added ladders from one level to the next," she told the workers. "Lady Miranda, they will be difficult to climb in your skirts. Use one hand to hold up the material and the other to hang onto the rungs."

The other workers exchanged glances as if they hadn't thought of that. "Maybe we could build stairs, your lordship," their leader ventured, pulling off his tweed cap to reveal russet-colored hair. "But it would take quite a bit longer."

"We'll give it a try as it is," he told them. "Excellent workmanship, by the way."

They all beamed.

Dawson brought them the basket of supplies, and Rosemary directed him to slip it up onto the platform.

"I'll go first," she said. "Lady Miranda can follow with Howland behind. Alex, we may need your assistance. Follow the earl."

Chance saluted her. "Aye, aye, Captain."

She cast him a look before starting up the ladder.

Drake could see what she meant about skirts. Even with her shorter hem, she had to gather the material in one hand to keep it out of her way. His daughter mimicked her, scrambling up to the next level with skill. Drake followed, with Chance at his back. The sailor made sure to reposition the basket to the next level as they climbed.

Like the other platform, the uppermost was about ten feet wide and five deep. Though they were only about a dozen feet above the beach, he felt as if he swung in the salty breeze. Every time Miranda veered toward the edge, he grabbed her back to his side.

"Probably should have built a railing," Chance mused, glancing down so close to the rim that Drake had to swallow.

Rosemary had opened her basket. "Take the brush, Lady Miranda," she instructed, positioning herself in front of the fossil with a hammer in her own hand. Now that the bone was at eye level, he could confirm it was no root, not with those telltale bulges at either end.

"Brush off the loose dirt, softly," she advised his daughter. "I'll see about opening up a little more of our fine fellow."

"It's a lady, not a fellow," Miranda informed her, but she worked the brush slowly and carefully over the bronze-colored bone.

"It's not generally possible to tell sex," Rosemary warned. Her little hammer tapped at the rock to the east of the bone, and chunks of limestone broke free to clatter down onto the platform at her feet.

"Well, I'm going to call it a lady," Miranda said. She stopped brushing to watch what Rosemary was doing.

He could only watch as well. Gaze focused, face glowing with intent, Rosemary worked at the stone for all the world as if sculpting a masterpiece. But then, God had already done that in her.

Now, then. He must school his thoughts. More bones were appearing above the original. Was that the curve of a shoulder? So near the leg? What sort of creature what this? He caught himself crowding closer.

"Fetch me the chisel, Howland," Rosemary said, voice breathless.

Chance's brows shot up. It wasn't every day the governess ordered the earl to fetch and carry for her. But Drake was as eager to see this done as she was, so he located the slim file in the basket and offered it to her.

Instead, she nodded to the west of the bones that had come into view. "Wedge it in there, if you please. Gently. I'd like to see if we can't break that entire face free."

Miranda caught her breath.

Drake slid the chisel into a gap and levered the tool out just the slightest.

Something cracked.

He froze.

"You broke it!" Miranda scolded, stomping her foot.

The platform swayed, but he couldn't care. "If I've damaged it…"

"You didn't," Rosemary assured him. "That was the rock. I know it. Set your chisel again."

Reluctantly, he did as she bid. She pressed close to him, hammer tapping at the end of the file. The space between the shoulder and the rock widened, and limestone rained onto his boots.

"Now there," Rosemary said, directing his gaze to the new crack along the top.

He repositioned the chisel. Together, they worked their way along the cliff as the sheet of limestone leaned out, farther, farther…

"Catch it!" Rosemary cried, and he dropped the chisel and put out both hands.

A massive chunk fell off into them, heavy in his grip. Light against the dark of the bone, two eye sockets gazed up at him from a jagged jaw.

He met Rosemary's gaze and saw his own awe mirrored there. "Is this a skull?"

Her nod was tremulous, as if she didn't trust herself to speak.

"But where's its long nose?" Miranda demanded, frowning at the bronze-colored bone. "And tusks?"

"It's not an *elephas*," Rosemary said. "I do believe we've found an ancient reptile. A crocodile, perhaps?"

"Oh," Miranda said. "May I hold it, Father?"

He wanted to clutch the ugly, glorious thing to his chest. "When we're safely on the ground," he said.

Miranda scurried for the ladder.

Rosemary pressed a hand to his arm. "There will be more. We're only beginning. But this is simply marvelous." As if inspired by it, she leaned against him and gave him a hug.

He nearly dropped the skull.

She was down the ladder before he could do more than gape after her. Only Chance remained beside him, regarding him as if he understood there was something in this world more amazing even than this discovery.

CHAPTER THIRTEEN

"CAREFUL," ROSEMARY CAUTIONED AS THE workers brought their prize into the great hall. "Set everything on the table, if you please. We can study and catalog things there."

The men lay the bones she, Howland, and Miranda had excavated that day on the long table that sat against the stairway and stepped back. Their gazes darted from the tapestry covering one wall to the massive stone hearth opposite. Very likely they had never been beyond the kitchen, if they had entered the castle at all.

"Excellent work," Howland told them, rubbing his hands together as he paced the table. "Jonas, see that these fellows are paid and add a shilling's bonus to celebrate our success."

Grinning, they all tipped their caps and thanked him before following the butler from the room.

"Where have you been?" the countess asked, starting down the stairs from the chamber story, silver hair piled up. "Jonas told me some story about digging rocks out of the cliff, but I knew that couldn't be right. Goodness, Miranda, what are you wearing?"

Miranda was too busy following her father along the table to so much as glance down at the worn blue frock, now covered in limestone dust and sand. "Old clothes, Grandmother, but they are ever so inconvenient. Father,

I want breeches like yours."

"Breeches!" Even the countess's black silk skirts protested in a fierce whisper as she hurried to the bottom of the stairs. "That is ridiculous. Miss Denby, I demand to know what you are teaching my granddaughter. Clearly not fashion." She looked Rosemary up and down, nose wrinkling as if she smelled something bad.

Rosemary refused to justify her choice in clothing. "I am teaching Lady Miranda that she can do anything she puts her mind to," she said. "Though, I agree, that breeches are regrettably out of the question, however convenient they might be."

Miranda made a face.

So did the countess. "And what have you put on the table? Is that a…skull?" She recoiled, paling.

"It is indeed, Mother," Howland said, crouching beside the table so that his eyes were on a level with the creature's. "And a shoulder, back, and one front leg. It's from an ancient creature. Miranda discovered it, and she and Rosemary excavated it."

The countess turned her baleful glare on her. "How very industrious of…*Rosemary*."

The use of her first name had raised the lady's hackles, but it was hard to care when a major scientific discovery sat in front of her in all its glory.

"If you'll excuse me," she said to Howland, one hand gripping her lorgnette, "I'll just go up and fetch my books. We may be able to confirm its age and genus from there."

"Excellent suggestion," he said, running his fingers along the ridge of the spine.

It was as if she felt his fingers along her back as well, soft as a caress. Shoving away the sensation, she started up the stairs.

"I don't see what all the fuss is about," the countess complained. "Nor do I see why you had to bring this thing into my house. Can you not simply give it a decent burial?"

Rosemary glanced back in time to see Miranda reach for the skull. Howland rose and took his daughter's hand. "Touch nothing, Miranda." He turned to his mother. "These bones are thousands of years old, Mother. They are coveted by collectors and museums around the world. I'm not certain what we will do with them, but we will most certainly not bury them."

Rosemary smiled as she reached the top of the stairs and headed for the schoolroom. Only her uncle had ever been as enthused about the work as Howland. Uncle Montgomery would have liked the earl and the way he guarded their discovery. She'd heard the countess call her son Drake, which must be his given name. From the stories told about his father, she could not imagine that the fellow had called his heir after the male duck. No, surely Drake stood for a dragon like the one depicted on their crest and various items of furniture. No dragon had ever been so zealous of his hoard.

As if to prove as much, he was still trying to convince the countess of the find's value when Rosemary returned with two of the books from her uncle's collection. Both purported to describe in picture and text every creature in the animal kingdom, but Maudie would have felt right at home reading them, for chimeras, mermaids, and dragons were included.

"Here, Miranda," she said, handing the girl one of the volumes. "Look in the chapter on reptiles and see whether these bones resemble any of the pictures."

The girl set the book on the edge of the table and began turning pages.

"Very well," the countess was saying to her son. "I can see these may have value to someone. What I fail to see is why my granddaughter should be involved in dealing with them."

"It's educational," Miranda said, gaze glued to the book.

"For a farmer," her grandmother argued. "Perhaps a mine worker or some other profession that grubs about in the dirt. You would be better served practicing the harpsichord, Miranda, or learning to embroider or paint."

Miranda glanced up, but her gaze went to the skull, which stared back at her. "Maybe I *should* learn to paint, Miss Denby, so I can paint this."

"That is not what I had in mind," the countess scolded. "You will paint sunrises, sunsets, fruit, and flowers, as a young lady should. If Miss Denby doesn't have the skill, we will find you a governess who does."

Rosemary's fingers tightened on the book. Could the woman not see any other role for her granddaughter besides painting bowls of fruit? Would Rosemary really lose her place because she'd never learned the fine art of watercolor and generally made holes in any fabric she attempted to embroider? No, it was not to be borne!

Drake's kind voice cut through his mother's diatribe. "I am more than satisfied with what Rosemary is teaching Miranda. If Miranda would like to learn to paint, we'll locate a tutor."

"Abigail Bennett, in the village," Rosemary offered, finding her voice. "She is an accomplished watercolor painter. I'm sure she'd be delighted to tutor Lady Miranda."

"Perfect," he said, turning away from the countess as if the matter was settled. "Any sign of our fellow in your books?"

"I told you, she's a lady," Miranda said, turning another page.

"Since we'll never know for certain, you may call her a female if you'd like," Rosemary said, all too aware of the countess's scrutiny. She attempted to turn her attention back to the book. Lizards, turtles, snakes. Nothing that remotely resembled that fearsome jaw.

"I begin to fear for the lot of you," the countess huffed.

"Here it is!" Miranda cried. She spread the book on the table, and Drake and Rosemary crowded close even as the countess stepped out of their way as if worried they'd dirty her fine silk.

"*Crocodylidae*," Rosemary read triumphantly. "That pointy snout, those interlocking jaws. The very likeness of a crocodile, though a rather large one! Well done, Miranda."

The girl grinned at her. Drake leaned closer, studying the picture of the low-slung creature. He was so close, she might have hugged him. Then again, she'd already done that at the beach. It had been a spontaneous display of delight. She refused to read more into it than that.

"Well, what a blessing," the countess declared. "That's over. We can write to some zoo or museum and have them take this thing off our hands. I'm sure we have a storage bin in the stable or cellar where it can wait."

"It stays here, Mother," he said, straightening, "until we decide what to do with it. With any luck, we'll have more of the skeleton to add in the coming days."

She choked. "More! Drake, really!"

"Really," he told her. "This is important. And while I agree with you that it should ultimately be placed where others can enjoy it, like the British Museum in London, I would hate to see our crocodile travel so far from where it was found."

"It's a nasty set of bones," his mother informed him. "It hardly cares."

But he did. Rosemary could see it in the way his jaw tightened, making him look a bit like his daughter, or the crocodile before them. He was utterly devoted to their discovery and not about to let his mother or anyone else bully him into disowning it.

How thoroughly marvelous!

In the end, his mother stalked off in high dudgeon, and Drake ordered Jonas to set a watch on the crocodile, both the remains on the table and the ones waiting at the top of the scaffolding on the beach.

"Under no circumstances are they to be moved or even touched by anyone except Miss Denby or myself," he told the butler. "If the countess attempts to countermand that order, send for me immediately, and I will deal with the matter."

Jonas inclined his dark head. "Yes, my lord."

"Crocodile," Miranda said dreamily, reaching out to stroke the bronze-colored snout. "I truly wanted an elephant, but you'll do."

Rosemary was gathering her books. "We should clean up before dinner, Miranda. And tonight's the assembly."

Her evening off. Something inside him urged her to stay. But that was selfish.

Besides, if she went to the assembly, he might have a chance to dance with her again. He followed them upstairs.

Rosemary's sister had apparently come for her, so only his mother joined him in the carriage for the ride to the assembly rooms that evening. A full moon lit the night in silver, and the breeze carried with it not only the scent of the sea, but the aroma of new-mown hay from the Downs.

"Harvest," he mentioned to his mother.

"And a fair, apparently," she agreed. "I suppose we will have to attend."

She did not sound pleased about the matter.

But no one at the assembly would have noticed. His mother blended in nicely with the spa Regulars in their silks and fine wools. Lord Featherstone claimed her hand right away. Mr. Donner followed. The fellow was younger than Drake, yet he seemed to hang on any word from his mother's lips. Even the Admiral roused himself to take her out on the floor.

Drake remained along the wall, watching from the shadows. He must not appear overly eager to dance with Rosemary. Tongues would wag. But after their triumph today, he wanted nothing so much as to have her at his side.

Others were not so hesitant. The Newcomers—Fenton, Nash, and Cushman—surrounded her and her sister for a time, as if basking in their glory. She danced with Mr. Chance, Lord Featherstone, and Mr. Carroll, the bookstore owner. Finally, Drake could stand it no longer. She had just returned to her sister and mother when he approached.

Her mother sighted him first. "My lord," she said, dropping a curtsey. Mrs. Todd, Rosemary's sister, followed suit.

Rosemary eyed him. "Ready to take your chances?" she asked.

"Rosemary!" her mother scolded. "What will the earl think that you talk of yourself in that manner?"

He held out his arm to Rosemary. "Your charming daughter wasn't referring to herself, madam. She has every reason to fear for her hem dancing with me."

"I'm persuaded you have learned," she said.

Her smile alone would have convinced him.

But, as the country dance commenced, he was more mindful of her than his own steps. The graceful turn of her body as she swept past him, the look that beckoned him closer.

"You are acquitting yourself well tonight," she told him when they stood out at the end of the line.

"Because of your teaching," he insisted.

He was only sorry when the dance ended, and he had to relinquish her hand.

"Until tomorrow," he promised, bowing. "I can't wait to see what else we discover."

Her mother frowned at him.

"Lord Howland, Lady Miranda, and I located a fossil in the cliffs below the castle," she explained to her family.

Her mother shook her head. "I'm very sorry she convinced you to join her in this obsession, my lord. I never liked that my brother encouraged her on the path."

"Why?" Drake asked. "I find it all fascinating."

Her mother started, but Rosemary beamed.

His mother was equally directive. She took him aside when the quartet called for an intermission.

"It is very kind of you to show an interest in Miss Denby," she said, "but you must dance with some of the other local ladies as well. Mrs. Greer has been attentive at the spa." She nodded to where the angular blonde was watching their every move. As if she noticed them looking her way, she stood taller and laughed gaily, setting her apothecary husband, the spa corporation president, to frowning.

"Then I will request her hand for the next available dance," Drake said dutifully. His gaze had other ideas, for it wandered about the hall, in search of Rosemary. Had she gone for refreshment? Was she promenading with her sister or a friend? Or had some other fellow importuned her hand for a dance?

Somehow, he made it through the rest of the evening, until his mother agreed to retire for the night. As they settled in the carriage, his mind drifted to the cliff and the way Rosemary had worked beside him to uncover the skull.

"Much as I am enjoying myself here," his mother said as they headed for the castle, "I cannot help wondering when we will return to Society."

He forced his attention back to her. In the light of the lanterns outside the carriage, her face looked more lined than he remembered.

"By Society, you mean London," he clarified.

She frowned. "Certainly I mean London. That is our home. Our sojourn here has been more pleasant than I expected, but you must admit it is a far cry from the capital. Bones, on my table." She shuddered.

He could not allow her to dream of something that could not be. "Forgive me for not making myself plain. We will not be returning to London."

"Before the spring?" she pressed.

Why did he feel so guilty? This financial mess was none of his making. Yet he couldn't help thinking that if he hadn't been so consumed with grief and busy attempting to fill Felicity's place with Miranda, he might have noticed his father's struggle sooner and been available to help.

"Not before spring," he said. "Perhaps not ever."

She stared at him, then collapsed against the seat. "No! That cannot be."

"I'm sorry, Mother. If we are careful, we can sustain ourselves here for some time, even build back our assets. But living in London is far too expensive. I hope to have enough put by to give Miranda a Season when she's ready."

His mother's lower lip trembled. "That's years away."

"Such are our circumstances," Drake told her.

"No." His mother sat taller, regained some of the dignity that had helped her attract one of the most powerful men in England. "I refuse to believe it. I will do my part to improve our lot."

His heart warmed. "Thank you, Mother. Any economy will help."

"Economy?" She spat out the word as if it tasted foul. "You mistake me. There is one sure path out of this. I mentioned it to you before, but now I must insist on it. You will marry an heiress."

Not that again! "No."

She knit her brows. "No? What do you mean, no? It is your duty to provide for this family. If it was in my power, I would wed a wealthy man to keep you and Miranda solvent, but any gentleman I marry would have no responsibility to support the Howland title. That only you can do."

Again guilt beckoned. Was he so selfish as to deny her and Miranda the status they deserved?

Did he not deserve to be valued for himself rather than his title alone?

"I hold my duty as earl seriously," he told her. "Which is why we are here, in Grace-by-the-Sea, where we can live comfortably without undue financial burdens."

She edged forward on her seat. "But, darling, surely you see the possibility of removing those burdens. You are fit, handsome, considerate. You can have a presence when you put your mind to it. If we were to return to London, let it be known you were seeking a bride, I'm certain we could find any number of families who would like to join with ours."

"Barter my title for a bride," Drake said. "We did that once before, Mother. It did not end well."

"I mourn Felicity's loss as much as you do," she started, "but…"

"No," Drake interrupted. "That's not possible. Felicity was everything right and good in my life, but she did not feel the same way about me. I will not put myself in such a position again. When I am ready to remarry, I will wed a woman I adore and who adores me in return."

She sighed. "I'm sure you could come to care for an heiress and she you."

"I'm not willing to take that chance. It isn't just my happiness at stake. It's Miranda's as well."

She sniffed. "And apparently Rosemary's."

"I requested the right to use Miss Denby's first name.

It's expedient."

She sighed again. "That is how it starts. Perhaps, if we are economizing, we can do without a governess. Marjorie and I can take Miranda in hand."

And squeeze every ounce of joy and originality from his daughter? "I have arranged other matters to cover the cost of a governess."

"But you said every economy helps," she protested. "We save her salary and her board."

And doom Miranda. "It's not such a great amount."

Her jaw was hard. He'd seen that look on Miranda and in his own mirror. "I knew it. You favor her."

"I admire her intellect, her determination," Drake said. "I see that she is good for Miranda. She encourages your granddaughter to spread her wings and fly."

"And deposit bones in my hall." She brushed off her skirts as if that would clear the table as well. "I will say no more on the matter for now. Just think on the possibilities."

He nodded, but he made no promises. As far as he was concerned, keeping Rosemary at Castle How was best.

For all of them.

CHAPTER FOURTEEN

THEY COULD NOT EXCAVATE ON Thursday because it rained, great buckets pouring down. From the windows of the castle, Rosemary could just make out a churning sea, black against the grey of the sky.

"My crocodile is getting wet," Miranda fretted as she stood beside her looking out.

"But the act of water on the cliff might make it easier to uncover the remaining pieces when the weather clears," Rosemary encouraged her.

She tried to maintain that attitude as the day wore on, but it wasn't easy. The countess was also confined to the castle and requested Miranda's company, first for tea late morning and then to play the harpsichord that afternoon. Neither amused Miranda or her grandmother. And Rosemary found herself looking at the door far too often, as if even her gaze sought the company of a tall, kindly earl.

Unfortunately, Drake remained sequestered in his study. Reports had been delivered that he must review, Warren said. No one seemed sure what those reports entailed, but many of the staff tiptoed around as if the house were in mourning. He seemed a bit grey when he joined them for dinner. Rosemary longed to ask him the problem, offer her aid, but she was all too aware of the countess across the table from her. Lady Howland would likely see such an offer as interference or worse, insubordination.

"We must go down to the shore tomorrow, Father," Miranda said around bites of roast beef in a mushroom sauce. "As early as possible."

"You saw the tide tables, Lady Miranda," Rosemary felt compelled to interject. "The water won't be far enough out until the afternoon tomorrow for us to excavate."

"And tomorrow is entirely inconvenient," the countess said, silver fork poised mid-air. "It is Friday, and I expect you and your father to accompany me to the spa. We will leave at half past eleven."

Rosemary thought Drake would refuse. His mouth was set, his gaze wary. But he nodded. "Very well, Mother. I know my duty. Rosemary, we will need you to join us as well, for Miranda's sake."

The countess did not look pleased, but she didn't argue either. She had to know the challenges of keeping Miranda entertained for the amount of time she'd wish to spend at the spa.

Rosemary was ready for those challenges by the next day. She'd had Warren locate a small satchel, which she loaded with pencils, parchment, her lorgnette, and a measuring stick. The countess frowned at the leather bag on Rosemary's lap as the coach set out, but she couldn't find fault in Miranda's pink muslin gown tied with a white satin bow, or the white straw bonnet perched on her golden curls.

She turned her complaints on her son instead.

"I do not know what has become of your wardrobe since we moved here," she said as the coach trundled down the drive. "That is the same coat you wore yesterday, and there is a button hanging on your waistcoat."

He glanced down at the textured waistcoat, patterned in gold and brown stripes. "Is there? I'll have to draw it to Pierson's attention."

"He should have discovered it himself," his mother

insisted. "I wish you would hire a decent valet."

"I'll take that under advisement," he said. "And who are you most looking forward to visiting at the spa today, Mother?"

The countess might be worried about his attire, but Rosemary was more concerned about the lines bracketing his mouth. Something was troubling him. She finally had a chance to learn more when they reached the spa, and Miranda and the countess were waiting for glasses of the mineral water.

"Is there something amiss?" she asked as she and Drake stood near the windows overlooking the sea. The spa wasn't crowded yet that morning, with only a few of the Regulars in attendance, so it was easy for her to keep an eye on Miranda as she scrunched up her face after taking a sip from the crystal glass Maudie had poured for her.

"Only the usual things an earl must contend with," he told her, gaze also on his daughter. "I am perhaps not as well versed as some in the responsibilities, so it takes me additional consideration to resolve."

Rosemary tore her gaze away from Miranda to frown at him. "How can that be? You were born the heir."

"To a father who preferred to hold things close," he explained. "Have no concerns, Rosemary. I will persevere. I too like learning. Speaking of which, I promised you a fortnight in your position as governess."

Suddenly, she felt as if she'd drank a glass of the mineral water too quickly. "So you did. I trust my performance has been satisfactory."

"Beyond satisfactory," he told her. "I begin to wonder how we got on without you."

His look was so warm she felt herself blushing.

"Perhaps you could assist in another area."

"Anything," she said before she realized she might sound too eager.

He nodded toward the chessboard, where Mr. Donner had challenged Lord Featherstone to a match. The younger man had his head bowed over the pieces, one hand stroking his chin, while the older baron smiled.

"What do you see when you look around the spa?" he asked her.

Interesting. Rosemary glanced around. Maudie and Miranda were engaged in conversation while the countess watched with a growing look of confusion. Jesslyn was instructing a husband and wife on the activities of the spa, in her grip one of the ubiquitous pamphlets Eva said Mrs. Greer rewrote on a weekly basis. The Admiral was seated on one of the wicker chairs, newspaper open and fallen over his paunch, head tipped back, and eyes closed. Dr. Bennett was in consultation with an elderly woman and her companion.

"It all seems a typical day at the spa," she said.

"Indeed," he agreed, sounding slightly disappointed. "My cousin tells me we should keep an eye out for French spies masquerading as spa guests. I can see no one who appears out of place."

Except perhaps Mr. Donner. He seemed too young to wish to tarry at the spa. As the summer waned, fewer and fewer people his age attended. Some might come with parents for the Christmas holidays, but most would not return until after Easter. Then there was Mr. Cushman with his curious questions and the shy Mr. Nash.

But to see them as French spies?

"If you truly want to discover whether anyone here is colluding with the French," she told Drake, "you'd need to follow their every movement, listen to their every conversation. That seems most uncharitable. I cannot think it worth the time or the risk to the spa's reputation. Who would visit Grace-by-the-Sea if they thought they'd be spied upon like that?"

"I'm ready to go," Miranda announced, skipping up to them. "Grandmother isn't. Can you hurry her along,

Father?"

He smiled. "I'll see what I can do." He inclined his head to Rosemary and sauntered over to where the countess was congratulating Lord Featherstone on his win while Mr. Donner frowned at the pieces as if he could not understand why he'd lost.

Rosemary sat on a wicker chair and motioned Miranda into the one next to it. "Let's work on sums while we wait. How many ships do you see in the cove?"

Miranda trained her gaze out the window for a moment. "Four, but another is coming in around the headland. Is that Captain St. Claire's ship?"

Rosemary started, then peered out the window, willing her heart to stop pounding at that ridiculous rate. Even if it was the *Siren's Call*, he couldn't possibly see her in the window of the spa much less attempt conversation.

"No," she said, drawing a breath. "But good for you for taking it into consideration in your count. What would happen if another dozen joined it?"

"We'd have seventeen," she said. "And I think they might bump into each other. It's not a very big cove."

Just then, Jesslyn hurried up to them. "Quickly," she said. "I'll be needed to make introductions shortly. What do you have planned for Monday?"

Monday? Ah, yes, the Women's Militia. In truth, she'd forgotten all about it.

"Tell the ladies to knock at the front door again," Rosemary said, thinking fast. "I believe Mr. Jonas would like to serve them tea this time. As soon as that's over, we'll all go to the kitchen to thank the cook, then claim the need to revisit the caves to see how they've fared after this rain."

She nodded, then leaned closer, sky-blue eyes widening. "And what's this I hear about bones in the cliff?"

Miranda was only too happy to tell her, but Jesslyn wasn't the only one asking. The workers from the village had evidently marveled to all they met about the strange sights they'd seen on the beach below Castle How. As the morning wore on, many found reason to visit the spa while the countess and Drake were in residence. Miranda was in her element, telling the story over and over again to all who would listen.

Mrs. Kirby, the titian-haired leasing agent for the village, came to ask how finding such things would affect property values. Rosemary's brother Lark stopped by to caution Jesslyn about allowing visitors to traipse down the shore. And Mrs. Greer arrived to toady up to the countess. Of course she took the lady's side and begged Drake to bury the bones immediately.

"Think what they could do to the reputation of our fair village," she insisted, as if the work somehow sullied the name of Grace-by-the-Sea.

Rosemary tried to focus on Miranda, but it wasn't easy. Her fingers tightened around her lorgnette.

"I have thought about the village," Drake told Mrs. Greer. "A discovery of this sort could attract collectors from around the Empire, around the world even."

Once more the lady struggled. Sycophant that she was, she could not bring herself to argue with an earl even if she found him quite mad. Rosemary fought the urge to raise her lorgnette and impale the woman with a look.

"Then you value such things, my lord?" she asked, hands worrying before her blue gown.

"I'm afraid he does," the countess said. "The foul things are lying on the table in the great hall this very minute."

Mrs. Greer gasped.

"The safest place for them," Drake assured them both. "Once we know the full extent of the discovery, I've no doubt we'll find others interested in them."

"How…fascinating." Mrs. Greer gazed up at him. "If these are so important, my lord, perhaps we should place their safe excavation into the hands of one of our fine gentlemen. It seems unfair to put such a responsibility on poor Miss Denby."

Rosemary stiffened, but Drake merely eyed the woman. "I have found Miss Denby to be more than competent at any tasks she undertakes."

The spa seemed brighter after that. She could hardly wait to continue their discoveries, together.

They did not have an opportunity to excavate the rest of the day on Friday, and it rained again Saturday. Drake thought Miranda would throw a fit when he refused to allow her to visit the shore. Rosemary looked nearly as frustrated, but she took his daughter's hand.

"We need to determine where best to house the discovery permanently," she said. "There are many rooms in this castle. I expect it will take some time."

Miranda's color subsided, and she nodded before allowing Rosemary to lead her from his study.

He could only be thankful for Rosemary. He had enough on his hands at the moment without trying to appease and entertain his daughter. That Rosemary had agreed with his assessment about the spa visitors gave him confidence, but he still had a boat waiting in his caverns.

Of equal concern were the reports James had provided. As his land steward, his cousin knew to the penny what each property cost to maintain and what it brought in quarterly income. The former still outstripped the latter. Some of the houses he owned in the village were currently unleased. Others needed new paint or repairs before winter set in. So how to balance his holdings? Should he invest in the properties he had in hopes of gaining more interest? Sell some? He'd already divested himself of his father's stocks. He was so close to managing income and expenditures, even a few hundred pounds more a month would do the trick. But where to find those pounds?

Miranda returned to his study that afternoon.

"My crocodile is waiting," she informed him, hands on the hips of her blue muslin gown. "I want to know she's all right. The rain's almost stopped. Please, Father, can't we go now?"

Over her shoulder, Rosemary sent him a commiserating look.

He pushed the reports away, wishing they were as easily forgotten. "I do not feel comfortable with you going down the cliff path until it has been confirmed not to have slumped. So," he continued when his daughter bridled, "I will check it myself. Give me an hour, and I should have news."

She darted around the desk and pressed a kiss to his cheek. "Oh, thank you, Father!"

"Thank you, Drake," Rosemary echoed.

Drake? The name sounded more powerful on her lips, as if the man behind it was bold, strong. He could get used to that.

Pierson managed to locate his caped greatcoat and a wide-brimmed hat, so he had some protection as he made his way through the drizzle toward the cliff path a short time later. Dawson, who accompanied him, had less.

"Are footmen generally supposed to survive the weather in breeches and tailcoat?" he asked as they paused at the top of the path.

"Yes, my lord," Dawson said, bulbous nose wrinkling as he gazed at the crashing surf below. "Wasn't so bad in London, when we didn't go out all that much. I'm sure Giles and I would be ever so glad if you could see your way to changing that here."

"I'll take that under advisement," he said, and his footman brightened. Apparently, Miranda wasn't the only one who thought that phrase was code for yes.

The path was muddy, and, here and there, small branches from the trees above had fallen over it. Dawson pulled those aside or tossed them over the cliff. More debris waited on the shore: floats from fishermen's nets, planks that had probably belonged to some jetty, bits and pieces of things he could not name. They picked their way down the beach to the Dragon's Maw, where the village lamplighter, had been stationed. He hobbled out from under the lowest platform and bobbed his grizzled head.

"My lord."

Drake nodded. "Mr. Drummond. Thank you for your diligence. Everything all right here?"

"Well, today," he allowed. "Rain was a bit unpleasant. So were those fellows last night."

"Fellows?" Drake asked with a frown.

"Yes, my lord. Came rowing around the headland just before the tide turned. Looked to be two of them, cloaks covering their heads. I waved my lantern, called for them to beware of the Dragon's Maw, and they heaved off. One didn't sound happy, but I couldn't understand what he said, only the tone."

Drake looked out over the waters, splashing against the massive boulders on either side of the cave's entrance. "Youths from the village, perhaps, attempting to prove themselves?"

Drummond snorted. "That sort generally sails in. They don't come a-rowing. Where's the adventure in that?"

Where indeed? And would village youths curse at the old lamplighter, knowing he could tell their families? They might be cloaked, but someone would know who'd been out last night.

Unless they had been Frenchmen using a stolen boat

again.

Drake thanked him for his time, made sure he was being brought meals and being spelled on occasion, then led Dawson back up to the castle. The path was clear enough for Miranda to follow, but he could only wonder who else thought to access their discovery on the cliff.

Or the caves inside it.

Just to be certain all was well, he sent word to James to look into their midnight visitors, then ventured down to the caverns. As far as he knew, Rosemary had kept Miranda too busy to visit the caves in recent days. The only person making use of them was Quillan St. Claire.

So why were there so many marks in the sand?

He gazed at them for some time, puzzling. The boat still waited, as did the triangle of rocks Miranda had spotted. Now footprints of various sizes marred the sand above the tideline. How many men was St. Claire bringing? And why did they cross the cave from one wall to the other instead of going from the shoreline up to the stairs to the castle? It was almost as if they had been pacing or marching.

He located Rosemary and Miranda in the schoolroom, sitting at one of the desks with the globe before them. Miranda looked up as he entered.

"Can we go now?" she asked.

Drake smiled to temper his words. "It's growing dark now, Miranda. Perhaps tomorrow, after services."

She glanced at Rosemary. "But Miss Denby won't be here then. It's her time off."

"Monday then."

She slumped in her seat, lower lip sticking out. "Monday, we have the ladies coming."

"After they leave," Rosemary promised. "We'll make sure we're all ready so we can go as soon as the tide allows."

Miranda drew in a martyred sigh. "Very well."

Drake moved closer, feeling as if he was coming in from the cold on a winter's day. "And what are you studying now?"

Miranda perked up. "India. They have elephants."

"So I understand." He paused beside Rosemary, who smiled up at him.

"Have you ever seen an elephant, Father?" Miranda asked.

"Once, at the Exeter 'Change," he allowed. "I didn't care for it. It was in a cage, and I couldn't help thinking something that magnificent should be free to do as it liked."

"Everyone should be free to do what they like," Rosemary murmured. "Within reason and laws, of course."

The sorrow in her voice told him not everyone had encouraged her. Something rose up inside him, fierce, protective. He wanted to slay her dragons.

He recognized the feeling. He had fallen in love with Felicity at first sight. That seemed to be his nature. The emotion was building slower this time, but just as strong, just as sure.

A shame he could no longer trust it.

CHAPTER FIFTEEN

DESPITE HER WORDS TO MIRANDA, Rosemary nearly stayed in Grace-by-the-Sea Sunday on her half day off. But her mother and sister commandeered her right after services and whisked her up to their home in Upper Grace. They too had questions about the discovery on the cliff. They had also shared a home with an avid collector, after all.

"I thought perhaps Flavius's fascination might have gone to the grave with him," her mother said as they sat sipping tea in the cozy withdrawing room. "Whatever possessed you to involve the earl and his daughter, Rosemary?"

"Lady Miranda craves just this sort of excitement," Rosemary told her, rose-patterned cup balanced over the lap of her grey silk gown. "She needs activities that stimulate her."

"Do not tell Rebecca," Hester advised, glancing up at the coffered ceiling as if she could see through the upper floor to where her daughter was playing with a nursemaid. "She'll ask to dig up the garden."

Like Miranda, Rosemary's niece was bright and inquisitive.

"I won't," Rosemary said. "Unfortunately, the story seems to have grown wings. It was the talk of the spa the other day."

"What do you intend to do with the skeleton?" her mother asked.

"I've already written to Uncle Montgomery's colleague Lord Belicent as well as the British Museum in London. I'm hoping one will want to mount a display."

The Women's Militia certainly would have applauded the idea. As planned, Rosemary and Miranda received them in the great hall on Monday morning. Jonas had tea ready to be served in the withdrawing room, but the women crowded around the table in the hall instead, bunched together and staring at the partial skeleton.

"A crocodile, you say?" Mrs. Kirby asked, taking a step back as if she thought it might snap at her.

"We believe so," Rosemary said. "But we'll know more when we excavate the remaining pieces."

"I don't understand," Mrs. Ellison said. "How did something like that end up buried in our cliff?"

"Fairies," Maudie opined. "They can be devious."

"Some believe the world was once warmer than it is now," Rosemary explained. "Parts of Britain may well have resembled tropical swamps."

Mrs. Catchpole glanced out the window near the front of the hall, where the rain was finally starting to taper off. "Sometimes I feel as if we live in a swamp now."

Knowing the countess might discover them at any time, Rosemary decided to forego the tea, ignored the frown that momentarily spoke of Mr. Jonas's displeasure, and ushered their guests straight to the kitchens.

"And I must commend to you our Mrs. Hillers," Rosemary told the women as Miranda pulled open the door to the caves. "The castle simply would not run efficiently without her."

Several of the women started applauding, and the others joined in. Mrs. Hillers turned a pleased pink.

"Our guests wished to know how the caves fared during this rain," Rosemary said when the noise subsided. "We'll be back shortly."

She led them down to the caves.

Abigail had them march for a bit, as they had before, then stopped them facing the boat.

"Well done," she told them all. "As we planned, I've asked Mrs. Catchpole to give us some advice on protecting ourselves."

The buxom employment agency manager moved up beside her.

"It's no secret that certain men are stronger than a woman," she explained, golden ringlets winking in the lamplight. "Very likely that will be true of many of the French. But we're not helpless. I have four older brothers, none particularly gentlemen, so I've learned how to duck a blow and where to strike back. Mrs. Bennett, if you please?"

Abigail drew herself up and swaggered toward her. "Surrender, you English wench."

Someone giggled.

Abigail scowled at them. "Pipe down you lot, or I'll be coming for you."

"I'm not afraid," Miranda declared.

"That's the spirit," Mrs. Catchpole encouraged her. "The best thing to do, of course, is run away. But sometimes that's not possible. Still, you don't have to let them know you intend to fight back." She put a hand on her chest and rolled her brown eyes toward the arching roof of the cavern. "Oh, my, a Frenchman! Whatever shall I do?"

"Spit in his eye!" Maudie cried.

"You have the right idea," Abigail said, breaking character. "The male anatomy has several spots that can prove vulnerable. The eyes, for one."

Mrs. Catchpole's fingers jutted out as if she meant to poke Abigail in the eyes.

"Ew!" Miss Pierce the younger hid her face in her sister's shoulder.

"It may sound horrid," Abigail said, taking a step back, "but the tactic could save your life."

"Three other spots can be useful," Mrs. Catchpole said, lowering her hand. "Though Mrs. Bennett tells me I should only mention two in this company." She glanced pointedly at Miranda, who was watching avidly. "One is the throat, just here." She cut the edge of her hand toward Abigail's windpipe.

Mrs. Ellison winced.

"Of course, if he's wearing one of those fancy thick collars or worse, a metal one, that won't do you much good," Mrs. Catchpole continued. "The other spot is the foot. You stomp your heel down near his instep. But only try this if you're wearing boots as thick or thicker than his. Dancing slippers won't break a bone."

"Then the French better not invade while we're dancing," Eva threw out, and the others laughed.

"We won't know when they'll invade," Abigail cautioned. "It could be while we're in church, or at the Harvest Fair, or simply going about our lives. We must be ready."

The women sobered, and Rosemary fought back a shiver.

Mrs. Catchpole nodded. "There's one more thing you should know. If you fight back, and he manages to get his arms around you, he'll think he's won. Go boneless, like this."

Abigail came up and wrapped her arms about her. "I have you now, my lovely."

Mrs. Catchpole collapsed so suddenly she slipped right through Abigail's embrace to the rocks. Then she sprang up and sprinted out of reach.

The women started applauding, then looked up at the ceiling and lowered their hands.

"There's another way," Miranda said in the silence that

followed. "I used it on the French spy."

Rosemary stared at her. All voices quieted; bodies stilled. All but one, that is.

"I told you the French were coming through Castle How!" Maudie declared.

Rosemary put an arm protectively around Miranda's shoulders, but Abigail held up her hands. "She's right. It isn't well known, but a guest at the spa, who called himself Owens and masqueraded as a physician, proved to be in league with the French recently. He tried to escape through this cavern, using the boat behind me. And he attempted to take Lady Miranda as his hostage. But she fought back. Come up and show them, your ladyship."

So that had been the horrid man Miranda had mentioned earlier. She glanced to Rosemary, who nodded, and the girl went to the front to join Abigail and Mrs. Catchpole.

"If I remember, he had you in his grasp." Abigail moved behind the girl and wrapped one arm about her chest.

"That's right," Miranda said. "All you have to do is this." She snapped back her head.

Even though Abigail had plainly been watching for the move, it still caught her on the chin. She dropped her arms, and Miranda ran to Rosemary.

Abigail rubbed her chin. "Very effective, as you can see. Pair up. Stop short of hurting anyone, but practice escaping threats."

"We ought to have invited the trolls," Maudie said as she turned to partner Eva. "They know how to fight."

"Perhaps you could ask them to join us next Monday," Miranda suggested.

They practiced for a while, then Abigail called them back together. "Next week, bring something you can use to fight with—a staff, a broom, a hoe, anything with a long pole will do."

"How are we to explain to the butler we came with a

hoe?" Mrs. Ellison asked with a frown.

"I'll think of something," Rosemary promised. "But come to the rear door in the kitchen, then, just to be safe."

They all trooped up the stairs.

"Fascinating geology," Abigail said as they exited the stairwell and once more stopped work in the kitchens.

"Perhaps next week I can explain how the forces of nature created the Dragon's Maw," Rosemary offered as she led them out of the room.

The ladies murmured their delight in the topic. They were almost to the front door when the countess caught them.

She was coming out of the withdrawing room, sheet music in one hand. Most of the women froze or glanced to Abigail or Rosemary for guidance.

Maudie stepped forward and dropped a curtsey. "Good morning to you, Countess. Any messages today?"

The lady's gaze widened as she took them all in. "Messages? From whom?"

As Maudie cocked her grey head, obviously thinking, Rosemary shooed the others toward the front door.

"The French?" Maudie suggested. "The Lady of the Tower? Mermaids?"

"Certainly not," the countess snapped. She lowered the sheets and stepped forward. "Miss Denby, what is all this? I don't believe I'm acquainted with any of these ladies, except for Mrs. Tully."

"I'll offer no favors," Maudie warned.

Rosemary managed to get the rest out the door before turning to meet the countess's outraged gaze. "A social experiment, your ladyship, for Lady Miranda's benefit. We didn't want to trouble you."

"And I doubt you know how to fight off the French," Maudie added.

"On the contrary, Mrs. Tully," the countess said, eyes

narrowing. "I am willing to brave much to protect my family. Where exactly did you conduct this social experiment, Miss Denby? You were not in the great hall, withdrawing room, or music room."

"Our visitors expressed interest in the caverns," Rosemary allowed, heart pounding as she rejoined Miranda and Maudie. "I know you dislike the place."

"Any lady of any breeding would dislike the place," the countess insisted.

Maudie puffed out her lower lip. "I don't know. It's rather fascinating if you like damp and dark."

"I do not," the countess told her. "And I do not want my granddaughter down there. It's dangerous."

Maudie nodded. "Kelpies dancing on the sand, French spies coming through."

"Kelpies are doubtful," Lady Howland told her, "but you are quite right about the French." She turned to Rosemary. "You would be wise to avoid those caverns, Miss Denby."

"I will take that under advisement," Rosemary said.

The countess peered closer. "I believe that was sarcasm." She straightened. "I will have a word with my son about all this."

Rosemary's stomach sank, but Miranda spoke up first. "Miss Denby asked Father. He said we could do it."

"Indeed."

Rosemary also knew sarcasm when she heard it. Time to try to mend bridges. "I'm very sorry if we concerned you, your ladyship."

"So concerned you refuse to assure me it will not happen again."

How could she make that promise? The ladies would be returning next Monday.

As if Rosemary had been silent too long, the countess shook her head. "You overstep yourself, Miss Denby. I have no doubt my son will see things as I do." She turned away from Rosemary to offer Maudie and Miranda a tight smile. "Mrs. Tully, I look forward to seeing you at the spa. Miranda, please escort your governess back to the schoolroom, where she belongs."

Drake had just finished laying out his proposed plan for the finances to show James when his mother sailed into his study.

"We must do something about Miss Denby," she said.

Drake slipped the pen into its crystal holder and leaned back, muscles tightening. "What's happened, Mother?"

She sank onto one of the dragon-seated chairs in front of his desk. "I found her with a number of women from the village. She had apparently invited them to call on Miranda, but not me."

"Ah." He smiled at her. "Rosemary discussed the matter with me. She is giving Miranda lessons on how to receive visitors. I thought you'd be pleased."

"Pleased?" She arched a brow as if he'd suggested she dance with the gardener. "I would be pleased if my granddaughter took tea like a lady with Marjorie and me, though even her aunt isn't her social equal."

"I doubt any of the women Rosemary invited saw a nine-year-old girl as their social equal," Drake pointed out.

"Miranda isn't any nine-year-old girl," she countered. "She is the daughter and granddaughter of an earl. I warned you this was no place for us. I'm certain some of the women today were in trade!"

"The horror," he drawled.

His mother's eyes flashed. "You will be horrified when Miranda elopes with some farmhand she met at the spa."

He rose and came around the desk. "I don't expect

Miranda to elope with anyone any time soon. And it would take a fairly educated, wealthy farmhand to have the interest and wherewithal to purchase a subscription to the spa."

His mother gazed up at him. "You refuse to heed my warning?"

"I refuse to see a visit from the local ladies as deleterious to my daughter's future. But if the matter concerns you so much, I'll ask Rosemary to include you in the visit next time."

His mother's posture relaxed just the slightest. "Good. Thank you, Drake. I knew you would understand if I explained myself."

She made it sound as if he had been particularly dense. Perhaps he was. His father would never have allowed the village women to visit or laid out an ancient skeleton in the great hall. Drake merely smiled, and she rose and sailed from the room, supremely confident in her ability to rule.

Would that he were so confident. He gathered his plans and went to request his coat and hat.

Pierson hadn't apparently finished dusting the mud from Drake's greatcoat after his trip to the shore on Saturday, but his valet offered him his black velvet opera cloak and top hat instead.

"I'm merely going to visit my cousin in the village," Drake tried. "Do I own nothing more…common?"

"Common?" Pierson squeaked. "But you are the earl, my lord."

Did the fellow think he had forgotten? "Perhaps I'll ask Giles where he put my old country coat," Drake said, heading for the door.

As if determined to fulfill his duty, Pierson followed.

"Might I recommend the tweed, my lord?" Giles asked, producing a perfectly suitable coat from the cupboard under the stairs.

"Tweed," Pierson said, drawing himself up. "My lord earl does not wear tweed."

"When he needs warmth and comfort, he does," Drake countered, turning so that Giles could shrug him into it. He left with the former footman and the current footman glaring at each other.

He found James also in his study in Butterfly Manor. The house had belonged to his cousin's maternal grandparents; Aunt Marjorie had been raised there. James and Eva had secured the lease when they'd married. The tall cases filled with books, the maps detailing the area, and the window looking out toward the spa bespoke a man of means and purpose.

"The income wasn't as high as you'd wanted, I know," James said after greeting him and nodding him into a chair. "The summer months are busiest here for leases."

"So I understand," he allowed. He handed his cousin the sheaf of papers he'd brought with him. "What would you think about selling Peverell the hillside down to the cove below his lodge? He's been wanting it for years."

James leaned back in his chair. "Ah, you haven't heard. The Lord Peverell you remember died recently and his heir with him. Boating accident. His younger son inherited."

Drake raised a brow. "The one you and I called Rob Rascal when we were growing up?"

"The same."

Drake chuckled. "Well, that should make things interesting."

"Indeed. But I can suggest to his steward you are willing to sell."

"For a fair price," Drake stressed. "That might give us enough to see us through the winter."

"Consider it done. And I asked around about your visitors the other night. No one will own up to it, but Jack Hornswag at the Mermaid Inn, who acts as our harbormaster, tells me he found one of his boats at the wrong mooring this morning. Someone could have used it and returned it."

"Then we still don't know who it was and whether they were making for the boat under the castle."

"I like it no more than you do," James said. "But I've set a watch on the cove. They won't slip away in one of our boats again."

"Good." He should go, but he couldn't make himself rise from the chair.

James cocked his head. "Was there another reason for your visit?"

Drake's gaze went out the window behind his cousin, where the white walls of the spa gleamed on the hillside. "In truth, I need advice about more than finances."

"I am always at your disposal," James told him.

"I find myself in an odd position, and I ask myself whether there's some flaw in my character that I seem to prefer women who already love someone else."

He returned his gaze to his cousin to see that James had paled. "I thought we agreed you were the better man for Felicity."

"You and my father agreed. Felicity and her parents agreed. I was never given a say in the matter."

James shook his head. "If you had known she was in love with me, would it have mattered?"

"I like to think so. I believe I loved her enough to let her go where she would be happiest."

"I suppose we'll never know, old man," James said with a sad smile. "Felicity is dead, and I wouldn't trade my Eva for the world."

Drake cocked his head. "And what if I'd been a different sort of man—more like my father: arrogant, focused on my own needs and ambitions. Would you have let Felicity go as easily?"

"Probably not," James allowed. "But why bring all this

up now?"

Drake took a breath. "Because I find myself falling in love with another woman whose heart may be already taken."

James started, then leaned forward again, eyes narrowing. "Who?"

He was surprised the entire village wasn't already speculating. "Rosemary Denby, my daughter's governess."

James leaned back, smile rising. "Interesting choice. The countess won't be pleased, and you'll face criticism from some high sticklers, but I see no real impediment, particularly if you make your home here."

"She's in love with Captain St. Claire."

James's smile popped. "You're sure?"

"She told me so herself. He refused to acknowledge any feelings in return, which hurt her badly, but he's asked enough questions, hovered about at the assemblies, that I suspect he may have changed his mind."

James chuckled. "Quillan St. Claire isn't the sort to suffer in silence. If he loved Rosemary Denby, she'd have no doubts on the matter."

Drake regarded him. "So you think the path clear, then?"

"Clear and open," James vowed. "The question is whether you are ready to take it."

It would always have come down to that. Even if Rosemary were free to love him in return didn't mean she would choose to do so.

Was he willing to risk his heart on the chance?

CHAPTER SIXTEEN

TUESDAY DAWNED BRIGHT AND CLEAR, so they could return to the cliff at last. Miranda chattered away as she, Rosemary, and Drake followed the footpath to the shore mid-morning. Miranda and Rosemary were dressed in their work clothes and bonnets. Drake, for once, wore the tweed coat and chamois breeches of a country gentleman. Giles and Dawson accompanied them, bearing supplies and sustenance, their black tailcoats making them look a bit like crows descending to the shore.

Miranda fairly bounced with each step. Rosemary's excitement nearly matched her charge's, yet she found herself all too aware of Drake just behind her. She heard every crunch of his boot against a rock, caught the scent of sandalwood from his soap, and anticipated each touch of his hand as he helped her over rough patches.

And there were many rough patches. The rain had washed the dirt off the path, leaving it rockier and more hollowed. Worse, as they stepped down on the beach, she could see where the cliff had slumped. Debris rose in mounds along the base, and gullies showed where waves had begun to carve and carry it away.

"It's a wreck!" Miranda cried as they neared the scaffold.

"It is," Alex Chance agreed, coming out from under

the lower platform to greet them. Breeze tugging at his dark wool coat, he knuckled his forehead to Drake under his thatch of tawny hair. "My lord. Mr. Drummond was about done in. I offered to spell him today."

Drake cast him a frown before grasping his daughter's shoulder. "Wait, Miranda. Giles and Dawson will go first to make sure everything is safe."

The two footmen exchanged glances as if they hadn't expected that duty, but they set their burdens on some rocks and began making their way up the ladders.

Drake transferred Miranda's hand to Rosemary's and nodded to Alex. "Any trouble?"

"Not a lick of it," Alex assured him. "But now that you're here, I'll take a walk to be sure."

Who did they think might trouble their discovery? Surely no one from the village would come down the shore with the weather so bleak. And any French agent would have more important matters to attend to than disturbing some scaffolding along the cliff.

Beside her, Miranda was pulling to be free. Rosemary turned her to face up the beach instead. "See there, Miranda, where the cliff has eroded? We may find more fossils exposed. We can look later, once we know the hillside is stable."

Miranda slumped nearly as low as the cliff. "The rain ruined everything."

"The headland has been crumbling for years," her father told her as Alex moved down the beach toward the Dragon's Maw. "Uncle James used to write to your grandfather, telling him when a particularly large piece had been lost. Thankfully, the castle is built far enough back that generations will pass before it's in any danger."

"My lord?" Giles called down. "There's a lot of dirt at the top, but I think you'll want to look at it before we remove it."

Drake frowned. "Why?"

"There seems to be a tail sticking out of it."

Rosemary felt as if a string had snapped inside her, sending her flying for the ladder. She gathered her skirts and started up. A scuffle sounded behind her. Drake. Miranda. What was she doing to have forgotten them? She stopped halfway to the next platform and peered down. He had caught his daughter and lifted her in his arms as if to keep her from scrambling after Rosemary.

"I know it's hard," he told Miranda as she kicked her feet, face reddening, "but wait until Rosemary tells you it's safe." He nodded to Rosemary to continue.

The two footmen made way as she reached the top. Easy to see why they were concerned. The hillside had broken free to pile on the platform in a jumble. Not a single fossil remained in sight on the cliff. But bronze-colored bones embedded in limestone, curving in a sinuous line, stuck out of one end of the mound.

"*Is* it a tail?" Dawson asked, coming up beside her.

"I believe it is," she told both footmen, and Giles puffed out his chest in pride.

Rosemary leaned over the edge of the upper story to where Drake had his arms full of a wiggling Miranda. "Bring her up. You must see this."

He set Miranda down. In a moment, they had reached her side. As if to give them privacy to enjoy their discovery, Giles and Dawson descended to the ground.

Miranda clasped her hands together. "That's the bottom of my crocodile. I know it."

"Based on how these fell, you may be right," Rosemary said. "But the drop may have cracked some of the bones or knocked others out of place. We'll have to go carefully. Drake?"

He was regarding the tail, eyes wide and mouth grinning. "Yes?"

"Would you ask Dawson to return to the castle and bring back any burlap sacks Mrs. Hillers might have handy? If we wrap the tail in them, we may be able to preserve the shape when we bring it back to the castle."

He nodded, then turned to call down to the waiting footmen.

Giles brought up Rosemary's basket of tools, and she, Drake, and Miranda set to work. They brushed off loose dirt and used the hammer and chisel to chip away chunks of limestone. Even after the fall, the bones seemed in good shape, dark against the rock.

"Look how long it is," Miranda said, eyes shining.

"All told, it may well be the largest such skeleton ever found in Britain." Rosemary's fingers trembled as she touched the sleek line. "Oh, Drake, isn't it marvelous?"

Not nearly as marvelous as Rosemary. Her hair was coming free of its pins, dirt smudged one cheek, and her gown was littered with chips of limestone, but she had never looked lovelier. He had to force himself to keep his gaze on the whip of a tail instead of her.

Then Miranda nudged him with her shoulder and pointed to the cliff to the east. "Let's see what else came down."

He didn't like leaving their discovery so soon, but Rosemary was craning her neck as if to spy the ground along the cliff's base.

"It will be a while before Dawson returns," she said. "Who knows what we might find."

With a smile, he led them down the ladder to the shore once more.

Humps of fallen material rose like waves along the slope of the cliff. Rosemary approached the first and showed Miranda how to sift through the debris with her fingers. They dug in the dirt like moles in search of grubs to discover Ammon's horns with their curly shells and delicate ferns etched in the limestone like copper on marble. Giles's brows rose a little higher each time they added another treasure to the pile to be returned to the castle. The sun on his back, his daughter happily occupied for once, and Rosemary glowing as she dug—what more could Drake want? Every concern, every doubt, fell away when they worked together like this.

"I have it," Rosemary said, and he looked up to find her beaming at him, fingers black with mud. "The castle's contribution to the Harvest Fair. We could display our discoveries."

"I don't want other people touching my crocodile," Miranda complained, clutching an Ammon's horn close.

"We can cover the items with a sheet of glass," he said. "Remember that display case on the third floor holding German drinking horns? It might be just the thing."

"We may have to reinforce the bottom, but I do believe you're right," Rosemary mused. "And Miranda can describe the history. The newspaper should be willing to print leaflets we can give out. We can call the discovery the Great Crocodile of Grace-by-the-Sea."

From the west, voices sounded. Drake turned with Rosemary to find visitors heading in their direction along the shore. Jesslyn Denby, in the lead, waved at them. Behind her, ladies lifted muslin hems off the sand. Gentlemen in tailored coats maneuvered their way between rocks and boulders. All of them paused to navigate the brook emanating from the Dragon's Maw. Mrs. Denby's brother, Mr. Chance, moved away from the cliff to join them.

Rosemary and Miranda met each other's gazes.

"Botheration," Rosemary said.

"Can't we ignore them and keep digging?" Miranda begged.

"I'll speak to them," Drake offered. "You two continue.

I'll be back shortly."

Rosemary's grateful smile made the walk easy.

He greeted the group near the scaffolding. "Mrs. Denby, a pleasure. How might I be of assistance?"

The spa hostess offered him a sunny smile, light glinting on the golden curls escaping her pink bonnet. "Good afternoon, Lord Howland. There was so much curiosity at the spa about your work here that we decided to take an outing."

Now that they were crowding around him, he recognized Mrs. Greer, Lord Featherstone, the Admiral, Mrs. Tully, Donner, Fenton, and Nash with her. Several other ladies must be Newcomers. All of them were gazing up at the scaffolding as if it were the Tower of London with the Crown Jewels hidden inside.

"You are all very welcome," Drake told them. "But I fear the scaffolding wasn't built to hold so many. Best to stay on the ground."

The Admiral tipped both his chins at the cliff. "Why climb to begin with, my lord? There appears to be no lack of dirt at this level."

"The recent rains caused some decay," Drake explained. "Miss Denby postulates that we may find fossils among the debris, which is why you see my fingers this color. The greater treasure lies a dozen feet above you, where the bones of an ancient crocodile have been deposited."

The Admiral frowned. "How'd it manage to insert itself up there?"

"Mermaids," Mrs. Tully supplied. "They always were fond of the beasts."

He could not quite imagine ancient mermaids tending a crocodile. "From what I understand, the land has risen since the time our crocodile lived," he told them. "When it passed, this cliffside may have been the shallow banks of a river."

"Still," Lord Featherstone said, rubbing his clean-shaven

chin, "crocodiles in England. The very thought enlarges one's imagination."

Mr. Fenton nodded down the cliff. "What about that hole? Do you intend to look for more crocodiles in there?"

"That hole, sir," the spa hostess informed him, "is known as the Dragon's Maw. On the highest tide, waves crash against the rocks with a roar."

"And only the finest sailors attempt to enter the caverns behind it," Lord Featherstone added. "Though I suspect attempts are less frequent now that you are in residence, my lord."

Unless one counted Captain St. Claire, but Drake certainly wasn't going to bring up his work. "We have no plans to excavate in the caverns. I rarely visit them myself, so I wouldn't know if a herd of Miss Denby's crocodiles was using them."

That raised a few chuckles.

They asked more questions that Drake managed to answer sensibly enough, he thought, then he promised them they could learn more at the upcoming Harvest Fair. Brightening at that, they all trooped back down the shore toward the village.

Rosemary came to join him as he watched them go. "Dawson has returned with the burlap. Excellent job answering their questions, by the way. Mr. Fenton seems to enjoy asking them as much as Mr. Cushman. He quizzed Hester and me mercilessly at the last assembly."

Drake smiled. "Likely he merely wanted an excuse to remain at your side."

"Perhaps. Still, I wonder why Mr. Cushman didn't join in the trip today."

So did he. Had Cushman been one of the ones to attempt to enter the Dragon's Maw by boat the other night? Perhaps he didn't know Mr. Drummond hadn't recognized him and had been afraid of meeting him again in daylight. But there had been two in the boat. If Cushman was one, who was his accomplice?

Rosemary glanced up at the platform. "I believe the tide is starting to come in. We should see to our prize."

Dawson had brought back a number of sacks. Rosemary first dampened them in the waters flowing from the Dragon's Maw, then Dawson carried them up to the top platform for her. Drake held one end of the tail piece, Miranda the other, while Rosemary wrapped the length in the clinging material.

"There," she said as she finished. "Now we need only carry it up to the castle."

That proved difficult along the eroded cliff path. Giles went first, walking sideways, with one end of the tail while Dawson followed with the other. Drake came next, ready to leap forward and save the thing should it start to tumble. Rosemary insisted on keeping Miranda at the back to prevent the girl from getting underfoot. He breathed a sigh of relief when they reached the castle safely.

"Absolutely not," his mother said when they all filed into the great hall. She must have seen them approach the front door from the withdrawing room window. "I will not have any more of these bones in my home."

The footmen looked to Drake.

"On the table, with the others," he said. "Gently."

His mother pressed her lips together and said nothing more until he dismissed the servants to clean up from their exertions. Rosemary was attempting to usher Miranda toward the stairs to do the same.

"I want to look at my bones," his daughter protested, one hand clutching at the newel post.

"Really, Drake, this is the outside of enough," his mother declared, silver head high over her black silk day dress. "Do you hear your daughter? What sort of lady will she grow up to be if you continue to indulge her this way?" As if she discounted his answer before he gave it, she turned to Rosemary. "Miss Denby, you must support me in this. Surely you heard the word hoyden often enough as a child."

Drake stiffened.

So did Rosemary. Hand still on Miranda's shoulder, she turned and met his mother's gaze. "Actually, the word I heard was bluestocking. I should be proud if it was applied to Lady Miranda. Now if you'll excuse me, your granddaughter and I would like to refresh ourselves before dinner. I was raised to be a lady." She turned and urged Miranda up the stairs.

"Well." His mother watched them go, then turned to Drake. "Will you allow her to speak to me that way?"

"Apparently so," he said. "I was raised to be a gentleman, and I cannot think of many words befitting a gentleman at the moment. So, I will take myself off for cleaning as well."

He left his mother gaping as he started up the stairs behind Rosemary and Miranda.

Guilt tapped on his shoulder. His mother may not appreciate what they were doing with the crocodile, but this would be her home for the foreseeable future. He should not treat her so cavalierly.

But she should not have treated Rosemary as if she were beneath her.

While he could not bring himself to openly berate his mother, he could surely find a way to apologize to Rosemary for such behavior. A gentleman should not offer a lady a gift without some claim on her affections, and simply commiserating didn't seem sufficient. But perhaps there was another way.

"Flowers, my lord?" Pierson squeaked when Drake asked him to see about procuring the same. "I'm sure I couldn't say where I'd find any this time of year."

It was late in the season. The Peverell's lodge was empty,

and he didn't recall that family having a conservatory in the sprawling manor house in any regard. But surely someone managed flowers for the spa and local events like weddings.

"Perhaps," Pierson said, as if thinking as well, "I might ask Giles. He seems to know things."

"Excellent idea," Drake told him. "See if he can have them delivered to the schoolroom before dinner."

Sometime later, he started down the stairs, smiling as he imagined Rosemary's pleasure when the flowers had arrived. He thought she might say something when they all met in the withdrawing room, but she kept her head down and took Miranda's hand to lead her in to dinner, leaving him to escort his mother.

"I must thank you, Drake," his mother said over the fish stew and crusty bread they often had on the cook's evening off. "The chrysanthemums were lovely. Such a pretty gold."

His *mother* had received the flowers? Perhaps he was working his new valet too hard that Pierson hadn't passed the right instructions on to Giles. Or was Giles overworked to make such a mistake?

"You're welcome, Mother," he said. "I had hoped to have some for the schoolroom too."

He smiled at Rosemary. She stirred the chunks of fish around in her bowl, gaze on the motion as if it were more fascinating than anything else on the table.

"Miss Denby doesn't like flowers," Miranda said. "She turned green when they came. We gave them to Grandmother."

Rosemary occupied herself with his daughter, fingers clutching her lorgnette as if it alone secured her at the table, but he couldn't help thinking that she still appeared a little pale. It seemed he'd misstepped, though he couldn't think why. If she did not like flowers, what else could he do to show his appreciation of her? New books for the schoolroom? They already had plenty. Additional time off?

"Will you be attending the assembly tomorrow night, Rosemary?" he tried.

Finally she glanced up, though her gaze looked more wary than usual. "Yes, my lord."

"Then allow me to send word to your sister that we will bring you and return you. Coming for you likely takes her out of her way. Delivering you to her is the least we can do to thank you for all your diligent work with Miranda."

She eyed him a moment, then inclined her head. "Thank you, my lord. I'll write to my sister. Perhaps Dawson can carry the note."

"I'll arrange it," Drake promised. He could hardly wait for Wednesday.

CHAPTER SEVENTEEN

WEDNESDAY MORNING, ROSEMARY SHOWED MIRANDA how to clean and position the skeleton. It was a relief to escape the schoolroom. It still smelled faintly of the earthy scent of chrysanthemums, and the reminder of the bright gold flowers brought back far less pleasant memories. Better to keep busy.

"A little vinegar will help remove the last of the limestone," Rosemary explained, dabbing it on the most crusted piece of the tail.

Miranda giggled. "It's bubbling!"

The limestone did indeed sizzle as it fell away. Once they had most of the rock removed, Rosemary repositioned the bones to form a skeleton.

"She only has one leg," Miranda said, lip starting to jut out.

"Yes, but she's still one of the most complete skeletons ever found," Rosemary pointed out. "If my uncle was here, I guarantee you he would be hopping about in delight."

Miranda grinned.

Next, they developed a plan for the display for Drake's approval. He praised it when Rosemary and Miranda brought it to him later that day in his study.

"I see you even provided a drawing of the fair's arrangement," he said. "These are where the various booths will be positioned on the fields above the spa?"

Rosemary had to come around the desk to orient herself properly. "Yes," she said, bending over the plan. "Farmers along the edges, displays of crafts and curiosities in the middle."

"Remind me of the timing."

His voice purred so near her ear. If she turned her head, their lips might meet. Her pulse seemed to find that a perfectly acceptable idea, for it kicked up like a colt in spring grass.

She drew in a breath and gathered her dignity. "The fair starts Thursday at one in the afternoon, is open from eight in the morning until nightfall on Friday, and Saturday until noon." She could have stopped there, but something made her continue. "There's a ball Friday evening at the assembly rooms. Everyone in the area attends, regardless of age or social standing." She could only hope the comment had not sounded like an invitation.

"May I go, Father?" Miranda piped up from the other side of the desk.

He started to shake his head. Rosemary could not seem to let the matter go.

"You will likely be asked to open the fair and the dance, Drake," she put in. "Those honors generally fall to the highest-ranking gentleman."

He slanted her a glance, as if he knew she was hoping for a dance, and her cheeks heated.

"We'll go to the ball for a short time, then," he allowed, returning his gaze to his daughter. "But you may not dance with anyone except me or Uncle James, Miranda, unless I approve first. I will not be disobeyed in this."

She nodded, face solemn. "Yes, Father." She pushed a cross-hatched piece of paper toward him. "Did you read my leaflet?"

"I did," he said with a smile. "It will do nicely for the handbills. My only concern is whether the newspaper will have time to print them."

"If I approach them today," Rosemary said, moving back around the desk to Miranda's side and finding the spot far less satisfactory. "If they affix a small advertisement about their services at the bottom, they may be amenable to printing them for free."

"Clever," he said. "I'll call for the coach. We can take the information to them now."

He must have more important things to do. Yet he seemed as eager for her company as she was for his, so she did not protest. A short time later, the three of them were riding for the offices of the *Upper Grace Gazette*. The countess might have been included, but she was down in the village visiting Eva and Marjorie.

The day was bright and crisp, the trees surrounding the castle beginning to shed their leaves in bright gold and dusky orange. As the carriage rolled off the headland, more scaffolding came into view on the fields at the top of the hill.

Rosemary nodded out the window. "See there, Miranda? They're nearly finished building the stands and animal pens for the fair."

"Animals?" Miranda pressed against Rosemary to see out the glass. "What sort of animals?"

"The sort farmers raise," Drake said. "Around here, that means sheep, goats, and cows."

"And perhaps a few horses," Rosemary added. "Pigs, chickens, ducks, and geese as well."

Miranda pulled back from the window. "Oh, Father, may I have a pig? I'm sure it would be happy running around the grounds."

"No," he said. "We haven't the space or staff to care for farm animals."

Miranda settled back against the squabs with a sigh, but Rosemary took heart that she did not pout or wheedle.

She remained a model of decorum as they alighted in

front of the newspaper offices on High Street in Upper Grace. Rosemary glanced up and down the familiar cobbled street, with the white-fronted bakery on one corner and the red-brick butcher's shop on the other. Giles hurried to open the door to the tall, narrow building housing the publisher for them.

Drake ushered Rosemary and his daughter into the building and introduced the publisher to them. Mr. Peascoat nearly bent double in welcoming them to his premises and readily agreed to Rosemary's proposal.

"And may I say what an honor it is, my lord, that you would patronize our establishment."

"It is a worthy endeavor," Drake assured him, and the bald-headed fellow beamed. He promised to deliver the leaflets to the fairgrounds the next morning, when they would be setting up their display.

Rosemary was congratulating herself on a job well done when they exited the building, and she spotted her mother, sister, and niece coming out of the baker's.

"Aunt Rosemary!" Rebecca pulled away and ran to her, yellow muslin skirts flapping.

Rosemary caught her in a hug even as Miranda frowned.

"Terribly sorry to intrude," her mother said as she and Hester joined them. "Your aunt is busy, Rebecca. Come away."

"No need," Drake told them. "I would very much like to be introduced to this charming young lady."

"She's not a young lady," Miranda protested. "She's a baby."

Her mother's face puckered, and her sister sucked in a breath. Rebecca reacted more strongly to the rude statement. She drew herself up to all of her forty-two inches, putting her eyes at a level with Miranda's breastbone. "I'm not a baby. I'm six."

Miranda put her hands on her hips. "Well, I'm nine,

which means I know a great deal more than you."

"Apparently," her father said, "not how to behave with civility."

Miranda's hands fell. So did her face.

"Lady Miranda," Rosemary put in, "Lord Howland, allow me to present my niece, Rebecca Todd; her mother, Mrs. Todd; and my mother, Mrs. Denby."

Hester and their mother dropped curtseys, and Rebecca followed suit.

"I don't have to curtsey to you," Miranda informed the girl. "I'm a lady, and you aren't."

A frown gathered on Drake's face. Before he could speak, Rosemary put an arm around Miranda's shoulders. "Excuse us a moment." She drew the girl a little way down the street.

"What did I do wrong?" Miranda demanded, eyes swimming with tears that Rosemary thought were no sham. "I do outrank her."

"Perhaps you can answer the question yourself," Rosemary challenged. "Do you enjoy the feeling when your grandmother tells you that you do not measure up to her expectations?"

Miranda reddened. "No. I feel as if someone dumped worms on my head."

"Then why," Rosemary asked, "would you inflict that pain on another?"

Miranda blinked. "I understand. May I apologize?"

"Please," Rosemary said, stepping aside.

Miranda moved back to join the others. Then she raised her chin, spread her skirts, and curtsied to Rosemary's family. "I'm terribly sorry, Miss Todd, Mrs. Todd, and Mrs. Denby. I am honored to make your acquaintance."

Hester and her mother smiled at her.

"I have a new doll," Rebecca told her magnanimously. "Would you like to see her?"

"I don't play with dolls anymore," Miranda said. "But

it's very nice of you to offer to share. We'll be sharing our crocodile at the fair. If you come by, I'll show her to you."

Rebecca glanced up at Hester. "May we, Mama?"

"We'd be delighted," Hester told them both. "Rosemary, I received your note about riding with the earl to the assembly tonight. Perhaps I might discuss this trip to the fair at greater length then, with Lord Howland."

It was all Rosemary could do not to frown at her sister. Hester never put herself forward. Why was she commandeering a moment of Drake's time?

And why did Rosemary have a sudden urge to tell her sister to go jump in the cove?

Drake tried not to show his surprise. Why would Rosemary's sister need a private word with him over a simple trip to the fair? Rosemary seemed just as bemused, for she hastily bid her family farewell and all but shoved Drake toward the waiting carriage as if protecting him from a highwayman.

Curiosity reigned, but he dared not give vent to it in front of Miranda. As it was, he and his daughter had a lengthy discussion about kindness and compassion as they rode home in the coach. Then he and Rosemary had to change into their clothes for the assembly. Afterward, they rode to the assembly rooms with his mother, who, at least, was on her best behavior. But he couldn't very well have a private conversation with Rosemary in front of her. He was only thankful that she went straight to where Aunt Marjorie, Mrs. Greer, and some of the other prominent older ladies of the village were gathered.

"Is there some reason your sister would need to speak to me?" he blurted out to Rosemary as soon as his mother was across the room. Well, perhaps Miranda wasn't the only one who needed to practice being civil.

Rosemary shook her head, setting the tantalizing curls along her face to bouncing. It was a softer arrangement than she usually wore, and he had to fight the urge to reach up and touch one of the shining locks.

"I have no idea," she said. "But I can promise you, I will have a few words for her myself."

Drake chuckled. "I hope you'll save me a dance or two."

She froze, and he realized what he'd just suggested. Two dances? She must know the statement that would make.

"Perhaps one dance and a promenade," she countered.

Yes, of course. That would be much more seemly. He couldn't understand why he was so disappointed. He inclined his head. "I'll await your good pleasure."

She managed a smile, fingers once more around her lorgnette, and went in search of her sister.

Hester Todd found him first.

He had greeted James and Eva and was making his way around the room to do the same with Lord Featherstone when Mrs. Todd materialized out of the crowd. Like Rosemary, she'd left tendrils curling against her cheeks, but those cheeks were already turning pink as she spread her green silk skirts and curtsied to him.

"Mrs. Todd," he acknowledged with a bow.

"My lord," she answered, one hand rubbing against the long glove of the other as she straightened. "Please forgive my boldness, but I must ask you your intentions toward my sister."

His brows shot up, and he took her elbow and steered her closer to a quiet spot along the wall, mind whirling. "Isn't that question asked by the head of the family?"

"It is," she agreed. "But my father and uncle have been gone for some time, and my brother, Larkin, may not have had as much opportunity as I have had to observe your interactions."

How ironic. He had not yet decided that he had intentions toward Rosemary, and her sister saw something he had been wary to name.

"I admire your sister greatly," he told her. "I would do nothing to cause her concern."

"Please remember that," she urged. "I have no doubt our company will grow tiresome after a while, and you will return to the excitement of London, where a fondness for one's governess is far less tolerated, I'm sure. I would not want to see her life made more difficult by her association with you."

She must not have heard the rumors about his financial constraints, or she had surprising faith in his ability to resolve them, to assume he would return to London. "Your sister is in no danger from me, Mrs. Todd. I commend you for your concern."

Still she regarded him, as if trying to see behind his words to the truth. He held her gaze until she looked away.

"Thank you, my lord," she said. She dipped another curtsey, then moved off.

Leaving him standing beside the wall, emotions tumbling over each other.

He had been determined to show more restraint this time. He'd promised himself he would consider Miranda's feelings. He was only a year out of mourning. Some might see that as too early to take a bride. And his mother urged him to marry an heiress.

He didn't want an heiress. He began to believe he wanted Rosemary Denby, with her quick wit, her clever care of Miranda, and the challenging smile that hovered on her rosy lips.

But her sister was right, and he could damage Rosemary's reputation if it appeared he was dallying with her. So, just to make it plain he wasn't showing her any favoritism, he made sure to dance with Mrs. Tully and his aunt Marjorie before approaching Rosemary again.

She and her sister had attracted a gathering in the meantime. He spotted Donner, Cushman, Fenton, and Nash from the spa, as well as young Mr. Chance and one of the officers from West Creech, resplendent in his crimson uniform.

"And why do you find these ancient deposits so fascinating?" Donner was asking as Drake strolled up to the group. "I suppose I could unearth the bones of some chicken devoured by the Romans, but I'm not sure anyone would care."

That elicited laughs, from everyone except Rosemary and her sister.

"This creature predates the Romans, sir," Rosemary said, raising her lorgnette to skewer him with her gaze. "It may predate British civilization. To imagine it and the world it inhabited takes intellect and vision."

"Both of which Miss Denby has in abundance," Drake put in.

Donner and Cushman bowed, and Fenton and Nash inclined their heads to a chorus of "my lord."

"Miss Denby must have courage as well," Cushman said as he straightened, "to venture to the shore so often when the French could invade any day."

Was the fellow that afraid? A sheen of perspiration was growing on his forehead under his curly blond hair.

Donner had no such concerns. He chuckled. "Perhaps Napoleon will come for your ancient creatures, Miss Denby. After all, they do call him Old Boney."

Fenton reddened. "I see no reason for jest, sir. The emperor is a serious threat."

"Was not a French vessel sighted off this very beach less than a month ago?" Nash put in.

"A vessel flying a French flag," Drake corrected him. "We believe it was an English ship stolen by French agents who had been abandoned on these shores."

"Captain St. Claire chased them all the way back to

France," Chance bragged.

Nash glanced around, brow furrowing. "Then you truly don't fear the Army massing on the other side of the Channel?"

"Anyone with any sense would be concerned, sir," Rosemary's sister put in. "But we trust our valiant English sailors and soldiers to keep us safe."

"Hear, hear," the West Creech officer agreed.

"And others," Rosemary added with a glance to where Doctor Bennett and his wife were moving out toward the dance being set up. She must be thinking of the Grace-by-the-Sea militia, though he had not heard the physician was a member.

Drake took the opportunity to step closer. "Miss Denby, I was hoping to claim the dance we discussed."

"Delighted, my lord," she said, lowering her lorgnette at last. The other men deflated as he led her away.

"Quite a devoted following," he commented as they crossed the floor and he tried not to preen to have her on his arm.

"Even a bluestocking might attract attention under the right circumstances," she allowed.

The music was already starting, so they must hurry into place. He did not have a chance to tell her it wasn't just her intellect that had made them seek her out.

The dance involved a great deal of hopping about, and they had little opportunity for conversation. Yet he could not help admiring her grace, her precision. It appeared he acquitted himself well, for she praised him as the dance ended.

"Much better. You followed every step."

Perhaps not quite in time to the music, but definitely an improvement since the last assembly. "I had an excellent teacher." She started to pull away, and he caught her hand, reluctant to let her go. "Perhaps that promenade you suggested?"

"Very well."

She sounded almost resigned, and he told himself not to be dismayed as they began their stroll along the edges of the long room. The visitors from the spa were clustered together now, laughing and talking. Mrs. Tully nodded to them as Drake and Rosemary passed.

Her hand tightened on his arm. "May I ask a favor?"

At the moment, it would have been easy to offer her the moon. "Certainly."

"Please don't send flowers to the schoolroom again," she said. "I cannot abide them."

A singular aversion. "All flowers or particular varieties?"

"Anything with petals," she said. She shuddered. "Hester and I found my father in a field of wildflowers we had gone to pick, you see. He was a Riding Officer for our stretch of coastline in Kent. He'd been out following a lead to a cache coming in the night before, and the smugglers found him first. He was lying among flowers, eyes on the sky, and there was blood on the petals."

She choked, and he only wanted to gather her closer. But that would raise too many eyebrows and questions.

He put his hand over hers instead. "I will never send you flowers again. No one should have to relive that."

"Thank you." She stopped, forcing him up as well. "I should return to my family. Please let me know when you and the countess would like to leave."

He released her, nodding, and watched her sweep across the ballroom, head high and steps once more graceful.

And he knew then he would have to decide what to do about these feelings, and soon.

CHAPTER EIGHTEEN

HOW KIND HE WAS. ONLY her family knew what had happened that dark day when her father had been murdered. Talking with him was like balm to her soul. She was reluctant to let him go, but their promenade had ended.

And she wanted to learn what her sister had said to him. She hadn't had a chance to ask before becoming surrounded by gentlemen. Now Hester was just returning to a chair after dancing with Lord Featherstone. As soon as the baron excused himself, Rosemary cornered her.

Hester took one look at Rosemary's face, and her honey-colored brows went up. "Are you all right? You look as if you'd lost your favorite book."

"Or found one I never thought to read." Rosemary dropped onto the spindle-backed chair next to her sister's. "I begin to think Lord Howland has taken an interest in me."

Hester pressed a gloved hand to her lips. "Oh, Rosemary, I feared as much. That's why I spoke to him."

"What!" Her yelp turned heads in their direction, and Rosemary hastily lowered her voice. "What did you say to him?"

"Nothing about your feelings," Hester assured her, dropping her hand and bending her head to hers. "I asked him about his intentions and warned him not to sully your reputation."

Rosemary snorted. "I'm surprised he didn't sack me immediately. What were you thinking?"

"I was thinking of you," her sister informed her, straightening. "An earl taking an interest in a commoner? You know where that could lead."

"He is no Rob Peverell," Rosemary insisted. "There's never been any stories of dalliances or flirting. He was by all accounts a devoted husband and remains a loving father."

Hester regarded her sadly. "Yes, I will grant you others claim him beyond reproach. But you are still in his employ, and he is an earl. It isn't seemly."

Suddenly, weariness fell like rain on the fire of her temper. "I know. I could tell you it is all in your imagination, but he sent me flowers yesterday."

Hester touched her arm, face sagging. "I'm so sorry. He couldn't know."

"Of course he couldn't know. I explained myself a few moments ago, so it shouldn't happen again. But it isn't simply a matter of the flowers. I find myself thinking of him constantly, always aware of his presence. I wondered what it would be like to kiss him. And that scares me."

Her eyes were probably as wide as her sister's. "It should scare you," Hester said. "Please, Rosemary, don't make the same mistake I did and fall top over teakettle. You are the logical one. Think of the ramifications."

Rosemary nodded. She was a bluestocking. She knew how to study a situation, think about it from various perspectives. A shame her heart kept countering every argument.

It wasn't easy riding home with him and the countess that night. She nearly jumped every time the carriage hit a bump and his shoe brushed hers. Oh, for a moment to think.

Unfortunately, Miranda was waiting, toes tucked under her flowered nightgown as she sat curled up on Rosemary's bed with a book across her lap.

"Crocodiles have strong jaws," she informed her.

"So I have read." Rosemary moved into the room. "I believe you should be in your own bed now."

Miranda snuggled against Rosemary's pillow. "It was chilly."

"Ask Warren to lay you a fire, then," Rosemary said, beginning to take the pins from her hair.

As if she'd heard her name, the maid bustled into the room. She stopped when her gaze lit on Miranda. "How'd you get in here?"

Miranda pointed to the connecting door. "That way."

Warren cast Rosemary a look. "Sorry, Miss Denby. I stopped using the basin ages ago, and I thought I had her settled."

"Help me change for bed," Rosemary said. "Then I'll see her back to her room."

A short time later, swathed in her flannel dressing gown, she escorted Miranda through the door and to her own bed. The girl crawled under the covers and shivered.

"It will warm up now that you're in it," Rosemary promised.

Miranda's look was doubtful. "You came home sooner than last time. Didn't you have fun?"

She couldn't answer that question directly. "It was an interesting evening. I enjoyed the dancing."

Miranda pulled the covers closer. "Did Father meet her?"

Rosemary frowned. "Who?"

"The heiress Grandmother wants him to marry."

Oh, that. "Not really," Rosemary replied.

"Good." Miranda paused to yawn.

Rosemary waited until her mouth was closed again. "Don't you want your father to remarry and give you a mother?"

"Another mother might be nice," Miranda allowed. "Mine was very kind and very beautiful, and she spent all her time with me."

Of course she had. His first wife was nothing if not perfect.

"But Grandmother said Father's new wife must give me a baby brother," Miranda continued. "We don't need a baby. They aren't much fun that I can see."

"Perhaps not," Rosemary said. "But a baby brother could grow up to be helpful. And you never know—the baby might be a girl. I love having a sister."

"Well, maybe a sister," Miranda offered grudgingly. "Though she'd have to do what I tell her."

Why not? Everyone else did.

Certainly it worked that way at the fair the next morning. Drake had arranged for Dawson and the stable hands to transport everything they would need for the display down to the fair in a wagon at first light. He, Rosemary, and Miranda followed not long after with the skeleton, once more wrapped in burlap and cradled in pieces across Rosemary's and Miranda's laps in the carriage. The weight of the thing only reminded her of its age and provenance. What an honor!

The stable hands had the plan she and Miranda had developed to go by, but that didn't stop Miranda from telling them what to do. They mostly nodded as they went about setting up sturdy poles and draping an awning to cover a space approximately ten feet square. They moved the display case to the front, facing into the fair, and Rosemary arranged the skeleton inside the case, with Ammon's horn and leaf fossils around it.

"She looks like she's crawling through the bushes," Miranda said with a pleased smile.

Drake was everywhere. He secured the awning into place, rubbed a sleeve against the glass to polish off a smudge, and positioned the table that would hold their leaflets at least a half dozen times.

"I believe you'll be wanted shortly," Rosemary told him with a smile and a nod toward the southern end of the fair, where the official entrance lay. Already a crowd was gathering. Most of the inhabitants of Grace-by-the Sea and their guests milled about on the grass, with more carriages and wagons approaching from Upper Grace to the north. The sea breeze pulled at bonnets and muslin. The gentlemen clapped their gloved hands against the arms of their coats. The magistrate, many-caped greatcoat draped about him, top hat on his golden head, beckoned to Drake.

"I'll be back shortly," he promised. "Miranda, do what Rosemary tells you."

"Yes, Father," she said, busy rearranging a fern specimen more to her liking.

The publisher brought the leaflets just before the fair opened.

"Fascinating account," he said. "Whoever thought there were crocodiles in England."

Rosemary finished filling the basket and set a rock on the lid to keep the wind from scattering the leaflets. Then she looked to Miranda. "Let's go hear your father."

Miranda slipped her hand into Rosemary's, and they hurried for the front of the fair.

His cousin, the magistrate, had just stepped out of the wide opening between the two rows of booths on that side. He held up his hands, and murmurs quieted. He looked to Drake.

The earl joined him. Like bookends, the two stood side by side, Drake an inch or two higher, his cousin an inch or two broader. They turned their blue gazes out over the gathering crowd.

"It is my great honor to welcome you all to the Grace-by-the-Sea Harvest Fair," Drake told them. "Please enjoy everything our area has to offer." He stepped aside and bowed.

Those in the crowd exchanged glances. What, did they fear him as much as they had feared his father? Enough of that! Rosemary drew Miranda around the side of the booths and gently wove her way back to the opening. Then they walked past him, all smiles.

"Thank you, my lord," Rosemary said.

He winked at her.

She refused to look back, but she heard others following.

She led Miranda past Mr. Ellison's booth, where the baker had spicy gingerbread available for a penny, and Abigail's display showing off the craft work of the ladies of Grace-by-the-Sea, toward where their booth held pride of place in the center of the fairgrounds. Miranda veered from one side of the aisle to the other, angling her head to see all around them.

"That tall booth is a puppet show," she reported. "I don't like Punch. He's mean to Judy."

"I quite agree," Rosemary said. She sniffed the air. "Oh, smell that? Someone's roasting nuts."

"Can we have some?" Miranda asked, pulling harder to escape Rosemary's hold.

"I imagine you'll want to sample a number of treats," Rosemary said, refusing to let go. "Apple cider, corn cakes, candy balls, pie, and pastries."

Miranda's eyes widened.

For now, she managed to convince her charge to settle in behind their display as various people streamed toward them. Their first visitor was Lord Featherstone.

"Good morning, Miss Denby, Lady Miranda," he said, tipping his top hat so that they caught a glimpse of his silver mane. "What an impressive display."

"It's a crocodile," Miranda informed him. "Even if a few bones are missing. You can read about it." She handed him one of the leaflets.

"Amazing," he said. "And how generous of you to bring it to the fair where we can all see it."

Guilt tugged at Rosemary, harder than Miranda's grip. If the British Museum refused and her uncle's friend made a good offer, the crocodile was likely headed for a private room at his estate. This might be the only time anyone else had the opportunity to view it.

"My father's very generous," Miranda said to the baron. "But I wrote those words."

"Most impressive," he told her, tucking the leaflet into his coat. "A keepsake to treasure with the memories of this fine day." He tipped his top hat again and moved on.

"I think he liked it," Miranda said to Rosemary with a wiggle of her shoulders in obvious pride.

Most of the people who stopped over the next hour seemed to like the display. They listened to Miranda tell them all about the crocodile and how it had been discovered. Some of the children asked her questions and gaped at her answers.

"They know I'm smart," Miranda told Rosemary at one point.

"Indeed they do," Rosemary told her, feeling a bit of pride herself.

Maudie was the most attentive. She came back three times to listen to Miranda tell someone else the story. When she came back a fourth time, Miranda frowned at her.

"You already know everything," she accused.

Maudie raised her chin, threatening the black ribbon that tied her bonnet around her face. "Of course I do. I'm glad to find someone who appreciates that."

Rosemary hid her smile. "I believe Lady Miranda is wondering if you'd like us to tell you something more."

She glanced both ways, as if expecting the crowd of harboring spies, which, apparently, could be possible, then leaned over the display case and lowered her voice. "I want to know if you'd let me touch them."

Miranda glanced at Rosemary.

"I don't want to open the case in front of others," she told them both. "But I'll take the matter under advisement."

"That means yes," Miranda confided in the older woman.

Maudie straightened with a smile. "I've always liked you, Miss Denby, no matter what the mermaids said."

More people pressed in just then, and Rosemary and Miranda each handled a group. Rosemary hadn't realized Maudie had slipped into the booth with them until she heard her telling a couple from the spa about the Ammon's horn and the fern fossils. She waited for the appearance of a mermaid or a troll in the tale, but the older woman stuck to the story Miranda had offered.

"It seems she really did listen to you," she told Miranda.

Drake returned to them in the middle of the afternoon.

"Sorry for the delay," he said, sliding past the display case to enter the booth. "Apparently, I am supposed to judge the sheep, pigs, and buttermilk."

That would explain the dab of white on his lips. She had to fight to keep from reaching up and stroking it away. Wouldn't that have been the talk of the fair!

"Miranda is keeping a tally of the visitors and the most asked questions," Rosemary told him.

"Forty-two visitors," Miranda declared triumphantly. "And they mostly asked why we care about old bones. So, Miss Denby, Mrs. Tully, and I tell them." She snapped a nod.

He leaned closer to Rosemary and lowered his voice, gaze on the woman in black who was dusting off the case. "We've added Mrs. Tully to our partnership?"

"She added herself," Rosemary murmured back. "And she's rather good at helping."

Miranda, who must have overheard the conversation, nodded. "She could take my part for a while so you could buy me gingerbread, Father."

He chuckled, straightening. "I suppose we could go in search of sustenance. Is there anything you'd like, Rosemary?"

To keep him at her side? Well, she certainly couldn't say that!

"Perhaps cider," she said aloud.

She watched as they moved off together, Miranda's hand swinging his.

"She's a clever one," Maudie said, coming up beside Rosemary. "Like you were at that age."

Rosemary smiled at her. "I didn't realize you remembered me at that age."

She tapped her bonnet near her temple. "I remember everything. How you put the other children to shame at the vicar's school we had then. How you crawled all over the cliffs with your uncle. The way you ran after Captain St. Claire."

"Oh, look," Rosemary said, cheeks heating. "Here come more visitors."

She made sure to keep Maudie busy after that.

Drake and Miranda brought them back savory meat pies and mulled cider.

"But we have to return the cups," Miranda warned.

"Rosemary and I will do that," Drake said. "If you don't mind helping for a while longer, Mrs. Tully."

She shrugged with a rustle of black crape. "What else am I to do? The trolls won't arrive until the dance tomorrow night."

Miranda stared at her. "There will be trolls at the dance?"

"Far too many," she grumbled. "Mind your toes."

"I'm glad you feel comfortable leaving Miranda with her," Rosemary said as she and Drake struck out from the booth, each carrying two empty tin cups. "She is harmless, but I can't promise you she won't fill Miranda's head with all kinds of fancies."

"We've already survived the Lady of the Tower and the Hound of the Hill," he reminded her with a smile.

"Hound of the Headland," she corrected him. "And don't forget Napoleon. She claimed to have seen him too."

The man in front of them stumbled just then, and Drake stopped to help him regain his feet. Rosemary recognized one of the spa guests.

"Are you all right, Mr. Fenton?" she asked as he pulled down on his waistcoat with trembling hands.

"Fine, fine," he assured her, face reddening. "Though you would be wise to avoid the brandy balls." He staggered off.

"I didn't expect that here," Drake said, frowning after him.

"Indeed," Rosemary said, frowning as well. "I don't recall anyone selling brandy balls at the fair. The spa council usually avoids any sale of alcohol to prevent just this sort of issue."

"Perhaps he came here straight from the public house," Drake suggested. Turning, he nodded Rosemary toward the next booth, which featured bushels of dusky red apples.

The farmwife behind the counter beamed at him. "More, my lord?"

"Just returning your cups," Rosemary said, setting them on the length of wood. "Thank you. It was quite refreshing."

"Anytime, your ladyship."

She must live farther out not to realize Rosemary wasn't a lady like Miranda. Rosemary started to correct the use of the term, but Drake took her arm and escorted her away.

"You've been working at the booth since it opened," he told her. "You should have the opportunity to enjoy the spectacle too. What will it be—the puppet show? Animal judging? Gingerbread to go with that meat pie?"

She should return to Miranda, but at the moment she could think of nowhere she would rather be than at his side. Perhaps she could indulge, just this once.

She linked her arm with his. "Let's see where our fancy takes us."

With her beside him, it was all too easy to let his fancy take him places he hadn't convinced himself to go yet. For now, he was content to wander past the booths with her, from where the blacksmith, Mr. Josephs, had set up a brazier and was demonstrating how he melted various metals to the bookstall Mr. Carroll's Curiosities had crammed with all matter of tomes. It was a while before he managed to extract her from that one.

At the back of the fair, where the Downs opened up, a telescope had been erected on a tripod, pointing out over the village and the Channel. An older woman had her eye pressed to the end, while her companion waited her turn.

"Why, I can see my house, as if it stood right there," she marveled.

"That is the beauty of the telescope, madam, and why our good sailors rely on it," Quillan St. Claire said, standing guard over his treasure. He glanced up, then stood straighter as he must have recognized Drake and Rosemary. "Care to take a turn, Miss Denby?"

"No, thank you," she said primly, turning Drake back toward the other booths. The speed of her steps proved the depth of her emotions, and he couldn't help the dip in his spirits.

"I see you still dislike our captain," he ventured as she stopped to admire a wool shawl crafted by one of the local ladies.

"I can find no reason for thoughts of him to darken so pleasant a day," she said, fingers stroking the russet-colored wool as the farmwife watched hopefully.

"Many of us end up with memories we would prefer to leave behind," Drake said, recalling her story about the flowers the other night. "But ignoring them, shoving them deeper into the darkness, only allows them to fester."

She cast him a glance as she moved on to the next booth, where soaps were on display. The aromatic scents of lavender and rose danced in the air. "Interesting supposition. You liken the practice to rot."

"I do." He waited until they reached a gap between the booths and some semblance of privacy before continuing. "I let the knowledge that Felicity loved someone more than me trouble me for too many days before realizing it did neither of us any good. If we were to be content in our marriage, I had to accept her as she was, not pine for what I wanted her to be."

She dropped her gaze to the trampled ground. "You are very good about accepting people for who they are. I find that refreshing."

And what a rogue he was for wishing she found it more than refreshing.

CHAPTER NINETEEN

HOW PLEASANT IT WAS TO stroll along beside him, marveling at the wonders. She couldn't remember a finer day, a better moment, than this. When they'd circled the fair, and neared their booth, she nearly asked him to keep walking. But that wouldn't be fair to Maudie and Miranda, who were even now explaining the display to more visitors from the spa. Rosemary recognized Mr. Donner and Mr. Nash among them.

"And when do you resume digging?" the latter was asking.

"As soon as we can," Miranda promised him.

"Tuesday at the earliest," Rosemary amended, squeezing into the booth to stand beside her. "The fair doesn't end until Saturday, then there's church on Sunday. And we have activities planned for Monday." She raised a brow at Miranda.

The girl glanced at her father, then fixed a smile on her face. "Yes, of course. Tuesday, then."

Drake frowned at them both, as if wondering what they had planned. She could only hope he would not ask her outright, for she could not find it in herself to lie to him.

A loud clang saved her, echoing through the fairgrounds, and every head turned toward the noise. Standing near the main gate, Eva Howland grinned at them, mallet in one hand and brass gong in the other.

"The fair is closing for the evening," her husband James called beside her, his magistrate's voice penetrating every corner of the grounds. "Please make your way to the nearest exit, and come back tomorrow for more of the fair and the ball."

As if to underscore his words, Eva banged the gong again.

"I must get one of those," Maudie muttered.

"Me too," Miranda said.

Not if Rosemary could help it. Much as she wanted her charge to try new things, the castle would never know quiet again.

Drake gathered up the leaflets. "We'll take these home to make sure they don't get damp."

Miranda glanced longingly at the display case. "I don't want my crocodile to get wet again."

"The glass will protect it," Rosemary promised her, putting an arm about her shoulders. "So will the awning. And I'm sure your uncle will have men guarding the grounds tonight, so everything will be as it should tomorrow."

Miranda nodded. They stayed a moment longer to allow Maudie a moment to touch the skeleton as she had requested. Her eyes glowed as she patted the jagged jaw. She and Miranda moved so slowly from the booth their feet might have been mired in the limestone as well. Rosemary's feet dragged too, but she knew it had nothing to do with the display and everything to do with the inability to spend more time with her handsome, kindhearted employer.

Drake had never attended the Harvest Fair before, but he found it difficult to leave behind. What he'd felt walking and talking with Rosemary, just the two of them, was what he'd always imagined marriage would be. If he could just be certain she'd left Captain St. Claire behind, that he had a chance of winning her heart, he would be more than delighted to court her, scandal or no.

Unfortunately, Friday was another whirlwind of a day. His mother insisted on his protection as she toured the fair, only to abandon Drake entirely when they encountered Lord Featherstone near the pie booth. He thought he might escape to the castle's booth, but James collected him to judge any number of contests, from jams to quilts to animals of various shapes and sizes.

"At least you had the hens," Drake commiserated as they left the cages for the chickens and he rubbed a spot on his hand where a rooster had pecked him.

James brushed at a smear of white on his coat. "I'll take knotwork over chickens any day. At least the spa council decided to stop the tradition of judging babies. It always led to fisticuffs. No parent is willing to accept second place."

Drake clapped him on the shoulder. "Wait until you have a child of your own. I warrant you'll think her the most beautiful baby ever seen."

James's gaze drifted to where his curly-haired wife was exclaiming over a tatted collar at the booth sponsored by Mrs. Bennett's art business. "I might at that."

As if she felt his gaze on her, Eva glanced up. The look she and James shared warmed Drake's heart. He didn't argue when his cousin excused himself to join his wife.

That was what he'd missed, he mused as he strolled toward the castle's booth. One look signaling affection, communion. One look and knowing you were everything to another.

Would Rosemary ever look at him that way?

He could imagine looking at her that way. It was hard not to look that way as he approached the booth, where she and Miranda were explaining the display to the spa corporation president's wife.

"These bones are remarkably ugly," Mrs. Greer was saying, head bent over the case and threatening her high, feathered hat.

"They are not!" Miranda declared, face reddening. "My crocodile is beautiful."

"Now, Lady Miranda," Rosemary said with a stern look, "you know it takes someone with a thoughtless disregard for their own ignorance to fail to appreciate them."

"Exactly," Mrs. Greer said, blithefully unaware she'd just been insulted. She must have noticed Drake, for she beamed as she curtsied. "My lord, here you are again. How kind of you to give us so much of your valuable time."

"I only wish my less valuable time wasn't already taken," he told her.

Rosemary's lips quirked, as if she was fighting a smile.

Mrs. Greer remained oblivious. "Dare I hope you'll stay after opening the ball tonight, my lord?" she asked, simpering. "The presence of a gentleman of your standing may deter the riffraff of Upper Grace from attending."

Rosemary glared at her.

Drake merely smiled. "I was counting on attending. There are several families from Upper Grace who are more than acquaintances. I want to make sure they know they are welcome."

"Any friend of yours will always be welcome," she hurried to assure him.

He glanced to Rosemary. "Thank you. I'll remember that, Mrs. Greer. Because tonight I hope to dance with the loveliest lady of my acquaintance from Upper Grace, Miss Rosemary Denby."

Rosemary stared at him. So did Mrs. Greer. Then she wagged her finger. "Oh, Lord Howland. How you enjoy teasing us. Until tonight, then." She sailed off.

"Are you really going to dance with Miss Denby tonight, Father?" Miranda asked.

"I certainly am," he said. "If she will allow it."

Rosemary's head was bobbing before she thought better of it. "I'd be delighted. And I'm sure you'll dance with Miranda and the countess as well."

"That's only fair," Miranda agreed.

His smile seemed to have stiffened on his face. "Of course."

She wasn't sure what the day might hold, but, once again, they were besieged by visitors, and the hours flew by. Eva must have relinquished her position, for it was Maudie, grinning brightly, who banged the gong to close the fair for the evening. Everyone hurried to go this time. They knew what came next.

So did Rosemary. She had attended the Harvest Ball every year since they'd moved to Upper Grace to live with her uncle following her father's death. Last year, she'd attempted to catch Quillan St. Claire's eye for the first time at that ball. He hadn't noticed, and she'd gone home thoroughly disappointed.

This time, anticipation fluttered inside her like a butterfly. If she took a little more care with her toilette that evening, asking Warren to fix her hair, choosing her prettiest gown, it was only to be expected.

As she was about to leave her room, she reached for the lorgnette case, then paused. Always the little pair of glasses had been a shield. Peering through them, she could keep people at a distance, a handy trait when those people were quick to find fault. Perhaps she didn't need the lorgnette tonight.

She swept down the stairs, apricot-colored silk dancing about her ankles. She must not look too eager to greet Drake, who waited at the bottom. She had to own that he looked rather fine as well in a deep green tailcoat and black evening breeches buckled at his knees, with his lighter-green waistcoat embroidered with palm fronds.

Miranda, in her blue silk gown, waited with the countess in her black silk. But Drake's gaze never left Rosemary, as if he would drink her in. A lady could become accustomed to such admiration.

As the coach set out for the assembly rooms, the countess gathered her wine-colored shawl closer. "I understand this event may be rougher than usual. I certainly don't recall attending with your father."

"You and Father frequently left before harvest," Drake pointed out from his place beside Rosemary, facing his mother and daughter. "I'm looking forward to an interesting night." He dropped his hand to the seat, where his fingers brushed hers.

It was all she could do to keep her smile no more than pleasant.

The assembly rooms were so full and joyfully loud Rosemary could only think this was what Londoners called a crush. But no London ballroom would have ever seen such attendees. Burly farmers moved among slender dandies, serving maids in their Sunday best brushed shoulders with the first ladies of the village. Children as young as six chased each other around their families.

"Stay by my side, Miranda," the countess instructed with a wrinkle of her nose as a little girl scampered past.

Miranda looked after the child and sighed.

"You stay close as well," Drake murmured to Rosemary. "If I lose you in here, I may never find you again."

She doubted that. He might lose her, but she would never misplace him. He was tall enough, important enough, that everyone gave way before him. His presence allowed them all to transverse the space and stop at the top of the room, below the alcove for the musicians.

"Wait here a moment," he told them before turning for the small podium where the magistrate waited.

"Where's Mrs. Tully and her gong?" Rosemary asked Miranda with a smile.

"I could yell," Miranda offered.

"You will not," the countess said, looking suitably horrified at the very idea.

In the end, the magistrate's call proved sufficient. "May I have your attention, citizens and visitors? Your attention, please!"

Once more, bodies stilled, voices quieted. Gazes turned toward the podium, where Drake stood waiting, the very epitome of a cultured gentleman.

"Friends, family, esteemed guests," he said, smiling all around. "Welcome to the annual Harvest Ball. This is an all-comers event. Ladies, please look kindly on those requesting your hand in a dance. The requestor likely screwed his courage to the sticking-place to dare approach such beauty. And fellows, be on your best behavior considering the treasures we have among us in our wives, sisters, and daughters. May the joy of our company long outlast the night."

Applause thundered. He inclined his head and started for her side. She only hoped she did not look as worshipful as some of the other ladies he passed.

She thought he might ask her to dance, but, as the musicians began tuning up, he bowed to his daughter. "Lady Miranda, may I request your hand?"

Miranda grinned, then schooled her face and dropped her gaze as she curtsied. "I would be delighted, my lord."

He offered her his arm and led her out onto the floor.

"Her manners appear to be improving," the countess mused.

"Their skill at the dance as well," Rosemary replied. Then she stood taller as Lord Featherstone approached.

"Countess, Miss Denby," he said with a bow, "you outshine the stars tonight."

"My dear Lord Featherstone," the countess said with a smile as he straightened. "How you do go on."

He offered the lady his arm. "Might I be so bold as to request a dance?"

"There is no one I would rather partner," the countess told him, and the two moved off.

Rosemary stood along the wall as she had at so many dances, watching as others partnered up. Mr. Donner was leading her sister out, and Lark had Jesslyn. A local squire claimed her mother. She dropped her gaze to the polished wood floor. Her lorgnette would have felt good between her fingers right about now.

Two black evening shoes moved into her line of sight. She knew who they belonged to before he spoke.

Her head snapped up, and she raised a finger. "Don't. I will have to refuse, and that means I must sit out. Find another lady."

With a bow, Quillan St. Claire moved on.

Rosemary collapsed against the wall.

"Not fond of sailors, then," Alexander Chance asked, coming up beside her.

She straightened. "I have nothing against those who sail, sir. Only a certain person who captains the ship."

"Then I hope my association with that person won't prevent you from accepting my offer of a dance."

"Of course not. My brother's marriage to your sister makes us family, after all." She accepted his arm and accompanied him out onto the floor.

The musicians had judged their audience well, or perhaps Jesslyn had encouraged them, for the first dance was a rollicking one with relatively few figures. Enough couples wanted to join in that they had to make two lines down the long hall. Rosemary lost sight of Drake and Miranda as she skipped and swirled with Alex. He was an athletic dancer, capering about with ease and earning him more than one appreciative glance from the ladies around them.

He escorted her back to her place when the set ended. Drake and Miranda were waiting. The countess seemed to have been absorbed by the spa group, which clustered on the opposite wall.

"My lord," Alex greeted him with a short bow. "Perhaps an exchange of partners, if the ladies are willing?"

Miranda hopped forward. "I'll dance with you."

Drake inclined his head, and Alex led her out.

"At last," Drake said, offering Rosemary his arm. "A moment with you more than makes up for any duty."

"Uneasy is the head that wears the crown," Rosemary teased, taking his arm. "Or, in this case, an earl's coronet."

With a smile, he led her toward the set that was forming.

But it was so much harder to dance with him than it had been before. Instead of her employer, Miranda's father, or the major landowner of the area, she suddenly saw a man, face worn but warm with regard for her, body lean and lithe, steps strong and stately. When they circled, his gaze was for her alone. When he cupped her hand in his to lead her down the line, she felt as if he held her heart instead. She was amazed she wasn't the one who forgot the steps!

As the dance ended, he closed the distance between them and offered her his hand. "That was energetic. Perhaps we should step outside for a breath of fresh air."

She raised a brow. The excuse had been used by every fellow seeking to steal a kiss since before the Romans first sailed into Grace Cove.

A kiss? From Drake?

"What a marvelous idea," she said calmly while her

heart slammed into her chest as if determined to go this very moment.

"Allow me to settle Miranda," he said.

Miranda. Of course. She'd forgotten all about her charge! Her skin tingled as he pulled away to speak to Alex and his daughter. The young sailor nodded, then began leading Miranda toward the countess's circle, where Mr. Cushman's curly blond hair caught the light. Miranda frowned back at her.

"Shall we?" Drake asked, and she latched onto his arm, trying not to cling like a barnacle to a ship.

Outside, the air was considerably cooler. Carriages and wagons waited at the edge of the light, the drivers taking turns seeing to their horses. Most who were staying in the village had walked the short distance to the assembly rooms. Closer to hand, a few other couples walked, heads together and arms entwined.

He glanced up at the crescent moon, golden against the velvety black sky. "Lovely night."

"Very fine weather for September," Rosemary agreed.

He dropped his gaze to hers. "Kind of you to even reply to that comment. It wasn't the most scintillating way to open a conversation."

Rosemary swallowed. "Did you bring me out here for conversation, Drake?"

"No," he said. And he bent his head and kissed her.

Joy and delight built inside her in equal measure, until she thought she might float up to touch the moon above. Perhaps that's why she clung to him as if she couldn't let go.

She was starlight, sunlight, warmth, and wit. He could not seem to release her, cradling her tight, murmuring her name against her lips. Who needed food, drink, breath, when this fire was possible?

He made himself pull back and gazed at her face, fingers tracing the curve of her cheek. "You're blushing."

"So are you," she pointed out.

He smiled. "I imagine I am. It has been more than ten years since I considered courting a lady."

She blinked so rapidly he was certain her lashes raised a breeze. "Define courting."

He could imagine his lovely bluestocking asking Miranda such a question. "A verb used to denote a gentleman's pursuit of a lady with the intent of matrimony."

"Oh." Her voice was low and breathless. "I was under the impression you intended to wed an heiress."

"Define heiress," he said.

She was watching him now. He could see the moon reflected in her dark eyes. "A woman whose family will provide her with a dowry sufficient to turn heads even if she herself might not."

"You turn my head," he said. "You open my eyes to things I'd never considered. You challenge me to be a better man. Riches enough for me."

"Are they?" she asked. "I want to believe that. But you confided that you fell in love with your late wife the moment you met. Your feelings apparently have grown over the course of three weeks this time, but I cannot help but question the duration. You are named for a dragon, and they are renowned for being attracted to shiny things. Might I merely be that shiny thing?"

Her analysis stung, and he took a step back. "I assure you my feelings are true. You are not the only one capable of observing and drawing conclusions. Your interactions with your family and Miranda tell me you care deeply. Your interactions with my mother tell me you stand up for your principles. No one would argue against your knowledge and intellect. You and I work well together.

We appear to want the same things for Miranda. What have I missed?"

She nodded slowly. "Your assessment is astute. My point is that you should be very certain of me. You loved your Felicity, but she hurt you. I care for you far more than is wise. I never want to hurt you."

He tucked her closer once more, relishing the feel of her against him. "And I hope to never hurt you either, Rosemary. Only promise me you will give our feelings time to grow. Allow me to court you."

She was silent a moment, and his gut tightened. Would she admit her emotions were still engaged with Captain St. Claire? He nearly shouted in relief when she nodded.

"Very well, Drake. Let's see what happens when the earl courts his governess."

CHAPTER TWENTY

A COURTSHIP. WONDER AND SKEPTICISM fizzed inside her like vinegar on limestone. She should not question her good fortune, yet something inside her refused to accept that Drake could truly love her. If the other gentlemen in the area, most of whom had known her for years, had turned aside from pursuing her, how could he claim love so quickly?

Some of what she was feeling must have shown on her face, for several of the ladies glanced her way with raised brows and fluttering fans as if they saw the change in her as Rosemary and Drake returned to the assembly. More likely, they too knew of the delights and dangers of stepping outside with a gentleman.

The countess might not have known, but she was waiting for them near the entry hall, Miranda's hand in hers. And it was a question as to who looked more flustered.

"I would like to leave," the countess declared, nose in the air. "We have done our duty and made an appearance. I'm sure Miss Denby would like to stay, but I insist on returning home. Now."

"Please, Grandmother?" Miranda begged. "The trolls haven't arrived yet."

"I could claim a few," her grandmother said with a glance toward the dancers, where Lord Featherstone was leading out a pretty Newcomer. "We will call for the carriage at once."

Drake cast Rosemary an apologetic smile. "Very well, Mother. Rosemary, would you prefer to ride home with your family?"

He and Miranda were becoming her family. "No. I'll join you."

The countess swept past her, dragging Miranda with her.

The ride back to the castle was chilly, and it had nothing to do with the night air. Miranda gazed out one window at the dark, shoulders slumped, and the countess gazed out the other, head high. Drake glanced between them and shared a puzzled look with Rosemary.

"Did something happen to upset you, Mother?" he tried.

The countess tore her gaze from the glass. "Nothing I care to discuss in present company."

Rosemary thought she might mean Miranda, but the countess's look was to her instead.

More distressing news awaited them at the castle. Most of the staff had been given the night off to attend the Harvest Ball, but Davis, Warren, and the earl's valet had remained behind so they could see to the family's needs. The earl's valet was waiting for them in the great hall.

"We had a bit of trouble while you were out, my lord," he said as he helped Drake off with his cloak.

Rosemary started, but Drake frowned at him as he turned. "What happened, Pierson?"

"With Giles and Dawson gone, I thought I should walk the floors," Pierson said. "Just to be certain all was well. I was passing the kitchen when I heard the rear door rattling, like someone was trying to force it open."

"What!" the countess cried, hand pressed to her chest.

"Was it the Lady of the Tower?" Miranda asked, eyes large.

Rosemary put an arm about her shoulders. Other governesses would have escorted the girl upstairs to protect against any unpleasantness. Miranda needed to know her home was safe.

And Rosemary wanted to know as well.

"I don't think so, your ladyship," Pierson said. "And no one got in. I made sure of that."

"This could have a simple explanation," Drake said calmly. "Perhaps Mrs. Hillers forgot something."

"She and Mr. Jonas have keys, my lord," Pierson said. "I knew it couldn't be them. I went for a pike from the armory to defend myself, but when I returned and opened the door, I found no one there. I thought you should know."

"Thank you," Drake said as the countess gave an audible sigh of relief. "And thank you for thinking to walk the floors while the others were out. Mr. Jonas will be back shortly. You should be able to resume your duties, but make sure you tell him what you told me."

Pierson inclined his head. "Of course, my lord."

Drake turned to his family. "I believe that's sufficient excitement for one night, don't you?"

Miranda nodded. The countess raised her chin and swept up the stairs.

Drake met Rosemary's gaze. How could one look convey so much information? In it, she knew herself valued, loved, that they had a future together if only she could find the courage to agree. It was all she could do to lead Miranda up the stairs.

Warren took Miranda in hand when they reached their rooms. While the maid helped the girl change, Rosemary went to her own bedchamber.

Two letters were sitting on the mantel. They must have been delivered while she was at the fair. In all her haste to change for the ball, she hadn't noticed them until now. The first was from the British Museum. The trustees regretted to inform her that they had sufficient curiosities from more renowned collections, including that of her esteemed uncle, and so on and so forth and thank you very much for writing.

"Philistines," she muttered as she opened the second from Lord Belicent.

My dear Miss Denby, of course I remember you. Your uncle was a great friend, and he often spoke fondly of you. I'm glad to know you continue his good work. For some time, I have been most desirous of obtaining a specimen just as you described. If it is all you say, I'm sure we could come to terms. Please write back at your earliest convenience, and let me know when I might view your discovery.

Rosemary set down the letter. It seemed they had a buyer, someone to take the skeleton away. Miranda would be bereft. The countess would be in alt.

As if conjured by her thoughts, the countess opened the door and swept into the room. Her chest was heaving, as if she'd run a great distance.

"Your ladyship," Rosemary said, taking a step toward her in concern.

The countess held up a hand. "Save your words. You have made your intentions known, and I will not have it. Pack your things. I want you out of this house by morning."

A man could smile forever after such a kiss.

Despite the news of their would-be intruder, Drake certainly found himself smiling as Pierson prepared him for bed. Even his valet seemed to sense his mood, for his fingers were far more deft than usual as he helped him off with his coat and cravat.

"Did you have an opportunity to take in the fair, Pierson?" he asked, sitting on the edge of the bed.

In the act of bending to remove Drake's shoes, Pierson looked up, eyes wide. "No, my lord. Should I, my lord?"

"You should," Drake said. "I'll see to my own needs in the morning. Take the day off and enjoy yourself."

His face held a look of awe. "I will, my lord. Thank you." He returned to his work.

Drake was in his nightshirt, splashing water on his face, when the door opened and his mother stormed in.

"I have discharged Miss Denby," she announced. "But she refuses to leave without speaking to you. I expect you to abide by my decision and have her removed first thing in the morning."

Drake turned in time to see his boots shaking in Pierson's grip. Then his valet hurried to gather up the rest of the discarded clothing and rushed to hide in the dressing room next door. Wise man. There was fire in his mother's eyes, a rigidness to her spine, that brooked no disobedience.

But he knew his own mind.

"And what," he asked, toweling off his hands, "has Rosemary done to displease you?"

"That you would have to ask proves how far things have gone." She swept closer. "I saw you—kissing. Miranda was restive, so I thought to seek you out. I am merely thankful I noticed you before she did and could prevent her from witnessing such behavior."

"I see." He hung up the towel on the stand and turned to face her fully. "You should know, Mother, that my intentions are honorable. I hope to make Rosemary my wife."

She gasped, taking a step back. Then her eyes narrowed. "Have you lost your senses? She is your daughter's governess."

"And a fine one," he reminded her.

She shook her head with a sigh. "I understand that Felicity's death distressed you greatly, but you cannot marry the first woman who looks your way."

"I can when that woman is Rosemary," he insisted. "I admire her intellect, her wisdom. I am in awe of how she encourages Miranda to use her own intellect. And, yes, I find her quite easy on the eyes."

She drew herself up, and he knew she was reaching for the largest weapon in her armory. "Your father would never have allowed this."

She probably thought he would admit defeat immediately, but the shot passed through him cleanly. "Very likely not. But if he were alive, I would still pursue Rosemary. He wasn't infallible, Mother, or we wouldn't find ourselves living here. I will never be his equal, and I thank God daily for that. I wish you could see the man I have become and accept me for it."

Her lips trembled a moment before she answered him. "You are my son. Of course I accept you. But you tell me we must live here now. How can you expect me to hold my head up in this place if you marry the governess?"

"Governess is merely her title, Mother," he said gently, going to take her hands. "There is a woman—a vibrant, determined, wonderful woman—behind that title. Try to take solace in that, for if Rosemary agrees to my proposal, she will be your daughter-in-law."

She peered up at him, as if she hadn't truly seen him before tonight. "You've changed. Loving her gives you such strength?"

He released her hands with a laugh. "Perhaps it does. Perhaps I'm merely growing into my own title. Either way, it is only to the good."

She nodded slowly. "I will take the matter under advisement. Good night, Drake."

"Good night, Mother." He bent and kissed her cheek. He waited only until she was out the door before calling for Pierson.

"Fetch my banyan. I have a call to make before retiring.

And you will accompany me."

"Yes, my lord," Pierson said, head bobbing. "Right away, my lord."

A few moments later, Drake knocked on Rosemary's door. Warren answered and paled at the sight of him.

"I'm glad you're here," Drake said. "That makes two witnesses. Would you ask your lady if I may have a word?"

She nodded and slipped back into the room, closing the door behind her. Drake stood calmly, though Pierson was shifting from foot to foot as if contemplating how easy it would be to run away.

"Are you happy being my valet, Pierson?" he asked.

His servant froze. "It is a very great honor, my lord."

"Not really," Drake said. "I would rather you served where you felt most comfortable. You seemed rather pleased to be walking the halls again tonight. Think about which position suits you best."

Pierson nodded.

The door opened again then, and Rosemary stood framed, pink flannel dressing gown wrapping her curves, and Warren peeking over her shoulder. Though her head was high, red rimmed her eyes. Had she been crying?

Everything in him shouted to hold her, comfort her, fight for her. He held himself in place with the utmost of will.

"Yes, my lord?" she asked.

"I understand the countess told you that you are discharged," Drake said. "She is mistaken. I have explained the situation to her. I simply didn't want the matter to concern you further tonight."

Her chin came down just the slightest. "Thank you. I hope you cleared up any misconceptions."

"I think it safe to say she knows where I stand now. I'm sorry if anything she said disturbed you."

"Mildly," she acknowledged. "Though this visit sets my mind at rest. Still, if she cannot value my service, perhaps it is best if I leave."

Both Warren and Pierson were regarding him with pinched faces. The longing to touch her was not to be denied. He settled on taking one hand.

"She is already coming around. I promise you, there will be no impediment to our plans."

They were his plans, but he took heart in the fact that she did not argue his phrasing.

"She will not be the last to question you," she warned. "You are in all things kind and compassionate. This… friendship between us may force you to be otherwise. I would not see you changed for the world."

"Nor I, you," he murmured, thumb stroking the back of her hand. "Give us a chance, Rosemary. Things will come right. I know it."

Her smile was soft. "Ever the visionary."

He grinned at her. "Is that a yes?"

"I'll take that under advisement," she said. "And you know what Miranda says that means."

He couldn't help himself. He leaned forward and brushed her cheek in a kiss. "Thank you, Rosemary. Sweet dreams."

Her look was sweet as he pulled back. "And you, Drake."

He nodded as she shut the door, Warren and Pierson both goggling, but he knew no dreams could be as sweet as the idea of a future with her.

Rosemary had a difficult time falling asleep that night. He'd countermanded an order from the countess for her. If that didn't show his belief in their future, she didn't know what did. Still, the countess would probably not give up without a fight. Rosemary wasn't looking forward to Saturday.

But the countess was nowhere to be found when Rosemary escorted Miranda downstairs the next morning.

"Fatigued," Drake said with a polite smile. "Apparently yesterday's exertions did her in. It will be just the three of us."

Miranda didn't seem to mind, for she bounced on the seat as the carriage started for the fair. "I want to try the corn cakes today, Father, and Mr. Josephs said he could make me a gong like Aunt Eva's."

He smiled. "I'll have a word with our blacksmith."

Rosemary should have a word with Drake as well, and not only about the gong. The Harvest Fair was nearly over. They would have to decide the disposition of their discovery.

She found her opportunity when Maudie appeared midway through the morning. Rosemary turned her duties over to the lady and took Drake aside with the excuse of going to see about Miranda's gong.

"Think about the peace of the castle," she urged him as they strolled past booths displaying shawls and quilts. "And think too of this. My uncle's colleague answered our letter. So did the British Museum. The latter declined the honor of hosting our collection, but Lord Belicent is keenly interested."

"And you don't sound happy about that fact," he noted as they neared the blacksmith's booth.

Rosemary made a face. "I should be. He will take excellent care of it. But I could wish that others might continue to enjoy it as well. If Napoleon wasn't breathing out his murderous threats, I'd write to my uncle's colleagues in Germany or America, but I cannot guarantee the safety of the skeleton while it is traveling or that of any couriers escorting it."

His gaze went out over the yellowing grass of the Downs beyond the fair, as if seeing something else entirely. "There may be a way." His look returned to her with his smile. "Leave this to me, Rosemary. We'll find the best solution."

He had given her no specific answer, yet she felt lighter. And even better when he commissioned a small, silver triangle and rod from the blacksmith for Miranda instead of the big brass gong she'd wanted.

"She won't like it at first," Rosemary told him as they headed for the booth. "But I believe the pretty sound will win her over."

They had reached a spot in the fair with few booths and fewer attendees. He brought her hand to his lips for a kiss. "Just as you have won me over, Rosemary."

She thought she sailed into their booth.

Once more the morning sped by, and all too soon, Maudie went to ring the gong for the last time. The fair had ended. Dawson and Giles came to help them load everything onto the wagon to return to the castle. Rosemary, Miranda, and Maudie had given out every last leaflet, but the display case must be moved, and the skeleton rearranged in the great hall. Rosemary thought the countess might use the reappearance of bones on her table as an excuse to mount another attack, but Drake's mother continued to avoid them all, going so far as to insist on taking a tray in her room instead of eating dinner with her son and granddaughter. And Sunday morning, when Rosemary brought Miranda downstairs to attend services, they discovered that the countess had already left.

"Her ladyship requested that the magistrate's coach come for her this morning," Mr. Jonas told them, nose up. "The estate carriage will be ready for his lordship momentarily."

"She'll have to acknowledge us at St. Andrew's," Drake predicted.

He was wrong. Even from the entrance to the chapel, Rosemary could see that the Earl of Howland's pew was nearly filled. The countess had apparently invited his aunt Marjorie, Maudie, and Mrs. Greer to join her. The spa corporation president's wife was preening, head turning as if to see how many others noticed this favoritism.

"You and Miranda might fit," Rosemary whispered to him.

He nodded to the other side of the aisle. "I believe there is room by your brother. I hope you'll allow Miranda and me to join you."

Oh, would that set rumors flying! Well, why not? Rosemary hid her grin as she led him and Miranda to join Lark, Jesslyn, and Alex. Her family welcomed him and Miranda into the box pew, and Eva and the magistrate nodded their approval from the row ahead.

Rosemary did her best to attend to the readings, the sermon, but her gaze kept wandering to the stiff-backed matron at the front of the church. With her husband gone, the countess only had Drake and Miranda left. Was Rosemary driving a wedge between them?

When her mother had urged her to find a husband, Rosemary had wondered what marriage would cost her. Would a husband expect her to give up her studies, take up domestic duties to which she was ill-suited? Would she be allowed no opinion but his? That was the way of many marriages she'd seen.

Drake seemed to accept her for what she had to offer. With him, she had no reason to hide herself, to try to be something she wasn't.

Yet, she began to see that he had an equally high cost in marrying. She had likened him to a dragon guarding his hoard, but a dragon could be equal part protector. He had to consider his mother, who hoped for an heiress, a quick solution to their financial troubles. Then there was Miranda, who wanted someone who would put her first and not prevent access to her father. And Drake only wanted someone who would love him for himself.

That, she was beginning to believe, she could do. But was she costing him the love of his family in the bargain?

CHAPTER TWENTY-ONE

"DID YOU ENJOY THE SERVICES, Mother?"

Drake asked when he drew Miranda over to join James, Eva, and Aunt Marjorie on one side of the churchyard. He would have preferred to have Rosemary with him, but he must honor their agreement about her time off. Already, she'd gone with her family, though he flattered himself to think it had been with equal reluctance to be parted.

"I have always enjoyed services," his mother informed him. "And the comfort of congenial companions like Mrs. Greer and Mrs. Tully is equally welcome."

By congenial, she meant people who agreed with everything she said. "True," he replied. "I quite enjoyed the companionship of the Denby family."

She sighed.

Drake turned to his cousin, who appeared to be fighting a smile. "I was informed someone tried to break into the castle last night while we were at the Harvest Ball."

All vestiges of humor vanished from James's face while Eva and Aunt Marjorie gasped.

"Did anyone catch a glimpse of the culprit?" James demanded.

"Alas, no," Drake said. "I went out on the grounds at first light this morning and checked the caverns as well, but nothing seems to be amiss. I have no idea who was at the rear door."

"Mr. Donner did not attend the Harvest Ball," Eva put in. "And Mr. Fenton and Mr. Nash left early." As if she noticed most of them were staring at her, she shrugged. "James asked me to keep an eye on them."

"Why?" his mother asked, glancing around at them all.

Marjorie put a hand on her arm. "French spies, dear. They are everywhere." She began to sound like Mrs. Tully.

"Frequently enough that we must remain on guard," James amended. "I'll ask around, but nearly everyone was at the ball. I should have realized it was the perfect time to strike."

Drake should have realized it as well. He would not fail his family again.

It wasn't easy spending the afternoon with her family at Shell Cottage and not blurting out her feelings. But she wasn't sure how to explain the situation to matchmaker Jesslyn, and she didn't want her mother to be disappointed should nothing come of the matter. Besides, it soon became apparent that Hester had other things on her mind as well. Her sister was sufficiently distracted throughout dinner that Rosemary drew her aside afterward.

"Has something happened?" she asked, noting the shadows under her sister's eyes. "Please tell me you are not worried about me."

"Of course I worry about you," Hester said. "You are my sister. But you are right that something terrible has happened." She glanced to where their mother was hugging Jesslyn goodbye, then lowered her voice. "He's back."

Rosemary had no need to guess who would put such a tremor in her sister's voice. "Rob Peverell has returned?

Are you certain?"

Hester nodded. "I quite literally bumped into him at the ball last night. Oh, Rosemary! He attempted conversation, and I was horrid to him."

"As well you should be," Rosemary encouraged. "He pretended to be something he was not, raised your expectations, then disappeared without a word. The fellow is a scoundrel."

Hester's gaze fell, and she fiddled with her glove. "I am not without blame. I pretended to be someone else too, thinking it wildly romantic. What a fool."

Rosemary took both her hands. "You are no longer that fool. He cannot weasel his way back into your good graces."

Her sister's smile was feeble. "No, of course not."

Rosemary gave her hands a squeeze before releasing them. "The Peverells rarely leave their monstrosity of a house on the few occasions when they are in residence. You probably won't have to face him again."

Their mother joined them then, and Hester dropped the matter. As far as Rosemary knew, her sister had only ever confided in Rosemary about her momentary passion for a passing stranger who had turned out to be the rapscallion younger son of Viscount Peverell. Her mother and Lark had no idea that Hester's marriage to Lieutenant Todd had been to salvage a wounded heart.

As it was, Rosemary did not reach the castle again until after nightfall. She found several reasons to remain in the great hall, dusting off the skeleton, warming her hands by the fire, inquiring of Mr. Jonas as to the plans for Monday. But Drake did not make an appearance, and she could hardly seek him out. In the end, she wandered up to her room to change for bed.

She was not surprised to find Miranda waiting.

"She refused to go to sleep without seeing you," Warren warned as Rosemary approached the bed, where

Miranda was curled up.

"Because Grandmother says you will be my new mother," the girl blurted out. "I told you I don't want another mother."

Warren grimaced.

"Stories downstairs as well?" Rosemary asked her.

The maid nodded. "He kissed your cheek, miss. That sort of thing gets noticed and talked about. Not by me, mind you," she hurried to add.

"He kissed you!" Miranda all but shouted.

Rosemary sat on the bed beside her and beckoned Warren closer.

"I am quite fond of your father," she told the girl, amazed at how easily the confession flowed. "And that means I want him to be happy. I want you to be happy too, Miranda. So, I would never do anything to come between the two of you."

Miranda nodded. "Good. So, if you marry him, no babies."

Warren's hand flew to her mouth.

"I can't promise that," Rosemary said. "Sometimes, when a husband and wife love each other, their love combines to form a baby."

Warren was turning red. Rosemary tried to focus on Miranda.

"Well," Miranda said after a moment, "I suppose a sister might be nice. But no brother!"

"I'll take that under advisement," Rosemary said before she thought better of it.

Miranda grinned. "Thank you, Miss Denby."

"I'll return her to bed," Warren offered. She held out her hand, and Miranda slipped off the bed and padded to her room.

Stories. Supposition. How long would it be before they spread beyond the castle?

She was up before Miranda the next morning and

dressed in time to escort her charge to the breakfast room. As her gaze met Drake's, he set down his cup, stood, and smiled her into the room. She felt as if she could breathe again.

"And how are my two favorite ladies this morning?" he asked as they were all seated.

"Miss Denby promised me no brothers," Miranda informed him.

He blinked.

"What do you want for breakfast, Miranda?" Rosemary asked.

Drake held up a hand. "It will have to be toast and tea. Butterfly Manor sent word about a problem in the kitchen there. I'm sending Mrs. Hillers and her staff to assist, and I thought I'd go down myself to see what else must be done. After that, I have an appointment with Mr. Greer."

"Oh," Rosemary said. She should not be disappointed. They had the ladies coming today, and it would be easier to cross the kitchen if it weren't occupied.

"By the way," Drake said as Giles came forward to help them to toast, "the countess has requested to be involved in your Monday visit."

Cold flooded her.

Miranda spoke first. "She can't. She doesn't have a hoe."

Once more he looked nonplussed. "A hoe?"

"Some of the women garden," Rosemary quickly explained. "I'm not certain the countess would enjoy meeting them. Perhaps a more select group next week."

He nodded. "I'll speak to her."

Better him than Rosemary.

They split up after breakfast. She and Miranda collected staffs from the armory and headed for the cavern to light the lamps. Then they waited for their guests.

"Clever of you to send everyone away," Abigail said, slipping inside the castle by the rear door a short while later, long pole in one hand.

"It wasn't me," Rosemary told her. "But I'm glad for the timing. Down you go with Miranda. I'll join you as soon as the others arrive."

Mrs. Catchpole was the last. She came panting into the kitchen, one hand pressed to her generous chest and the other clutching a hoe. "Sorry. Bit of a to-do in the village this morning. Lord Peverell has returned and is wanting to hire staff."

"Then he and his family intend to stay for a while?" Rosemary asked, thinking of her sister as she closed the door behind the employment agency owner.

"For the winter, at least." She handed Rosemary the hoe and started unbuttoning her redingote, then looked around. "Where is everyone?"

Rosemary explained on the way down the stairs.

"Set aside your weapons for now and line up," Abigail was saying as they reached the caverns. "We'll start by marching. Knees high, heads up, ladies. Right face. Forward, march."

The crack of muslin sounded like musket fire echoing in the cave as they crossed the beach.

Rosemary marched beside Miranda. The movement was welcome, for the cavern air was cool and moist. Still, she was glad when Abigail called a halt a few moments later.

"Nicely done," she said. "And I see you brought your staves, as I requested. We'll learn a few tricks with them shortly. For now, we'll try…may I help you?"

"Which drill is that?" Mrs. Catchpole asked.

But Abigail's gaze had gone past them. Turning, Rosemary spotted Mr. Fenton and Mr. Nash, stepping down from the stairs. They stared at the women.

The women stared back.

The two men exchanged glances, then squared their shoulders, lowered their heads, and barreled down the beach. Rosemary grabbed Miranda and pulled her out of their way.

"Here, now," Abigail protested as the other women scattered like leaves in the wind.

The men shoved past her and splashed into the water to grip the sides of the boat.

The boat.

"They're French!" Rosemary shouted, and the cave took up the cry.

Fenton and Nash didn't deny it. Heaving and grunting, they broke the boat free of the sand and threw themselves inside as it began to bob on the outgoing tide.

"They're getting away!" Mrs. Ellison cried.

"The mermaids will stop them," Maudie predicted.

"I'm not waiting for mermaids." Abigail picked up a rock, balanced it in her hand, then swung hard. It splashed in the water beside the floating vessel.

"Let me," Mrs. Catchpole said. She picked up a bigger rock with both hands, spun in a circle and let fly. One of the men cried out.

"Let's sink them," Miranda told Rosemary.

Something wasn't right. Rosemary couldn't put her finger on it, but the other women certainly rallied to Miranda's suggestion. All around them, women snatched up rocks. Others lifted their staves and hurled them like spears at the boat. Fenton and Nash ducked and yelped.

But they were on the oars now, and they began to pull away. Once beyond the cave, they could lift the mast into place and raise the sail. If they weren't stopped, they might make it all the way back to France.

To France. And Napoleon.

"Wait!" Rosemary cried. "Let them go!"

The women lowered their weapons to frown at her.

"Let them go?" Abigail asked, voice incredulous.

Rosemary pushed her way to the front of the group, then raised her voice. "I know you can hear me, Mr. Fenton, Mr. Nash, or whatever your real names are." The cave kindly magnified her words as if to prove it. "We are choosing to let you go. Return to your emperor, and tell him the women of Grace-by-the-Sea are ready for him. We will not be defeated."

Abigail let out a defiant yell at that, and every woman joined in, until the cave trembled with the noise. Rocks plummeted, splashing in the water, and the boat rocked as it shot out the Dragon's Maw.

"That showed them," Mrs. Catchpole said when the echo faded.

Everyone exchanged smiles. Out of the corner of her eye, Rosemary saw a movement by the stairs. Oh, not another one! Donner, perhaps?

She turned, face set, ready to fight.

Drake stood at the foot of the stairs, mouth agape.

He'd never seen anything like it.

He'd gone to Butterfly Manor, only to learn that there was nothing amiss.

"We're perfectly fine," his aunt Marjorie had assured him, smile gentle. "I can't imagine how things became so crossed."

"I can," James said. "Someone wants you out of the castle."

"Out of the kitchen and the caverns," Drake realized. "I'll head back. Gather your militia and follow."

"Right behind you," James promised.

The kitchen was empty when Drake entered, but simply opening the door to the caverns filled the room with noise.

"Jonas!" he shouted.

Although his tread was sedate, his butler appeared in

the doorway to the kitchen remarkably fast. "My lord?"

"Open the armory. Equip Giles, Dawson, and Pierson, then follow me to the caves."

"At once," he said, backing away from the hubbub echoing up from below.

Drake had crept down the stairs, listening and trying to understand what was happening. He'd stepped out into the cave in time to see Fenton and Nash make off with the French vessel while a good dozen women attempted to sink them, with hand-launched rocks as cannonballs and hoes as lances.

Then Rosemary had stood, head high, voice ringing with conviction, and scared them right out of the cavern.

"Father!" Miranda wiggled away from the rest now to run up the beach to him. "Did you see us? We fought off the French."

"Apparently so," he managed, for he could think of no other reason for the two men from the spa to take the boat. "Introduce me to your friends, Miranda."

She led him down the beach as the women began to lower their gazes and drop curtseys. Only Mrs. Bennett and Rosemary remained upright, both with looks verging on the defiant.

"This is Mrs. Ellison," Miranda said of a blond-haired matron. "Her husband makes the best rolls. She's very good at marching." She nodded to the woman beside her. "This is Mrs. Josephs. She hit Mr. Fenton on the head with her broom. Her husband is making me my gong."

"Triangle, I believe it was," Mrs. Josephs said with a fond smile.

"And this is Mrs. Catchpole," Miranda announced, glancing up at one of the sturdier looking women. "She tells people what to do."

"I manage the employment agency, your lordship," Mrs. Catchpole explained with an apologetic look.

"And I manage this meeting," Mrs. Bennett said, as if

determined to take the blame off them. "With Napoleon ready to invade at any moment, every man, woman, and child must be prepared to protect their family, their village, and their country. We are the Women's Militia of Grace-by-the-Sea. And we are at our service." She saluted him. A moment later, the other women mimicked her.

"Abigail is right," Rosemary put in, "about everything except this. She envisioned the Women's Militia, but I volunteered the caverns. They are secluded, impervious to harm, and big enough to shelter us all. I've been the one letting them in every Monday. I allowed you to believe it was a social gathering. I'm sorry."

He glanced around, and, once again, gazes danced away or dropped to the rocky ground. They expected his censure, perhaps even his wrath. His father would likely have held them up on charges of trespassing.

"No need to apologize," he said. "I can see the merits of the endeavor. I simply don't understand why you must hide down here."

Just then, Giles, Pierson, Dawson, and Jonas poured out of the stairwell, pikes and maces in hand. The women bunched together, raised their own makeshift weapons, those that weren't floating on the tide.

"Stand down," Drake ordered his bristling staff. "Our guests have already protected the castle."

Several of the women grinned as they lowered their brooms and hoes. Drake looked around at them all, from Eva's earnest smile to Mrs. Tully's proud head to Rosemary's wary look.

"I thank you for your valor, ladies," Drake said. "Know that you are welcome here. The castle grounds are at your disposal, as is the great hall when the weather proves fickle. And if you require instruction in something more than rock throwing, please avail yourselves of the armory. My butler, Mr. Jonas, likely knows how to work each weapon there."

He glanced back in time to see Jonas incline his head.

The women, however, were all staring at him again.

Abigail Bennett recovered first. "Thank you, my lord, for your enlightened view. It is refreshing. If we are questioned about our efforts, may we say we have your patronage?"

"I would be honored," he said. "We should always do all we can to share our gifts with others."

Applause broke out, and he bowed. Another rock fell with a splash.

Rosemary stepped up to him, eyes shining in the lamplight. "Bravo, my lord. This kind of response is exactly why I love you."

He was reduced to gaping again for a moment, but this time, he had enough thought left to pull her into his arms and kiss her. If she could make such a brave stand before the French, he could take a stand here and now, before most of the families in the village.

Sighs and squeals echoed around them.

"Miss Denby is going to be my mother," Miranda told them all.

Drake leaned back to eye Rosemary. "Is that right?"

"You know I assume nothing," she said, cheeks rosy and voice prim. "Besides, there is something very important I must attend to before we have this conversation. If you and Abigail could make the arrangements about practice days and times going forward, I have an urgent errand to run."

CHAPTER TWENTY-TWO

CAPTAIN ST. CLAIRE'S MANSERVANT ANSWERED Rosemary's knock. His craggy brows rose at the sight of her in her cloak and bonnet, but he stood taller. "Yes, miss? How might I help you?"

"I must speak to Captain St. Claire immediately. Tell him Rosemary Denby will brook no delay."

Perhaps he was used to females arriving at odd hours and begging entrance, for he merely nodded. "Yes, miss. If you'd be so good as to wait in the entry hall…"

"No need," the captain said, coming down the paneled corridor behind him. "There's no mistaking Miss Denby's educated drawl." He cocked his head, sending black hair spilling along his clean-shaven cheek. "And with no maid, mother, sister, or friend in attendance. My, my. Tongues will wag."

"They will wag far less if you let me in and hear me out," Rosemary told him.

He nodded to his manservant, who stepped aside and allowed Rosemary to enter.

As he shut the door behind her, the corridor dimmed dramatically, and she had the vague sensation she'd just been trapped. She shook off the feeling.

"I must speak to you, alone," she said to the captain.

He chuckled. "Oh, you are courting trouble. But how can I, as a gentleman, refuse a lady in distress? This way."

He turned, and she followed him just down the corridor to where a door led into a cozy paneled room with a view out over the village and the cove. Two leather armchairs nestled near the wood-wrapped hearth, where one of Abigail's paintings of the sea held pride of place. The only other furnishings in the room were a sea chest along one wall and a triangular wooden table between the two chairs.

"I'd offer you refreshment," he said, going toward one of the chairs. "But it seems your errand is urgent."

"It is," Rosemary said, refusing to sit. "The French have returned."

She had the satisfaction of seeing him start, but he turned to wander toward the window. "Interesting thought. I've seen no ship on the horizon."

"You will. Mr. Fenton and Mr. Nash, who have been visiting the spa, broke into the castle, took the ship anchored there, and rowed out the Dragon's Maw this morning. I expect they will attempt to cross to France or abandon their prize to seek passage on a larger ship headed that direction tonight."

He turned to face her, jaw set. "Very likely. And you want me to stop them."

"No," Rosemary said. "I want you to let them go."

He frowned. "You dare to tell me my duty?"

Clearly, no one else ever had. "Absolutely," Rosemary said. "We at the castle almost made the same mistake. But these men must escape. We want them to carry a message back to their master. Do not land in Grace-by-the-Sea. The villagers will be waiting, and they are formidable."

He watched her a moment, then his brow cleared, and he nodded. "Very well. I'll chase them back to France, but I won't impede their escape. Will that suffice?"

"Admirably," Rosemary said with a nod. "Thank you, Captain."

"Thank you, Miss Denby." He moved closer, with all

the grace and power of a cat prowling. "It took courage to bring me the news. Why didn't the earl send one of his servants or come himself?"

Rosemary raised her head. "Because I wanted to tell you."

"Ah." He closed the distance between them. "I'm glad to hear you're willing to be in my company again. The last time we had a private conversation, I was curt with you, and I've been regretting it ever since. Is it too late to start over?" He ran a finger down her cheek.

And she felt nothing—no anticipation, no exhilaration. Whatever influence Quillan St. Claire had exercised on her heart was gone, to be replaced by something deeper, something lasting.

A desire to be with Drake, always. He was her dragon, the one who protected, who cherished, who believed in their future together even when she doubted. She needed no other.

"Yes," she said. "I have found someone far better suited to who I am and what I believe."

His hand fell. "Then I envy you."

"Thank you, Captain," she said, inclining her head. "I wish you the same fortune."

His sad smile said he couldn't believe he'd be so blessed. "Allow me to see you to the door. May I at least know the name of this paragon of men who managed to eclipse me in your regard? No small feat, I imagine."

Rosemary smiled as they started back toward the entry. "No small feat indeed. Rest assured there are easily a dozen hearts still pining. But I regret I cannot tell you his name, not until arrangements have been made formal."

"Of course." He opened the door for her and bowed her through. "Give my regards to his lordship, and remind him that faint heart never won fair lady."

He was too clever by half. But, until she'd had a chance to talk with Drake, she wasn't about to claim him as her own.

It had taken a bit to set the castle to rights. First, Drake had seen the members of the Women's Militia out the door amid profusive thanks for his patronage. His mother had come downstairs in the middle of that, shot him a wounded look, and disappeared into the withdrawing room. Then he'd had to explain everything to James and the Men's Militia, who had come charging up the hill in time to see the women calmly marching away from their victory. Finally, he'd settled Miranda in the schoolroom with Warren attending her.

"Draw up a plan for how the ladies might best use the castle," he instructed her, and she bent her head over the parchment, pencil already moving.

Jonas met him as he returned to the great hall, long nose pointed accusingly at Drake's forehead.

"You understand my position about the Women's Militia?" he asked his butler.

That impassive face did not so much as flinch. "Of course, your lordship. Will Miss Denby and Lady Miranda be joining them?"

"They will," Drake said, unable to keep the pride from his voice.

"And the countess?" Jonas inquired.

"The countess is welcome to observe. I'm sure she'd be welcome to join as well, but that's probably too much to ask of her."

"Agreed, my lord."

Still his face betrayed nothing. Drake couldn't let the matter lie. All this time, he'd been comparing his every action against what his father might have done. Castle How and Grace-by-the-Sea were his home, and these were his people. He must do what he thought best to protect and encourage them.

"If I have given you the impression I intend to allow the countess, Miranda, or any other person in this castle to run roughshod, please disabuse yourself of the notion. My father and I disagreed on many things, but I am the earl now. I welcome wise counsel, but the decisions are mine. Those who cannot abide by those decisions are free to leave."

He inclined his head. "Of course, my lord. Will there be anything else?"

"Yes," Drake said. "I believe Pierson will admit that he prefers being a footman. What would you think of him swapping places with Giles? Leveling out their salaries, of course."

"I believe Giles to be an excellent choice, my lord. I'll make the arrangements." He started to move away, then paused.

"Something else?" Drake prompted.

Jonas seemed to stand taller, as if that were possible. "Only this, my lord. Most of the staff worked under your father before following us to Dorset. I think it safe to say that not one would prefer to go back to the way things ran under him. You have won their respect and devotion. Forgive me if I overstep myself by saying so."

"Not at all," Drake said, fighting a grin. "Thank you for telling me."

His butler bowed and returned to his duties.

So, the staff approved of the way he was handling things. He took it as a good sign. Now, to deal with his mother.

He found her in the music room, giving a Haydn sonata savage treatment. She did not so much as glance his way until the last note faded.

"They walked through the castle with brooms in their grips, as if they had come to clean the village public house," she said, gaze on the keys. "Have you no spine?"

Drake came around to face her. "I'm a Howland, Mother, which means my spine is always stiffer than most."

She sighed, glancing up at him. "Then why allow this affrontery, this demeaning of our station? We are the first family of the area!"

"The first family in an area where the inhabitants fear for their future," he reminded her. "I refuse to allow such fear to rule me. The women of the village appear to feel the same way. They have chartered a Women's Militia. I have agreed to serve as patron. Rosemary and Miranda will take part."

Her face bunched. "I don't understand you. You have embraced this place, these people, as if you weren't meant for more."

He spread his hands. "What more, Mother? I will take my seat in Parliament, seek to help guide our king and country. I will support the church, the dame school, and endeavors like the Women's Militia that attempt to protect the coast from invasion. I will make sure that you and Miranda are provided for. What else would you have of me?"

She heaved a sigh. "I suppose that is, in essence, the duty of an earl—to see to the wellbeing of those entrusted to him."

Drake lowered his hands. "Have I failed in that duty?"

"No," she admitted. "Never. Oh, it's all so difficult!"

Something else was at play here. He could see it in the tremor in her shoulders. Drake took her hand and helped her up off the bench. "Why is it so difficult, Mother? This may not be London, but no one would doubt that you rule Society here."

She sniffed. "There will always be someone new at the spa, ready to turn heads."

"No Newcomer could ever supplant the Countess of Howland," he argued.

Her smile was a shadow. "You would be surprised. I certainly was. I thought he cared."

Ah. Drake nodded. "Lord Featherstone has proven fickle."

"Slippery, more like," his mother lamented. "He was so attentive, and then Marjorie mentioned how proud she was of the way you were resolving our financial difficulties. He promptly told me he fears he isn't good enough for me. Rubbish."

"I'm sorry, Mother," Drake said.

She shook herself. "A momentary setback only. But I let my pain lead me into hurting others, and for that I must apologize. Miss Denby is a fine young lady. She has done a world of good for Miranda, and for you, I think. Will you make her your countess?"

"If she'll have me," he said, tucking her hand in his arm and turning her for the door.

She raised a brow as they moved toward the withdrawing room. "If she refuses you, she is not the bluestocking she claims. Anyone with any sense could see you are an excellent catch."

He could only hope his mother was right.

As it was, he had to wait another hour before Pierson brought word that Rosemary had returned to the castle. Jonas had wasted no time in reinstating the fellow to his former position. Pierson seemed to have grown a foot now that he was back in uniform, his head high, his brow clear.

"Miss Denby is in the schoolroom with Lady Miranda, my lord," he announced, and he went to hold the door open. Drake probably walked entirely too fast, but he couldn't care.

"Look, Father," Miranda called when he reached the schoolroom. "Miss Denby is going to teach me to read German, so I can learn from their scientific papers."

"An excellent notion," Drake said, coming into the

room and hoping he didn't look like a moon-struck calf. "Perhaps I should learn too."

"Miranda can learn a lesson, then teach it to you," Rosemary suggested with a smile. "That should help you both learn."

"An inspired idea." He nodded to the maid. "Warren, may I ask you to watch Lady Miranda practice her sums while I have a word with Rosemary?"

Warren's head bobbed. "Yes, my lord."

"Don't be long," Miranda said, as if she were an aged chaperone scolding a lad on his first Season. "I want to know how to ask Grandmother for more biscuits in German before tea."

"I'll attempt to be concise," Drake promised. He ushered Rosemary out of the schoolroom.

But once in the corridor, the words left him. She'd said she loved him. He was ready to admit he loved her. Could it be so simple?

"I take it your errand went well," he said. *That* was his opening?

She had to know he wanted to ask her something more important than that, but she answered readily enough as they strolled down the wing. "I went to see Captain St. Claire."

He thought the floor had tilted. Surely the castle was crumbling around him. "Indeed," he managed with some semblance of normalcy. "May I ask why?"

She moved along beside him as if she hadn't a care in the world. "I wanted to warn him about the Frenchmen, so that he wouldn't attempt to capture them. We want them to take the message to Napoleon."

He nodded. "Sensible."

She slanted him a glance. "And I wanted to prove to myself what I felt for him."

She had thrust a knife in his heart. He swallowed the building pain. "And?"

"The experiment was a success," she said. "I felt nothing. I suppose that shouldn't be surprising. How can there be room in my heart for Quillan St. Claire when my heart is overflowing with love for you?"

He jerked to a stop, stared at her. "Rosemary! What are you saying?"

"I love you. You are kinder, more considerate than anyone I've ever met. You always look for solutions that allow others to keep their dignity. You love fiercely, with the utmost devotion and dedication. And, no matter what life has dealt you, you still hope for, strive for, a better future. I find all that beyond admirable."

The light in her eyes confirmed her words.

"In that case." He went down on one knee in the middle of the corridor, where anyone might have come upon them. Why hide? His heart was overflowing too.

"Rosemary Denby," he said, "I love you. You are brilliant, passionate about whatever task you undertake. Your example inspires me. Would you do me the honor of accepting my hand in marriage?"

"Yes."

He rose, laughing. "That's it? One word?"

She raised a brow. "Do you require more?"

"No," he assured her, gathering her close. "Now that I know you love me, I require nothing more. I am utterly content to be the governess's earl."

Rosemary leaned her head against his chest, listening to the sound of the heart that beat in time with hers. How extraordinary!

She pulled back to meet his gaze. "If we're to be married, I should move out of the castle. It's not seemly that we live under the same roof."

He chuckled. "Anyone who knows Miranda, or my mother for that matter, would realize there's little chance of us being alone together for long."

As if to prove it, Miranda stuck her head out of the schoolroom doorway. "Hurry, Father! I need Miss Denby."

Rosemary took his hand. "Not everyone knows Miranda's unusual schedule. I'll see if Lark and Jesslyn will allow me to stay with them at night while I come teach during the day."

"I'll take that under advisement," he said, and she started laughing as they headed for the schoolroom.

"If you're that sure of yourself," she challenged, "let's tell Miranda now."

Suddenly *he* was the one towing her. Warren looked somewhat alarmed as he strode into the room.

"Miranda," he announced, "Rosemary has agreed to marry me."

Warren collapsed on a chair to fan her face with one hand.

"My feelings exactly," Drake told her before turning to his daughter again. "I know this may be difficult to become accustomed to, Miranda, but…"

"No," Miranda interrupted. "I don't need to become accustomed to the idea. I like Rosemary. She promised not to come between us."

"And I will abide by that promise," Rosemary said as he looked her way, brows up. "Just remember that there are things a husband and wife do together. Alone."

Miranda frowned. "Why?"

Warren fanned herself all the faster.

"I'll explain at a later date," Rosemary said and turned the girl's agile mind to the matter of planning the wedding and reception to follow.

"Stay a moment longer, Warren," Drake said. "We'll be back after we speak to the countess."

She couldn't help the hitch in her step as she accompanied him from the room. "Are you certain you're ready to beard the lioness in her den?"

He tucked her arm closer. "With you beside me, what fear have I of mere lions?"

She clung to his courage as they were admitted to the countess's suite. The lady was sitting by her fire, blanket across her lap as if she were chilled.

"I suppose it's too much to hope we might hold the ceremony at St. George's Hanover Square," she said with a sigh after Drake had announced their intentions.

"We'll be married here, at St. Andrew's," he told her. "It's more convenient for all our friends and family."

She sighed again. "I suppose it's best to keep the wedding small and quiet."

He smiled at Rosemary. "I doubt it will be either. I'm quite ready to make a statement about my beautiful bride."

And when he looked at her that way, she could not doubt that she was beautiful, cherished, valued for who she was. The gift was more than she had ever thought possible.

"I will do all I can to be a credit to this family," she promised the countess, who unbent enough to offer her a cheek to kiss.

"You make Drake and Miranda happy," she said as Rosemary drew back. "And that cannot help but make me happy as well. I will do my best not to vex you in the future."

Her mother was more effusive when they drove to Upper Grace to see her with Miranda that afternoon.

"Oh, my dear, such wonderful news! I'd almost given up hope." She hugged Rosemary close. Over her shoulder, Rosemary saw Drake trying hard not to grin.

"I couldn't be happier for you both," Hester said, hugging Rosemary in turn. "This exceeds all my expectations."

"Then, perhaps," Rosemary said as she disengaged, "your expectations are too low."

Hester tipped her head in wry acknowledgement.

Their next stop was Shell Cottage, but they found no one home.

"The spa, then," Rosemary suggested. "If Lark is out riding, we can ask Jesslyn to relay the news."

Her sister-in-law was overjoyed, and they accepted well-wishes from the spa guests too.

"You're a fortunate fellow," Maudie told Drake. "I understand the King of the Trolls has had his eye on her."

Rosemary also took a moment to tell Jesslyn what had happened at the caves earlier and her visit with Quillan St. Claire.

"Abigail reported as well," Jesslyn explained. "I'll make sure Lark and Alex know too. We can only pray that Napoleon heeds this warning and gives up on his plans to invade."

Their last stop was Butterfly Manor, where Eva hugged Rosemary, and James clapped his cousin on the shoulder.

"I'm delighted for you, old man," he said. "You deserve every happiness. I have good news as well. Peverell agreed to purchase the land below the Lodge. You should be solvent through the winter, at least."

Drake was still smiling as they climbed into the coach to return to the castle. Jesslyn had readily agreed to let Rosemary stay, so she planned to move her night things down that very evening.

"You have made me the happiest of men," he said, threading his fingers with hers while Miranda gazed out the window at the sea.

"And you have made me the happiest of women," she told him. "I only wish…"

"What?" he asked eagerly. "What can I do for you? Sail through the Dragon's Maw by the dark of night?"

Miranda turned her face toward them. "May I come

too, Father?"

"No," Rosemary said. "To you both."

"Challenge Napoleon to combat?" he suggested.

Miranda scrunched up her nose. "The Women's Militia can do that."

"Precisely," Rosemary agreed. "No, I need none of that. The only thing that distresses me is that we never found a way to keep Miranda's crocodile."

Miranda glanced between them, lower lip starting to tremble. "My crocodile is leaving?"

"No," Drake promised her. "I spent most of the day Sunday crafting a proposal that Dawson delivered this afternoon to Mr. Greer for the spa corporation council to review. I have no doubt they will endorse it."

"I don't understand," Miranda said, and Rosemary nodded agreement.

"It isn't only the spa waters that attracts visitors to Grace-by-the-Sea," he explained. "Our shops are without parallel, our assembly rooms without peer. I proposed another establishment that would attract and delight visitors. A museum."

Rosemary pressed her hands to her cheeks. "Oh, Drake, how perfect!"

"Where?" Miranda asked.

"I'll set aside a suite of rooms at the castle. Other great houses give tours. Why not ours? The Howland Museum would be open by appointment only, arranged through the spa. A member of the Howland family will personally conduct each tour."

Rosemary raised a brow. "A family member?"

"You, me, Miranda, or some combination," he allowed. "The exhibits would display items related to the unique geology, flora, and fauna of the area as well as the ancient creatures discovered here. We could also conduct invitation-only outings to the cliffs below the castle to show where the fossils were found. I guaranteed them that no other spa will have its like."

"Oh, they'll agree," Rosemary predicted. "Though some might balk at the cost."

"The cost is ours, but so are the rewards," he acknowledged. "I proposed a reasonable fee for entrance, more for a tour of the cliff. The income will be used to preserve the displays and the castle, which houses them."

"Brilliant," Rosemary breathed. "This could be the making of Grace-by-the-Sea."

"And you are the making of me." He took her hand, brought it to his lips. "I feel it, Rosemary. Together, there is nothing we cannot do."

"I know it too," she agreed, and she leaned forward to seal the matter with a kiss.

DEAR READER

Thank you for choosing Drake and Rosemary's story. I share a lot of traits with Rosemary, and I have always wanted to delve more into the history of the fossils along what is now called England's Jurassic Coast. If you missed how Jesslyn and Lark fell in love anew, see *The Matchmaker's Rogue*. Eva and James found each other in *The Heiress's Convenient Husband*, and the redoubtable Abigail met her match in Dr. Linus Bennett in *The Artist's Healer*.

If you enjoyed this book, there are several things you could do now:

Sign up for a free email alert at *https://subscribe.reginascott.com/* so you'll be the first to know when a new book is out or on sale. I offer exclusive, free short stories to my subscribers from time to time. Don't miss out.

Connect with me on Facebook at *www.facebook.com/authorreginascott*, BookBub at *www.bookbub.com/authors/regina-scott*, or Pinterest at *http://www.pinterest.com/reginascottpins*.

Post a review on a bookseller site or Goodreads to help others find the book.

Discover my many other books on my website at *www.reginascott.com*.

Turn the page for a peek at the fifth book in the Grace-by-the-Sea series, *The Lady's Second-Chance Suitor*. Hester Todd hoped never to run into her first love, Rob Peverell, again, until she does just that at the Harvest Ball. A tragedy has propelled the rapscallion younger son to the title of viscount, and Rob is struggling to become the man his sister and tenants need. Could a second chance at love make the difference in his life, and Hester's?

Blessings!

Regina Scott

SNEAK PEEK:

The Lady's Second-Chance Suitor,

Book 5 in the Grace-by-the-Sea Series
by Regina Scott

Grace-by-the-Sea
Dorset, England, September 1804

WHY DID SHE COMPARE EVERY man to him?

Hester Todd smiled up at the silver-haired baron who had requested her hand in the dance. Lord Featherstone was a Regular at Grace-by-the-Sea, meaning that he could be found daily at the spa that supported the village and was a well-known figure among the shops and at assemblies like this one. He was old enough to be her father and then some, though he danced with the elegance and grace that fellows half his age might envy. He was well dressed, well spoken, a gentleman in all ways.

But he would never be as dashing as Rob Peverell. There was no spark of excitement when his gaze brushed hers, no giddy anticipation that their fingers might meet.

She'd learned there was something to be said for a lack of giddy anticipation. Peace and stability were not unwelcome, particularly as she had her daughter, Rebecca, to think of now.

Of course, peace was at a premium at the moment. The Harvest Fair ball was one of the most crowded of the year. Anyone from kitchen maid to lord of the manor might attend. The lovely pale blue walls of the assembly rooms were all but invisible behind the throngs of attendees. Muslin and cotton skirts swept past those of silk and fine wool. Rough-spun coats bumped shoulders against tailored velvet. It was a wonder the candles in the crystal chandelier didn't start melting from the rising warmth alone.

The music stopped; the dance ended. She curtsied to Lord Featherstone's bow, and he offered her his arm to escort her back to the wall, where the other widows waited similar kindnesses.

"You are an accomplished dancer, Mrs. Todd," he said. "I appreciate you honoring my request, particularly when you have so deservedly attracted such a train of followers."

She and Rosemary, her sister, had attracted their fair share of late. Newcomers at the spa, such as the dapper Mr. Donner, who had been her first partner of the evening; curly haired, curious Mr. Cushman; shy Mr. Nash; and determined Mr. Fenton; as well as Alex Chance, younger brother of their sister-in-law, Jessica, the spa hostess, and an officer or two from the camp at West Creech. It ought to be gratifying.

Why did she persist in seeking a tousled, dusky blond head among them?

"You are too kind, my lord," she told Lord Featherstone. "I would be delighted to dance with you whenever you have a free moment. But you too have amassed quite a following." She nodded to where Lady Howland was gazing in their direction. It was not quite a glare—the widowed countess was far too polished for that—but the look was decidedly chilly. It seemed the lady thought the gentleman hers.

He, apparently, did not. "No one who could eclipse my affections for you," he said with a gallant bow to Hester. "I envy the gentlemen who will beg for your hand in the next dances."

She inclined her head, and he strolled off, away from the countess, who huffed and stalked in the opposite direction. Well, at least Hester wasn't the only lady who made the gentlemen run.

She took a seat on one of the only open chairs, trying to shake the feelings that crowded her more surely than the other attendees. It had been seven years since she'd laid eyes on Rob. She'd been a wife, widow, and mother for most of them. If she thought of anyone with longing, it should be Lieutenant Todd, her late husband. She must do better.

She drew in a breath and glanced around the room, only to spy Rosemary strolling away from the dancefloor on the arm of her employer, the Earl of Howland. How proud her sister had been to win the position of governess to the earl's daughter. But Hester had seen more in the way the handsome widower gazed at her sister.

Rosemary was brave, working with their uncle to learn all manner of things, scurrying about the cliffsides searching for evidence of ancient life. Hester was not brave. She'd accepted that her nature was one of commiseration and propitiation. But she had emboldened herself to speak to the earl about the matter of Rosemary recently.

"What!" Her darker-haired sister had yelped when she'd heard of it at one of the weekly assemblies in this very room. "What did you say to him?"

"I asked him his intentions," Hester admitted, "and warned him about sullying your reputation."

Rosemary snorted. "I'm surprised he didn't sack me immediately. What were you thinking?"

"I was thinking of you," Hester informed her. "An earl taking interest in a commoner? You know where that could lead."

"He is no Rob Peverell," Rosemary insisted. "There's never been any stories of dalliances or flirting. He was by all accounts a devoted husband and remains a loving father."

Hester regarded her sadly. "Yes, I will grant you others claim him beyond reproach. But you are still in his employ, and he is an earl. It isn't seemly."

Rosemary sagged, as if all the fire had gone out of her. "I know. I could tell you it is all in your imagination, but he sent me flowers yesterday."

Which only proved how little Lord Howland understood the tragedies she and her bluestocking sister had survived. Hester touched her arm. "I'm so sorry. He couldn't know."

"Of course he couldn't know. I explained myself a few moments ago, so it shouldn't happen again."

She should hope not. She hadn't the aversion to the blossoms her sister had, but she would never forget finding their father dead among the wildflowers. He had been attacked by the smugglers he had sought to apprehend as a Riding Officer for the Excise Office. She and Rosemary had relied on each other then, while their mother and older brother dealt with moving the family to Upper Grace from Kent to live with their mother's brother. The only thing that had ever threatened to drive her and Rosemary apart had been Rob Peverell.

She shook herself now. Enough of these thoughts! She must find her next dance partner. She rose and set off around the edge of the dancefloor, as if she were intent on some errand. Still, memories chased her.

Rob, racing her down the road on horseback.

Rob, laughing as he spun her in a circle among the waving grass of the Downs.

Rob, meeting her on the shore to watch the sun set in a glory that was as fiery as his kiss.

Rob, disappearing with only the most casual of farewells, leaving her hurting.

No, no! She had made a fool of herself over a handsome stranger who had turned out to be the younger son of Viscount Peverell, one of the two local landowners. It had been humiliating, heart-breaking. But good had come of it. Because of her wounded heart, she had carefully considered the proposal by the dashing Lieutenant Todd, who had been home between assignments in the Navy. Because she'd married her lieutenant, she now had a beautiful six-year-old daughter who brightened her life. Because of Rebecca's birth, her mother had opened her home to her, so she always had somewhere safe to live. Because she'd been widowed, she'd been accepted as the teacher for the dame school in Upper Grace, helping young minds to grow. And because of that, she could live with her head high, a pillar of the community, respected wherever she went. Truly, it was all a blessing.

"Excuse me, dearie." A farmwife shoved past on her way to the door. Hester stepped back to avoid her and collided with a solid frame.

She turned to apologize, and the words dried up in her mouth.

Rob Peverell stared at her, light-hazel eyes darkened by his evening black, hair as tousled, chin just beginning to hint of stubble.

"Gwen?" he asked.

She wanted to shoot into the sky like one of Mr. Congreve's rockets, explode in a flash of lightning, sink to the bottom of the cove and never be seen again. Her cheeks were hot, her muscles frozen. Somehow, she managed to find her voice.

"You are mistaken, sir. I do not know you."

Then she turned and fled as fast as dignity allowed.

"Who was that?" his sister asked.

Rob, the recently elevated Viscount Peverell, shook his head. "I thought I knew, but perhaps she's right. Perhaps I was mistaken."

Elizabeth's hazel gaze, so like his own, followed the honey-haired beauty as she hurried away from them, ruby-colored silk skirts swaying. "She certainly didn't care for you. That was nearly the cut direct."

It had been. Over the years, he'd deserved it on any number of occasions. His dalliance with Guinevere Ascot had been one of them. Yet surely someone so lovely, so warm and giving, as Gwen would have been long married. It had been, what, seven years now? She would have changed.

He was doing his best to change.

"Lord Peverell, Miss Peverell." The pretty hostess of the spa smiled at them as she approached, the curls at the sides of her face glinting like gold. "I've been asked to introduce you to several of our Regulars. Would that be permissible?"

Mrs. Denby had been a dewy-eyed miss, helping her hostess mother and physician father at the spa, when last he'd visited the area. His father and brother had been alive then, and he'd let them carry most of the conversations. He'd needed more than the spa, the village shops, and the assembly to enliven him.

Gwen had been all in all.

Now he inclined his head. "We'd be delighted. Perhaps first, you could answer a question for me. Do you know Miss Guinevere Ascot?"

She tapped her chin with one finger. "I don't believe we've ever had a guest by that name, and certainly no one locally."

He nodded across the room, to where a young military officer in scarlet regimentals was escorting Gwen out onto the floor. "What about that lady?"

She followed his gaze, and her smile warmed. "My sister-in-law, Mrs. Todd. But her first name isn't Guinevere. It's Hester."

"And her husband?" Elizabeth put in with a glance to Rob. "A stalwart sort, protective of his lady, perhaps?"

Did she think he intended to carry Hester Todd off? Once, perhaps, but not now. Too much depended on him finding a way to pretend he knew how to be the viscount.

"He was a valiant lieutenant in the Navy," Mrs. Denby assured his sister. "Gone now these past six years. Mrs. Todd teaches at the dame school in Upper Grace. Did you wish an introduction, my lord?"

Elizabeth's eyes narrowed at him.

"No, thank you," Rob made himself say. "But we will await your good pleasure on the others."

She nodded and swept off to find those desirous of making his acquaintance. Mrs. Todd would not be among them.

He couldn't have mistaken her. She had to be his Gwen.

She'd been rather proud of that name. "Guinevere," she'd said with a toss of her silky mane when he'd asked the intimacy of using her first name. "Like Arthur's queen."

"Then you shall be mine," Rob had vowed.

If she had given him a false name instead of her own, it had been only his due. He certainly hadn't advertised his name. His father would have had apoplexy if he'd known his younger son was improving a boring summer by romancing a local lass.

Beside him, Elizabeth's feet shuffled under her lavender silk skirts. "After Mrs. Denby makes these introductions, can we go? I'm not as ready as I thought to rejoin Society. I'm finding this all a bit much."

It was. And it was exactly the sort of evening he normally enjoyed. Dozens of people from all walks of life, mixing, laughing, conversing, dancing. Constant movement, constant buzz. No fellow could be bored in such a place.

But he was the head of the family now. He must think of more than his own pleasure. The act was still foreign, but necessary.

"Of course," he promised.

A short time later, he skillfully extricated himself and Elizabeth from a scintillating conversation about the shocking price of grain and left the crowded assembly rooms behind. His coach was waiting. They had only to step inside before they were swept out along the headland to the west of the village. He peered out, thinking of how many times he'd raced along these roads, but the sight of his triumphs eluded him. In fact, the carriage lamps made it difficult to see more than his own reflection out the window. And he'd had entirely too much time to reflect on himself of late.

"So," Elizabeth said, crossing her arms over her chest as he turned to face her. "Who is she, Rob?"

He did not want to have this conversation. "The goggle-eyed Mrs. Greer who gushed all over you? I distinctly remember our charming hostess saying she is the wife of the spa corporation president, who is the village allegory? No, actuary?"

"Apothecary," Elizabeth reminded him with a small smile. "And you know very well I wasn't referring to her."

"Glad I am to hear it. I would not want to think you had fallen into the habit of encouraging a sycophant, unless it is me, of course. Though, if you have, I might bring to your attention that pimple-faced youth who kept staring at you."

"Rob." Her voice hinted of both reproach and laughter. "Who is Hester Todd to you?"

He looked away. "Apparently someone who would prefer not to renew our acquaintance."

She lowered her arms. "And why? Is there some scandal involved? You said you would like us to stay here through the winter. If I am to associate with people here, I should know if there's a matter best left unspoken."

"Precisely why I would prefer not to speak of it."

She rolled her eyes. "I will have the truth. You know that. You never could keep anything from me."

Far more than she realized, but Rob merely smiled at her. "Yes, you can be quite the sleuth when you put your mind to it."

She leaned forward. "And my mind is entirely engaged with thoughts of this Mrs. Todd. Where did you meet? What were you to each other? Are you intent on pursuing her now?"

Rob sighed. "Very well. You're right that someone else may know the tale, though we both tried hard not to share it."

"Oooh," she said, leaning back, eyes kindling. "Secrets. Do tell."

"It is not to my credit, I assure you."

When she still regarded him, waiting, he knew there was nothing for it. "You may remember the summer you were finishing your first Season. Father, Thomas, and I came out to the Lodge to escape the London heat. They were quite content to while away the days reading, playing at draughts, and visiting the spa. I wanted more."

She nodded. "Of course you did."

"Since I found the spa set insipid, I sought better game afield. Thinking to throw Father off the scent, I dressed like a commoner and took to strolling through Upper Grace until I fell in with a group of fellows about my age who knew how to have fun."

"Fun," she said, as if the word was foreign to her. "Racing horses, gambling, seducing women?"

"Certainly plenty of the first two, though not much of the last, I'm sorry to say."

She raised an eloquent brow.

"It's true," Rob insisted. "You will find the ladies of the area a clever lot. They were proof against even my considerable charms."

"How refreshing."

"I found it a challenge," Rob admitted, "and never more so than when we happened upon a young lady talking a walk out from the village. The others treated her with all deference and urged me to be off, but I was instantly smitten and demanded to know more about her. She was reticent at first, but I soon won her over. She told me she was the daughter of a well-to-do merchant, who closely watched her comings and goings. She had barely managed to escape the house that day by climbing from her bedroom window."

"And that only made her more of a challenge," Elizabeth guessed.

"Of course. Nothing like a little subterfuge to whet the appetite."

"We can skip the part about your appetites," she informed him.

"Nothing more than a few stolen kisses," he assured her. "She was in all ways the epitome of a lady in my eyes. She could do no wrong, and she felt the same about me. We spent part of nearly every day together."

She sighed, face softening in the lamplight. "How wildly romantic."

Was that envy in his little sister's voice?

"I thought so at the time," he said, "but I must caution you against attempting the feat. Someone always gets hurt."

Her face saddened. "Apparently Mrs. Todd."

"She was unmarried then," he said. "But yes, I have no doubt my defection hurt her. That is the saddest part of the tale. When Father was ready to return to London, I rather blithely told my angel that I would be leaving the area, but thank you very kindly for making my summer bearable. I doubt she knew who I truly was until then."

"Oh, Rob." She shook her head. "You're right. It is a sad tale. You truly were reprehensible. At least you are trying to change."

The word *trying* stung, but he could not denounce the truth of it. He'd been born the coddled second son, with no expectations of greatness, no pressure to perform. He'd done what he'd liked, and money or charm had resolved most of the consequences.

One tragic afternoon on the Thames, one vessel with everyone aboard lost, had changed all that. Now his sister, his tenants, and their family fortune depended on him doing the right thing, every time. A dozen duties awaited him at the Lodge on the headland.

Yet, the thoughts foremost in his mind were those of Hester Todd and how he could go about seeing her again.

Learn more at

www.reginascott.com/secondchancesuitor.html

OTHER BOOKS BY REGINA SCOTT

Grace-by-the-Sea Series
The Matchmaker's Rogue
The Heiress's Convenient Husband
The Artist's Healer

Fortune's Brides Series
Never Doubt a Duke
Never Borrow a Baronet
Never Envy an Earl
Never Vie for a Viscount
Never Kneel to a Knight
Never Marry a Marquess
Always Kiss at Christmas

Uncommon Courtships Series
The Unflappable Miss Fairchild
The Incomparable Miss Compton
The Irredeemable Miss Renfield
The Unwilling Miss Watkin
An Uncommon Christmas

Lady Emily Capers
Secrets and Sensibilities
Art and Artifice
Ballrooms and Blackmail
Eloquence and Espionage
Love and Larceny

Marvelous Munroes Series
My True Love Gave to Me

The Rogue Next Door
The Marquis' Kiss
A Match for Mother

Spy Matchmaker Series
The Husband Mission
The June Bride Conspiracy
The Heiress Objective

And other books for Revell,
Love Inspired Historical, and Timeless
Regency collections.

ABOUT THE AUTHOR

REGINA SCOTT STARTED WRITING NOVELS in the third grade. Thankfully for literature as we know it, she didn't sell her first novel until she learned a bit more about writing. Since her first book was published, her stories have traveled the globe, with translations in many languages, including Dutch, German, Italian, and Portuguese. She now has had published more than fifty works of warm, witty historical romance.

She loves everything about England, so it was only a matter of time before she started her own village. Where more perfect than the gorgeous Dorset Coast? She can imagine herself sailing along the chalk cliffs, racing her horse across the Downs, dancing at the assembly, and even drinking the spa waters. She drank the waters in Bath, after all!

Regina Scott and her husband of more than 30 years reside in the Puget Sound area of Washington State on the way to Mt. Rainier. She has dressed as a Regency dandy, learned to fence, driven four-in-hand, and sailed on a tall ship, all in the name of research, of course. Learn more about her at her website, *www.reginascott.com*.

CPSIA information can be obtained
at www.ICGtesting.com
Printed in the USA
LVHW052209080321
680888LV00015B/2888